UNTHINKABLE

SHAKIR RASHAAN

nebu
publishing

This book is a work of fiction. Names, characters, places and incidents are either products of the author's imagination or are used fictitiously. Any resemblance to actual events or locales or persons, living or dead is entirely coincidental.

This book is for sale to mature audiences only. It contains substantially sexually explicit scenes and graphic language which may be considered offensive by some readers.

Cover Design by Woodson Creative Studio

Published by NEBU Publishing, LLC

Printed in the United States of America

ISBN 978-0-9986640-6-4

To my Beloved…and my Beauty

For loving me so deeply,

The sound of your voices silence my demons.

I was wondering maybe…
If I made you my baby…
If we do the unthinkable, would it make us look crazy?
Or would it be so beautiful?
Either way I'm sayin'…if you ask me, I'm ready

Un-Thinkable by Alicia Keys

ACKNOWLEDGMENTS

12 May 2018
2345hrs (11:45PM)

Happy Springtime! I've been working so much lately that I hadn't even realized that the seasons had changed. Good grief!

Oh well, such is life, I guess. I need to stay busy so I can keep showing of things a bit, you know?

Anyway, I'm getting off script a bit, so, let me let you know what to expect with this novel you're about to read, okay? Cool!

This particular project has gone through a lot of different versions and incarnations. I originally wrote and released this book way back in 2011 as a period piece, of sorts, but then I took it out of publication when I went through a revamp of my catalog. Funny how life works, huh?

I'm gonna keep it "one hundred" with you: the things I write as Shakir are just a little rougher around the edges than what you are about to read, even though I will admit there is some heat in this book, too, but I'm in the midst of going through a bit of a growth spurt with regard to my platform. If you've read any books in my catalog, then you know that this journey you're about to embark on is softer by comparison than the journey you've been on inside my Underworld.

Okay, let's be honest, nothing I write as Shakir is soft and sweet (at least, not yet), so don't expect this to be your typical romance, either. I don't do conventional, but I might surprise you along the way.

I do hope you like this project, though; this was something that I dug out of my old manuscripts from years and years ago when I was writing for the hell of it. I updated the time frame to about a year or so ago, and I think this latest incarnation turned out pretty good, but don't take my word for it, take a look for yourself.

So, without further ado, the usual shout outs and recognitions and such like there must now commence. ☺

To my Beloved, there's nothing more to say that hasn't already been said so many times over. Thank you for being the center of my universe, and being strong enough to be the anchor in the storm that is my world. I love you more than life itself.

To my Beauty, thank you for coming at a time when things were at their most hectic, and helping to be that other anchor when the storm was at its most fierce. I love you.

To my mother and father, thank you for everything. Enough said. I love you.

To my sister, Rae Lamar, you know how we do. Thank you for always being there and for being my hero as much as I've tried to be yours. I love you, girlie.

I'm going to end this in my usual fashion (I think you all know how I do this by now), so, let me say it anyway:

I'd like to thank _____ for the support and love. I hope to continue to put books out there that you will want to tell fellow readers and friends about.

Thank you for reading, and God Bless you.

UNTHINKABLE

Devin

Chapter One: One Last Cry

"It's over. I can't do this anymore."

I looked at the phone like touching it would infect me with an incurable disease. "What do you mean, it's over?"

"I need something different, Devin," she explained. "What we had was good, but we want different things now."

The voice over the phone, the one that only a week ago sang in high octaves to any deity who would listen over how much she loved me while I was digging in her yoni, now sounded like poison, making my ears bleed.

"You're really serious? Yeah, this is a joke," I spat. "You want to make me beg to keep you and what we have or something? Yeah, that's it, that's got to be it."

"Don't make this harder than it has to be," she pleaded. "I'm not the woman that I was a couple of years ago when we met. Our dreams are different now. The paths that we're taking are, too."

There was no doubt in my mind where this conversation was headed. She wanted to throw the "marriage and kids" thing in my face again. We'd been arguing about that the last few weeks, but it seemed like she was almost adamant about it over the past few days, nearly popping off an ultimatum.

As I listened to her drone on about her so-called evolution, it dawned on me. She'd upgraded me. She thought doing this would let me down easy. She could have dropped me off a cliff and it would hurt the same way.

"I know this isn't easy, but hopefully we can still be friends, baby." Her voice was calm, but I didn't want to be. "It doesn't have to be bad between us, baby."

Friends? Really? No thanks, not in this lifetime. That was the final straw. I wasn't about to be anybody's emergency option in case things didn't go well with the upgrade. Nope.

"You're right, this is over, and no, we can't be friends." I felt the need to regain some semblance of dignity, despite the fact that my heart was breaking. She was not about to hold any power over me. "And don't call me baby, you've lost that right. In fact, lose my number and don't call me anymore."

That conversation was weeks ago, but the wounds felt fresh every time I thought about it.

All the signs were there, but I didn't see it coming. If I was honest, I didn't *want* to see it coming. If I'd stuck to the rules and stayed on my game, I wouldn't be looking so stupid, but my nose was too wide open, thinking she was the "one". Under normal circumstances, my instincts would have been hypersensitive enough to warn me of the impending blindside hit.

I looked back on everything I'd done, all the sacrifices I

made for this relationship, more than my fair share. But I guess that wasn't enough for her. That's what I got for ignoring my base instincts and letting her get so far inside that I couldn't tell which way was up.

The one thing that gnawed at me was a decision that would have stunted my growth if I wasn't associated with my employer. I gave up big money about a year ago, turning down some overseas photo shoots that would have made me a superstar in the fashion industry. Being an up-and-coming photographer, turning down jobs wasn't an option unless there was a damn good reason. I thought that she was that damn good reason.

That was my first strike.

Hindsight was 20/20, with the laser focus of an FBI sharpshooter.

I was lucky that it didn't kill my career and I was able to parlay my skills to become one of the most sought-after video producers in the industry, with the prospect of being able to be the next Ryan Coogler. Now that he'd gotten *Black Panther* trending so hot that it had the whole industry buzzing on a whole other frequency, there was no doubt that it would earn a cool billion-plus at the box office in the next few months. *That* was where I wanted to be, and *that* was where I was going to be. Thanks to the filmography classes I took at USC when I was younger, I might be well on my way to doing that, and it didn't hurt now that I was situated in "Hollywood South".

I had fallen victim to the spell that love had cast over my heart—a heart I thought I'd protected. Cupid's a dead motherfucker, God as my witness.

Being the logical thinker that I was, I had to be honest with myself and check my own ego at the door. Maybe I set myself up for this fall. After all, I had my rules, and my number one rule was to never fall in love until they fell in love with you.

I thought I had that rule covered. I should have thought twice to be sure. But, that's what I got for thinking I had all my bases covered.

Okay, so I wasn't all the way innocent. I mean, who jumped out of a plane without a parachute? I kept a few women who were still in my corner, and some continued to make passes at me, despite my relationship. All of them knew who she was, and for the most part, they were okay with that.

Could it have been that Karma was making me pay for not being "all in" with my relationship? I could have waxed philosophical for the next few days playing the "what if" game, but I no longer cared. As far I was concerned, my game was still on point; I allowed my feelings to get in the way. It was her loss, regardless of whether I thought she was worth letting all of the side pieces fade to black in order to make her the center of my universe.

The moral of this story? Never make someone a priority when they saw you as nothing more than an option. The problem with that moral was that I didn't make sure I was not an option.

That was my second strike.

There was no room for strike three because I got tossed out of the game for arguing the call.

Jenna Whitmore was everything that I thought I wanted in a woman: ambitious, aggressive in her business dealings, sensual to a point to where she could have any man eating out of the palm of her hand. She knew what she wanted, and she knew how she was gonna get it. She had the type of drive that made me want to match hers tit-for-tat, and the way my life was set up in that moment, I needed someone who fit what I needed from my woman.

Despite all the pros of the situation, she did have her downside; that damn hindsight thing again. She was never affectionate away from the bedroom. She was nonchalant at times, and the words "I love you" didn't have the same effect as I thought they should have. I tried to convince myself that none of that mattered. I loved her, or at least I thought I did.

My friends and family had a fit when they found out. My best friends, Anton and Quinn, couldn't believe that I'd chosen Jenna in the first place. In their eyes, there were other women in my "harem" that were much better suited for me. Natalia, my best female friend, never liked her, and in retrospect I saw the reasons why.

I wasn't trying to hear any of them, though. I'd made my choice, I had to live with it, and that was what I told my friends and family. There was no point in going back on my word at this point, and I didn't have time to hear the "I told you so" speech from anyone.

I charged all of that to the game. I made myself a promise that I wouldn't let my heart make any more decisions from now on—once it mended. Until then, I had plans to treat my body like an amusement park roller coaster, and you had to meet certain requirements to ride.

It was an unusually warm Saturday evening when Anton called me. He had the bright idea of rolling through the clubs downtown and midtown club circuits, since we both had the day off tomorrow. It figured he'd wanted to go out more now. He was in the midst of a bad dry spell and he'd picked up on my old habit of picking up a new bevy of beauties every few months or so, and this time of the year was prime feeding time.

At the beginning of the year, I entertained around four or five women, depending on my mood and what I had a taste for. After that, the war of attrition bore out who the weakest links were until one remained. I had no problems getting back to that plan, but there was no motivation anymore because I was still healing from losing Jenna.

"Yo, D, we heading to the Havana Club, you down?"

"I don't know, bruh, I'm not feeling being around people tonight."

"Come on, bruh, I'll even come through in the Yukon and grab you. I got a sweet tooth for some chocolate, and Quinn's coming, too. It will be like old times."

Anton made a very strong case, and I couldn't argue. I didn't have to drive, either? Man, listen!

"I'm down, bruh, I'll see you at my place in thirty."

"All right, bet. See you in thirty."

I hung up the phone and my mind began to think back to what my father told me when I was in high school and I lost my first love.

My father was old school, last of a dying breed of players from back in the day. You know, the ones that had a "mistress" that the wife knew about, but as long as he was taking care of home, the wife didn't care too much about who else he was fucking with. He'd had me and my brother later in life after he'd gotten all of his love of random women out of his system and decided our mother was the one for him.

He saw me trying to look like I wasn't crying in my bedroom after the "love of my life" at that time decided that she wanted to be friends.

"Son, it only takes thirty seconds to get over a girl." I could still hear him laughing as he said it. I didn't find it so funny since my heart was hurting as much as it as. "You lose one, pick up a few more. It ain't nothing like a few new dime pieces in your pocket to make you feel like a new man."

I took that lesson and ran with it for as long as my heart and body would let me. For a while, it worked, and I didn't have to worry about my heart being broken until I felt like I wanted to bother with putting it out there to be broken again.

Pops said it took thirty seconds.

Well, looking back on it in the midst of my current pain, I realized that it took a lot longer than thirty seconds—a *lot* longer. Jenna was not some random chick on the street that I'd been playing around with. She was supposed to be my forever. This one was going to take a long time to get over.

But like he told me, the best way to forget about the last one was to pick up on the next one—or a few next ones. But I didn't want to forget about this last one. It hurt too much.

Devin

Chapter Two: You Don't Have to Call

The Havana Club was the spot on a Saturday night.

The ladies were looking everywhere from classy to trashy, and no club was immune to having them all in between, not even the Havana Club. All flavors were on full display, from French vanilla and caramel, to mocha latte and chocolate. The bruhs were at the bar, trying to spit game at any woman who paid attention for more than five minutes.

It wasn't like the ladies weren't feeling it tonight, but they were too busy trying to get the male bartenders' attention, sweet-talking them into giving up free drinks for a peek or two. If a few were adventurous enough, perhaps a quickie in the bathroom or something like that would be on deck.

If they weren't doing that, they were popping off on any social media platform that would have them, anything that would whip their "followers" into a frenzy. I was already over the scene before I had a chance to sit down at the bar.

Still, this was the spot to see and be seen by some of the most well-known people in the entertainment industry, and this was where a lot of the top-level talent came to show, including some of the hottest deejays in the A…but none of them were hotter than my dude, Quinn. Even though he wasn't going to be spinning tonight, it wasn't hard for the groupies to start filing in once they saw that he was in the spot.

Quinn was the light-skinned, pretty boy between the three of us. He and I balled against each other back in the day in high school, and when we ended up playing together in college, we managed to find out that we had a lot in common and stayed tight ever since. He was around six-foot-one, a couple of inches shorter than me, and he was thin and wiry as hell, but the ladies seemed to love that. He decided to keep the outfit he wore casual in case he decided to put in some work in the deejay booth. He was good for showing off what the great DJ Infinity could do when other deejays were in the spot, and the Havana Club was the prime spot to show who was the best in the city.

Anton was on the other end of the spectrum, the dark chocolate one among us, but he was also the shortest. He always felt that he had to overcompensate for his height, which was weird to me. He was one of the biggest names in the adult entertainment industry, but he always felt like the ladies were always checking for me or Quinn, when nothing could be further from the truth. He came out in some crazy-ass bronze suit to show off the contrast in his skin tone, and the ladies were feeling it, whispering over his physique the minute we stepped through the door.

I read somewhere that dressing in certain colors was a direct reflection of the mood that you were in. Tonight, black was appropriate for the mood I was in. I didn't want to be bothered, but at the same time, I would have gone crazy at home. It was yet another oxymoron that I didn't feel like explaining, so, I had it made up in my mind that if a woman approached me—and they would, trust me—with the "Why aren't you smiling?" questions, I would tell them I got off work a few minutes ago.

Don't get me wrong, I wasn't supermodel material, I made my living taking pictures of them. I was easy on the eyes, and from the looks I got from the women who were trying to get my attention, it was going to be an interesting evening.

I hoped that they didn't catch attitude if I chose not to fall all over myself to find out if their legs were opened for carnal business after the club closes later tonight. It wasn't my fault that I dealt with beautiful women on a daily basis, so I could get it whenever I wanted to bother, and tonight, I wasn't trying to bother, unless the convo was that stimulating.

As I expected, my boys dropped me and started on the hunt in the club, picking up the vibe on the dance floor at moment's notice. That didn't take long at all, as one little cutie with hazel eyes and a blonde weave grabbed Quinn and pulled him on the floor so quick that I didn't get a chance to blink twice.

A chocolate honey over in another corner of the spot was already in full flirt mode, blowing kisses and licking her lips in Anton's direction like he was the next Idris Elba or something, and he was off in her direction as quickly as Quinn was. I stood there, dumbfounded, trying to figure out exactly how I became the odd man out. That never happened to me. I guessed I was giving off a "get away from me" vibe after all.

Hell, I couldn't blame them. If I was in a better mood, I would have done the same thing to them. But I was hoping that my boys would have had my back for at least a half hour before pussy would be on the menu. I barely got ten minutes.

Sitting at the bar while nursing the Hennessy and Coke in my hand, I watched my boys have the time of their lives. I was good with that; someone needed to have a good time. I flowed with the music, zoning out for a minute or two, feeling my mood improving as the baseline of each song seemed to breathe life back into me. I even started smiling and nodding at different women passing me on their way to getting a drink from one of the bartenders.

I was in such a zone that I didn't flinch when I noticed out of the corner of my eye that a thick little brown-skinned sexy walked over and sat next to me. I didn't pay attention to her at first, but the way she let the skirt rise up as she sat in the chair, she wanted to make sure I would be soon.

I heard some new songs that weren't getting any radio play, and I wanted to check out who they were in case my bosses might be interested.

She shifted her body toward me, crossing her legs to close off the space between us.

I exhaled. This was about to be an encounter I wasn't trying to have right now. It was only a matter of time before she would try to holla, and the first words out of her mouth would determine whether or not I would want to further the conversation or not.

"So, are you gonna buy me a drink or what?"

I gave her an incredulous look, trying to figure out how many dudes she's tried that line on tonight. "You can't come any better than that? Can a bruh at least know your name before you start running through his pockets?"

"Well, excuse me, I'm just trying to get to know you. And my name is Jemma," she retorted, tapping her finger on the counter top. "And why you already thinking I'm trying to run your pockets? Damn, a sista can't holla without you thinking I'm digging for gold or something?"

Yep, her routine had worked before, her irritation showed. I wasn't the one for tired-ass lines and routines, and if she had kept her mouth shut, maybe she could get it. The fact that her name was too close to my ex's name was not going to work, either.

Why she decided to try me I'd never understand.

I needed to make change out of this dime piece…she was killing my vibe, and she needed to be dealt with fast.

"The conversation is free, Jemma, but the drink is optional," I fired back. I glared at her, no longer caring about her feelings. "Is this how you approach men that you are interested in? If so, you can hit the bricks. I'm not hearing it."

"Oh, I'm sorry, maybe I had you confused for a baller, instead of these other fuckboys up in here tonight." She twisted her lips and moved away from me. I didn't know who she thought I was, but that move only worked on wannabes that still wanted that booty regardless of her stank attitude.

I'd had better, and she was not about to be the start of my renaissance.

I straightened up at the spot I sat in, ready to pop off and let the chips fall where they may. "You must be kidding?

Listen, miss, the game you're spitting is weak, and calling me a fuckboy before you even found out my name lets me know that you need to get back to the lab and work on your people skills some more."

She gave me a look like I'd grown a third eye. She was raring up for a scathing rebuttal when Kirsten, one of the models I used to work with, walked up on us.

She surveyed the situation for a few moments before she spoke to me. "Devin Lowery, I see you're busy as usual, not that I'm surprised, with your fine ass. Do you think you can find a spot on the dance floor with me before the night is out?"

The funniest thing happened in that moment. This woman, the one who not thirty seconds ago thought I was a "fuckboy", began to light up like my name rained money from the heavens. We weren't at an industry party or anything like that, but it's nice to be recognized. "You're Devin Lowery? D-Lo? I mean, for real, for real?"

D-Lo was the moniker I switched to when I progressed from the photography scene. Everyone in that industry knew me as Devin Lowery; I wanted something different when I got ready to shoot videos in the music industry, so I used D-Lo. The name stuck, and that's how I moved in that world. I had thought about going back to my given name when I went to filmmaking, but I figured it was more unique moving forward.

"Wow, Devin, if this girl had to ask who you were, I need to get you out on social media more. You'd have at least a half-million following you on the 'gram right now." Kirsten winked at me, turning to the young lady to lay the accolades on thick. "Girl, this man is magic behind the camera, I can tell you that much. I've seen him turn regular girls into video vixens and video vixens into stars. That reminds me, D-Lo, are you going to be at the *Pleasure* album release party this weekend?"

Pleasure was a hot new girl group that topped the Billboard charts last week. I did the album cover for them and took care of some other promotional work before their label asked me to shoot the video for their hit single.

Jemma tried to find her way into the conversation as best she could. "I love that group! They can give Fifth Harmony and Little Mix a run for their money!"

Kirsten slipped in the space between us, turning her back to Jemma to give me her undivided attention. She had Jemma blocked from my view, and the change of scenery was much more inviting to my eyes. "So, you were saying about being at the release party, sexy? If you do, I promise to wear something slinky and sensual...*only for you*."

To say I was tongue-tied for a brief moment didn't do her proposal justice. Kirsten had the most mesmerizing, smoldering eyes I'd ever seen on a woman, the type that could bring any man to his knees. I no longer noticed Jemma trying her best to slide around Kirsten, desperate to have my attention again.

"Oh, absolutely, Kirsten, I will see you there, and you better wear something sexy for me, too. As good as I make you look on camera...not that I have to work that hard to do it."

I took her hand and made my way to the dance floor, intent on putting Kirsten to work in more ways than one.

Jemma grabbed my arm, slowing me down for a moment. "I'm so sorry, I should have...can we start over? I mean, you're a cutie and all, I really would like to know you better."

If I was in a better mood, I might have given her a second shot. She had about a snowball's shot in hell of success now. "Sorry, sweetness, looks like my dance card is full, and besides, I was a fuckboy a few minutes ago, remember?"

Kirsten laughed as she kissed my lips in front of Jemma, staking her claim. Her lips tasted like mixed exotic fruit, no doubt from the drinks she'd consumed tonight, and her perfume was light and airy, threatening to dull my senses and make me her for the night. "Damn, she called you a fuckboy, too? Later for that trick, D, real women know a decent man when they see one."

Before Jemma could form a response, Kirsten had me on the dance floor and in a sweat in minutes. It was fun to see the dejected look on her face as I looked back before the sea of people closed off my line of sight. Maybe I wasn't supposed to take pleasure in the misery of another person, but I couldn't help it. It almost made me feel better—almost.

After shaking it up with Kirsten for a few songs and setting up a rendezvous for later in the evening, I picked another spot in the club to chill out for a few, when my boys finally remembered that I was still in the club.

They walked up on me to check on me, and I already figured out that Quinn was high within seconds. The rank odor of the Kush in his system was on his breath, his bloodshot eyes confirming my suspicions. Anton was drunk, although he usually got high, too. The alcohol was needed whenever he needed to get loose and keep his courage while spitting game with the ladies.

"Come on, son, I know you got better game than that?" Anton said, looking around like I was supposed to be surrounded by multiple representatives of the fairer sex. "You supposed to have juice, playa."

"Yo, he got a point, D-Lo. This ain't you, what's really going on?" Quinn added.

I was about to explain the incident with Jemma and Kirsten when I saw this caramel-skinned goddess walk towards us. She was tall, and the skirt that she wore gave her legs all kinds of purpose. Thick thighs save lives. It really didn't matter that she had crimson streaks in her hair—I didn't care for that on a woman—my body needed attention.

To hell with the promise I made, I needed to have the validation I was looking for, and this might do the trick. Kirsten could wait; that deal was already sealed. This was the type of challenge I needed.

She slipped between Anton and Quinn, sat down next to me, crossed her legs, and extended her hand out to me, "Hi, I'm Yvonne."

I took her hand and kissed the back of her palm, "My boys call me, D-Lo."

I guess the night wasn't a total loss after all.

"So, what should I call you?" She licked her lips as she asked.

"For now, call me Devin." I felt the need to slow her down. It wasn't that kinda party, but she was sexy and bold with her flow. I liked that in my conquests. From the way that my boys were gawking at her, I decided to take this outside on the deck. "Can we head outside, you know, talk a little more without shouting?"

She nodded and took my hand to lead me outside to the deck area.

Now, my instincts would have given me a reason to stop

and think. *Something's not right with this one, D, she's too aggressive.*

Yeah, like I cared at that moment.

I caught a glimpse of a woman mean-mugging me as Yvonne continued to make her way through the crowd with me in tow. I dismissed her as nothing more than a lesbian trying to throw shade. I guessed she tried to holla at Yvonne earlier and got shot down.

Once we were out on the deck, Yvonne hopped up on the railing, spreading her legs wide enough to make things interesting, and motioned with her finger for me to come closer. "I was hoping I would be able to talk to you. I didn't think I'd get the chance."

"Oh, really now?"

"Yeah, I was. You've got this thing about you. Your eyes, they're pretty. You're really sexy." She continued the ego stroke, and I wanted her to keep feeding it.

"You're pretty sexy yourself, sweetness, showing off those thick legs of yours." I couldn't help but peek at the fact that she wore a thong. Easy access was the special of the night. "So, tell me, when do they open?"

"They might open later tonight if you say the right things. You wanna touch them? I mean, I know you want to be sure they feel as thick as they look, right?"

"Is that all I get to do?"

"Why don't you come closer and find out? You might be surprised what I might let you do." Yvonne leaned forward, grabbing at my arm to pull me in. "Or how long my legs might stay open for you."

She was working her way into becoming the first of my new harem. I couldn't wait to see where this episode would end.

I felt the intense heat between us, which was only enhanced by the mild sixty-degree weather. She didn't care, and I damn sure wasn't about to argue, not with the way that her body felt in my arms at that moment. She kissed me, moving my hand so that my fingers could move the fabric out of the way.

That made me weak. "Damn, girl, what are you doing?"

"I'm trying to get you to fuck me, Devin. Are you telling me it's not working?"

"What makes me so special? You could have had anyone." I tried to keep my composure, but I was failing by the minute.

"Nope, you are a special case, Devin." Yvonne kissed me again. She looked over my shoulder for a brief second, and her face reflecting pure lust when her eyes met mine again. "Let's go to your place, I need some more space to do what I want to do to you."

"How much more space did you need?" I teased. I wanted to know how far she thought she wanted to go.

"I think a king-sized bed might be enough space to do what I want, among other areas." Yvonne kept up the cat-and-mouse, licking and biting my neck before we walked through the club to get to the exit.

I stopped in my tracks, holding her in place. I forgot that I didn't drive tonight. "Hold on, sweetness, I need to let one of my boys know I'm bouncing so we can do this."

I couldn't locate Anton for the life of me, so I went on the hunt for Quinn. I found him near the deejay's booth with some female snuggled up under him like she was trying to be the next jump-off for the evening.

I walked up on him and, since we were so close to the speakers, I yelled in his ear that I had a ride home and I'd catch him later. He barked that he'd let Anton know I was already gone whenever he had the chance to find him. Knowing Anton, he'd already caught one, too, ready to smash at the first available opportunity.

I didn't worry about it too much; I had better things to do now, and she stood about five-foot-eight and had a body to die for.

Alexia

Chapter Three: Late Nights and Early Mornings

Keri yelled at the top of her lungs over the music, trying to get the rest of us in line. We had been rehearsing for the past few weeks, but we were out of sync tonight. We'd had the routine down at other events in the past, but the next few days were different.

Ever since we found out that we had attracted the attention of the executives at RPK Entertainment, it caused us to press harder than usual. We weren't in the right spots, the harmony wasn't as sharp as we were used to, and Keri was not pleased with our effort. None of us were.

"Look, I know you think that this deal can be wrapped up, but you need to get your heads right," Keri continued, turning the music off so she didn't have to yell.

"Relax, Keri, it's just an off night, that's all." Camryn leaned against the wall, taking sips of her bottled water to cool down. "We'll be fine later tonight. *Envyye* will be the talk of the industry once we're done."

We named our R&B girl group *Envyye* because, well, other groups always envied us once we were onstage. There were three of us: Keri, me, and the other member of the group, Camryn. Our manager, Laura, thought it would be a good idea to get us together as a group even though we were all solo artists.

We fought like sisters, but were as tight as sisters were, too. I guess in her mind she felt we could be a TLC-type of group, but in my mind, there would never be another group like them. But it would be nice to have their level of success, though.

"That's your problem, Cam, you think that we can have an off night and everything will go smoothly," Keri fired back. "Well, what if we have an off night tomorrow? All this practicing that we've been doing will be wasted."

"Would you calm down, please? We've been down this road before, and we were on point and still didn't seal the deal. What makes this one any more or less different than the other times?" Camryn's temper was getting the best of her, and it felt like we were two more exchanges away from a full-blown argument.

"Okay, ladies, relax, let's try to concentrate." Laura watched us the whole time, trying to find the right moment to get us back on track. "This time will be different. A lot of the work you've put in has attracted the attention of the real decision makers, not just the A&R reps. Mr. Richton will have his representatives, including his staff photographer, in attendance for the showcase."

That got our attention. Word in the industry was that neither Mr. Richton nor Mr. Parker attended the showcases except on rare occasions. In the event that they do, they are accompanied by the company's top videographer, who worked primarily within the company's media and film department, but he was now handling a lot of their video production. He had found a couple of platinum-selling acts for RPK, but he insisted on staying in the media and film department, with designs to become the company's Director of Photography.

The updated information about Mr. Richton's attendance took things to another level. Someone close to him must have really liked our last performance for him to take time out to take a look at us. Knowing this, I felt the need to find a five-hour energy drink or something to perfect this routine.

"All right, I'll tell you what, let's relax it for tonight, we have been pushing a little bit." I looked at the clock, and realized it was one in the morning. There was no point in pushing to exhaustion. We needed the energy for tonight. "We know the routines, and we know the songs, let's just execute and get this contract, okay?"

"Lexi, you've been right before, we'll cut for tonight." Keri backed down, realizing she might have been pushing a little too hard. She could be a hothead at times, but someone needed to keep things in line at times. I loved her for that. "But we need to be on it for the showcase."

"We got you, Keri, damn. Now, I don't know about you two, but I've got a taste for some wings," Camryn announced, patting her stomach. "Are you rolling with me, ladies?"

The idea of eating wings did not appeal to me in the slightest, but I needed to eat something. I hadn't eaten much, so I was good with making a stop by there to grab a chicken salad or something, maybe grab a wine cooler to help me sleep. "I don't know, I'm not about to eat that heavy tonight. I don't have your cast iron stomach, Cam."

Keri shook her head. "I can't do it tonight, ladies. I don't have the ability to gorge and keep my figure like you, Cam."

I laughed at Keri, but she did have a point. Camryn could eat damn near anything and not gain a pound. If either one of us even looks at a cheesecake wrong, five pounds showed up with the wave of a magic wand.

Still, I couldn't let her hang by herself. Downtown Atlanta could be a bit rough for women after a certain time of night. "Cam, I'll roll and meet you there. Keri, we'll catch up with you in the morning."

Deion

Chapter Four: What Goes Around Comes Around

"You have a beautiful place, Devin."

Yvonne perused the erotic art on my walls, pieces I purchased from my art school friends that had gone on to bigger and better things. She looked at everything in my space—except me. It didn't make any sense; she was all over me at the club, damn near ready for me to smash in the warm air of the night on the deck at the club, and now she wanted to stall like she was a born-again virgin?

Something's up, I could feel it. "So, why are you acting shy on me, Yvonne?"

"I'm not shy, Devin, but I haven't really done this before."

I moved behind her, and while her hips didn't lie, her eyes spoke a different truth. "Are you having second thoughts? I understand if it's too much."

"Just fuck me now, please." She took my manhood out, dropped to her knees and took me in her mouth before I could protest about the weirdness of her vibe.

She pulled me down on top of her, trying to slide me in before I could get the condom on. I'd be damned if she was going to succeed in that endeavor. There was no way in hell she was gonna trap me into some Plan B conversation the next morning. My body was at war with my mind, and my body was winning that war once the condom was on and the other head was ready to do battle.

Something's wrong, D, she's too quick about this shit.

My body had other ideas. *Do you see the dime piece under us, begging to be fucked right now? Are you mental, bruh? We're about to have this bitch walking sideways by the time we're done, with or without you.*

Yvonne bucked her hips, urging me to slide a little deeper, her body reacting like there was something I needed to erase from deep within her essence. I drilled into her, kept pounding her even after she came.

I took her in the kitchen.

I bent that ass over in the shower doggie-style while we were washing off from the interlude in the kitchen.

I got her one more time in the bedroom, making her ride me so we could both pass out. I wasn't about to put in all the work; I needed to see what them hips could do, and I had every intention to find out what that mouth did the minute I was ready to take the condom off and erupt down her throat.

She was already spent, trying her best to catch her breath, and there was nothing more that needed to be said. I couldn't fall asleep fast enough, and the way she began to slumber, I knew I'd gotten exactly what I needed, and it was needed.

If I was lucky, she'd want to get worked over again in the morning, and I couldn't wait to put that work on her. Much to my chagrin, sleep would be the last thing I would be getting, thanks to a series of determined knocks on my door minutes later.

"Vonne, bring your ass out here now!" The voice on the other side of the door was female, there was no doubt about that, but I couldn't understand why she was knocking on *my* door. "Get your ass out here before I break this goddamned door down!"

I reached in my nightstand for my Glock, but Yvonne stopped me. I gave her a look that could melt iron. "What the fuck are you stopping me for? If this keeps up, my neighbors are gonna be out trying to figure out what's going on."

"Devin, don't…she's…it's complicated."

I was already looking for my jogging pants before I grabbed for my piece to head downstairs. "The hell it is complicated. How did whoever the fuck this woman is even know you were here?"

Yvonne hesitated a moment before she confessed…well, sort of. "Look, she and I were together."

The words wouldn't come out of my mouth, no matter how much I wanted them to. "Were together? Wait a damned minute, the knocking I'm hearing does not sound like a woman who you used to be with."

Yvonne was ready to go on the defensive, like I was going to go in a whole other direction. "You hate me, don't you? I knew you would hate me."

"I don't hate anyone, but you're not making it easy to like you right now." I rubbed my hands over my face, but I kept my gun in my lap. Whoever I would be facing in a minute would have malicious intentions the moment I opened the door. In a flash, it dawned on me, in light of the advancement of technology. "Let me guess, find my iPhone app on your cell, right?"

The pounding persisted, and it was only a matter of time before this woman would make good on her threat. "Vonne, get out here, goddammit!"

"You got three seconds to explain to me why a woman you claim you're no longer with is pounding on my door like she's fucking APD or some shit before I get out of bed and find out for myself." I needed to go see about things before my neighbors would. This had the potential to go left in a heartbeat.

I gave the silent count of three and stood up to slip on my pants. Yvonne grabbed for my arm, flinching as I snatched it away from her grasp. She looked up at me, the guilt evident in her eyes. "I'm married. That's my wife downstairs making a fuss."

I felt like I'd been shot with a twelve-gauge shotgun. "Anything else you want to declare?"

She hesitated for a moment, trying to reach out to me to help drive home her original thought. "I didn't tell you before because…you looked so damn good, and…I didn't think you would have slept with me if you knew beforehand."

Her instincts were dead on. Of course, I wouldn't have fucked her if I'd known she was married. Sure, even in the advent of gay marriage, I still wouldn't have if she was married. I didn't want that kind of karma in my life.

In the span of a couple of hours, due to my game and instincts being way off, I had done exactly what I had no plans of doing. Now I had drama I didn't want to deal with staring at me with bad intentions. All in the name of validation.

Nice one, D-Lo, real nice.

"I can't believe this shit. Out of all the women I could have had tonight, and I go and fuck a lesbian with dick on the brain." I bemoaned my fate, irritated that I had to prove I could pull a new piece of ass instead of enjoying a stress-free night of carnal dancing with Kirsten.

"None of the others were sorry about fucking me, what the fuck makes you so special?" She huffed, her "sorrow" in getting busted no longer evident on her face. The fact that she was pissed that I was irritated about fucking her under false pretenses was enough to make me go nuclear.

In the midst of my growing anger at a situation that would have been a good one for the *WorldStar HipHop* website, one word cut through the murky fog with laser precision. Others? There were others?

"Damn, I should have known better, but that's cool, too. I wanted it as bad as you did, but I'm not the one fucking around on my mate, either." I laughed at myself on that one, ignoring the scowl on her face. "You're right, this ain't happening again, and you need to bounce."

I dragged her down the stairs toward the pounding door, not even caring that she had yet to get dressed. I opened the door, coming face to face with the woman who gave me the evil eye in the club earlier tonight. I slung Yvonne in her direction, no longer in the mood to have this drag out any more than it already had. "She's all yours, *bruh*."

Yvonne hurried to get dressed as her wife continued to berate her for betraying her yet again and falling for another weak-ass man who couldn't take care of her the way she could. She tried to bring her vitriol in my direction, looking like she wanted to catch a fade. I laughed; lesbian or not, if she stepped to me like a man, she was gonna catch this fade like one if she even thought about swinging on me.

Sure enough, she advanced toward me, fists balled like she had malicious intentions on her mind. One glance at the Glock in my hand made her reassess her situation. Instead, she continued her verbal assault. "Do you even feel bad about fucking my wife?"

"Nope, I'm not, although I should be. She lied to me to get back at you for whatever you did. I'm not the one you should be coming for."

"You're a sorry ass brotha!"

"And you obviously need to treat your *wife* a little better, or she wouldn't have been begging to get run-through the way she did tonight." I smirked. I felt like being a jerk after all I'd been put through.

I caught a glimpse of my neighbors coming out of their houses, trying to figure out what all the fuss was about. My neighborhood was quiet for the most part, and this would be the most excitement they would have for at least another few months. I could only imagine what the next HOA meeting would look like, but it was a good guess I would be one of the topics of conversation.

As a last effort to get her to turn up, I offered one more unsolicited piece of advice. "You might wanna give her a few days before you stroke that again. She's gonna be a little sore after being handled by something other than polyurethane."

"Bastard! You can go to hell!"

"I don't do requests, love. Now, you and your woman can leave, okay? My neighbors won't be happy about you disturbing the peace like this, and I already have to smooth things over as it is."

As I watched Yvonne pick up her clothes and hurry after her significant other while calling me everything but a child of

God for throwing her out of my condo, I'd reached the point to where there was nothing more to say.

I assured my next-door neighbor that all was well and I apologized to her for causing the disturbance. I was fortunate that I hadn't had any incidents before tonight, so there was no need to bring the police into the mix. The fact that I even had to say anything was enough to keep me in a high state of irritability. She was gracious in her acceptance of my apology, though, and an offer to cook dinner seemed to be a cure-all for the inconvenience she'd dealt with.

I needed some air. The walls were closing in on me, and the sooner that they could leave the subdivision, the sooner I could head out and get some food. Dealing with this not only made my head hurt, but it gave me one hell of an appetite.

Some wings or some barbecue was the perfect cure for all that ailed me. I grabbed my keys and headed out the door, intent on heading to the one spot that I always went to whenever I needed to take things off my mind.

Alexia

Chapter Five: Crown Royal on Ice

It was a crazy night for a Saturday, despite the time we walked into Fox Brothers Bar-B-Q in Northeast Atlanta. There wasn't a seat to be had in the place, and we did what we could to find any space in the place while we waited for our orders. We got lucky, finding barstools up front after ordering, and Camryn was already in rare form, flirting with one of the college football players to pass the time while I ignored his friend, who thought I was supposed to fawn all over him once we found he was projected to be a first round pick in the upcoming NFL Draft. He was cute, but he looked like trouble, and that wasn't what I wanted right now.

Camryn didn't care either way; she liked being a tease, it was part of her newly-formed persona she'd wanted to use when we leveled up. The way I saw this scenario playing out, she'd have that boy eating out the palm of her hand, promising him that the gold between her legs would be worth waiting a couple of weeks until the Draft so he could fly her out to Dallas and give him the time of his life—until her order came up.

While I was listening to the game that Camryn was taking in from her temporary object of desire, this man walked into the place like he owned it. The arrogance was evident in his walk, but his presence could not be denied. Even the wait staff acted like he deserved their full attention, making sure that they spoke to him the minute they passed him. Even the other patrons noticed, and they couldn't stop whispering amongst themselves, trying to figure out who the mystery man was.

To command that type of attention and all he had on was jeans and a polo shirt? I couldn't front, it had my attention— along with every other woman in the restaurant. I didn't know how to feel about that, but I wasn't there for him, I was there to pick up my chicken salad and leave. Despite my best efforts, I couldn't resist being nosey and trying to ear hustle a little bit to see what the fuss was about.

He stared in my direction for a brief moment, flashing a smile before he turned his attention to the bartender to get something to sip on while waiting for his order. There was something about him that screamed for me to want to see about him. His demeanor told me that he could have given a fuck whether I noticed him or not. That unnerved me, not so much that he should have noticed me checking for him, but that I cared one way or the other if he did.

Camryn caught his attention, too; the youngster she was all into at the time faded to black. "Girl, what's up with that fine piece of sexiness over there? The one trying to be all casual GQ and everything."

"Who, him?" I feigned interest, but I didn't stop looking in his direction. "Ain't nobody worrying about him, Cam."

"Well, maybe you're trying to not look like you ain't

checking for him, but the rest of these women in here are definitely trying to see about something," Camryn replied, turning my head in his direction after I had taken great pains to do otherwise. "I wonder what the deal is with him. He's got all these folks snapping and moving like he's got investment dollars in the place."

"He's got playa written all over him." I snapped my head out of her hands, making sure my body didn't give me away. "I don't need to see nothing these other tricks are trying to see."

Camryn had other plans as she locked eyes with him the minute he turned away from the bar. She gave a quick smile and waved at him to come over. The sense of dread I felt was enough to have me bolt for the first exit I could find.

The moment he moved in our direction, it took everything in me to keep from vacating the area and leaving Cam to deal with this madness. I wasn't in the mood to dealing with pretentious jackasses tonight when I was hungry and tired from rehearsal.

The cologne he wore was the first thing to consume me the moment he entered our area. It caused my other senses to open to him, aroused the curiosity that I didn't want to have at that moment. No matter what I thought I wanted, my curiosity had to be satisfied.

I hated when that happened. I wanted to believe I had more restraint than that, but at the end of the day, I was on a self-imposed hiatus from relationships. Despite my intended resolve, a girl had needs, and it was only a matter of time before someone would have the swagger to break down my defenses. Still, if they had to be broken, he was worth the reason for them to be broken.

"Good evening, ladies." His smile was enough to make me melt. Damn, even the tone in his voice was commanding. "How are you doing? Suffering from late night munchies, too, huh?"

"Hello, *gorgeous*." Camryn noticed the change in my body language, and she laid it on thick, asking questions she thought I wanted the answers to, when she was the one whose curiosity needed to be satisfied. "We couldn't help noticing, you know, with all these people giving you all this attention. Are you one of the owners or something?"

"I'm sorry, you have me at a disadvantage, Miss?"

"Goodness, where are my manners? I'm Camryn, and this is my girl, Alexia." Camryn put on the full act of being interested in him. "And no, we don't have you at a disadvantage, sexy, but now that you know our names, what's yours?"

"You have a good point there. I'm Devin, and no, I'm not the owner." He chuckled, amused by the assumption. "I've been coming here since I was little, and they know my father pretty well. Best barbecue in the city, hands down."

I still couldn't look at him, but I felt his eyes on me. I gathered myself as best I could, turning in his direction to speak and not be rude. "It's nice to meet you, Devin."

I had to get some control over this feeling that he brought out of me, so I forced my eyes to meet his. It was a risk; I had an affinity for confident men who bordered on the arrogant. He fit the description to the letter, and I was already prepared to dismiss him with all due haste.

I looked in his eyes, and as much as I wanted to see what I'd expected to see, I saw something else. I saw hurt and vulnerability mixed in with the confidence and swagger. He wasn't egotistical, at least not on full-tilt, and I think that's what drew me in. He was irresistible, there was no doubt about that, but it was this complication within him, the fact that I couldn't figure him out at face value, it captured me, with no chance of escape.

By the time Camryn had a chance to say another word to him to see how much further she could probe, the sound of his name over the loud speakers interrupted the flow.

"Well, it was nice meeting you, Camryn and Alexia." Devin stood up from his stool, extending his hand to both of us to shake our hands. "I hope that the rest of your night treats you well."

"There's no need in rushing off without getting your number, Devin." Camryn batted her eyes at him, shifting her weight in his direction so he could get a good view of her chest. "Maybe one of us—or both of us—can call you sometime, invite you to one of our performances. In fact, we have one later on tonight. We're a part of a singing group."

"Oh really?" Devin's interest seemed to pique for a short minute before he went back to being his smooth and nonchalant self. "Well, how about we do this: why don't you tell me when and where you're performing later, and I'll make sure I stop by with some of my boys, see if you girls can blow."

I tried to hide my annoyance over his reluctance to give up his number, but I was intrigued that he had two fine ass women trying to get at him and he didn't even flinch. Any other man would have been frothing at the mouth if they were in his position.

As much as I needed to dismiss him, there was still something in his eyes that told me there was more to him than the swagger that seemed to sweat off of him. I wanted to find out what that was.

"We're performing later tonight, at the Masquerade," Camryn offered up the details of the showcase without a single thought, ignoring my glare as she continued her pitch. "And bring your boys, we have a third girl in the group who wouldn't mind a little attention after the set, too."

"Fair enough, I'll make sure of it." Devin pulled out his smartphone, and I noticed he had the new iPhone X, and typed the information in. "Okay, you said the Masquerade, right? And you'll be performing around what time, again?"

"Eleven."

"Cool, locked in, and my boys have been texted on it, too." Devin grinned after receiving a text back from someone seconds later. "Ladies, would you mind posing for a picture? One of my boys wants to see who we're supposed to be supporting."

I hesitated. He was taking control and we were only talking about the showcase. I wanted to stand firm and tell him we weren't about to sit pretty for some random dude that we'd never met before. Who does that?

I got poked in the side a few times, Camryn's universal sign that she wanted to go along with the idea. "Okay. Come on, Lexi, I'm sure his boy's no slouch, either."

After we posed for the picture, Devin opened the FaceTime app. I assumed the dude he was connecting with was the one that wanted to see us. A few seconds later, Devin lifted the phone to adjust for the lighting. "Yo, Q, these are the girls I just texted you about."

Devin turned the face of the phone towards us and said, "Say hello to DJ Infinity, ladies."

"Hi, DJ Infinity!" We yelled toward the phone. At first, I

didn't want to believe it was him, but there he was, in the flesh! I was convinced he was pulling some bullshit since we said we were in a singing group.

"Hi, ladies," he replied back through the video feed. "Damn, you sound as sexy as you look. My boy's telling me you'll be performing at the Masquerade tonight."

"Okay, are you really *the* DJ Infinity?" Camryn was incredulous, and I couldn't blame her. DJ Infinity was one of the biggest deejays in the country. We couldn't believe that we were that close to someone who knew him. No one could be *that* lucky.

"Yeah, it's me, ladies, in the flesh. I know it might not sound like it right now, but, if you know the sounds I'm dealing with, then you'll understand why I don't sound like myself." He sounded like he was switching tracks in the studio. I recognized the sound and realized that Devin was telling the truth. "My boy wasn't playing. We'll be there, no doubt."

"All right, bruh, I'll get at you in a few." Devin disconnected the video feed. He gave a nod, recognizing our skepticism. The grin on his face gave away his satisfaction that he'd proven us wrong in our assumption. "So, ladies, will we see you tomorrow?"

I wanted to scream on the inside. All I wanted to do was get something to eat, and now thanks to Camryn, we had added pressure, performing for one of the deejays that might be spinning our tracks one day soon. I did everything I could to make it look like I wasn't impressed, but nothing could have been further from the truth.

If he kept this up, I was bound to be in more trouble than I could handle, and for once, I didn't care. I offered my hand,

and after watching Devin kiss the back of my palm, there was no denying that he could get it the first chance he got.

I found my voice to respond to him, thankful that our names sounded off over the loud speakers to let us know our orders were ready. I used that opportunity to shake off the lust in my heart and the heat rising from my body. Grabbing our food, I stopped to look up at him once more, realizing that if I stood there any longer, my body would betray me. "See you tomorrow, Devin."

The smoothness of his tone threatened to turn my legs into gelatin as he responded to me, insistent on getting the last word. "I'm looking forward to it, pretty girl. Be safe getting home, I wouldn't want anything to happen to either one of you."

"Such a gentleman, too. Do you want us to swap numbers so we can text you when we get home?" Camryn was in total slut mode, dragging me into the madness with her.

A smirk crossed his lips, a sure sign that he was enjoying this way too much. "That won't be necessary, I'm sure you know how to handle yourselves. Besides, I'm sure there are some gentlemen who don't mind making sure you get home in one piece."

"There's nothing wrong with having another one to ensure we're safe. One look at you and I feel safer already." Camryn continued to ignore me as I tugged at her arm to get her out the door. "I guess for now, we will have to find a way to have you earn that spot."

"I have to want to earn that spot, but I see where you're going with this." He raised his eyebrow, looking like he was losing control of the situation. "I'll see you two Saturday night. Enjoy the rest of your evening."

The minute we got outside to our cars, I was ready to smack the taste out of her mouth. "Did you just have to serve it up on a platter, woman?"

"Well, since you didn't want to, I wasn't about to let all that fineness go to waste," Camryn huffed. "I'm gonna need you to stop with this born-again virgin mess, it's bad for business. We aren't a gospel group, we're R&B and Pop, okay?"

"What I plan to do and who I plan to do it with is not part of the group's narrative, okay?"

"Well, you better figure out something and soon, or else we're going to have to figure it out for you. If you don't wanna get at him, I'll have no problem handling that, for real."

I narrowed my eyes as I got in my car, not sure whether I wanted to acknowledge what she was saying or not. What I did know was that, in her own annoying way, she might have been right. And I hated when she was right, but I didn't want to do anything about it in that moment.

Maybe I should have been more aggressive in seeing about him. My body was all for the plan, but my mind and heart had other ideas.

All I wanted was to eat my dinner in peace and process, and I was going to do that, even if I was doing my best not to think about the handsome stranger who insisted on making me swoon.

Alexia

Chapter Six: Too Gone, Too Long

"Why are you here? What do you want? I'm not in the mood for your BS tonight."

Seeing the reason why I swore off men standing at the doorway to my apartment was the last thing I needed. I was still trying to calm down from the heightened state of arousal I'd subjected myself to from trying not to flirt with Devin, and I did not want to take out my fuckstrations out on this fool.

My ex-boyfriend Troy had this silly grin on his face as I walked toward him, opening his arms in an attempt to welcome me with a hug. That grin faded when it was met with stone-cold contempt. "Come on, Peaches, I know you're not still mad at me?"

He tried to close the space between us, but I placed my palm against his chest and straightened out my arm to let him know my personal space would not be invaded. He no longer deserved that right. He raised his eyebrow, resigning himself to the obvious. "Okay, I think that answers my question."

"I hate repeating myself. What do you want, Troy?" My food was getting cold and this wasted conversation threatened to piss me off. "I have a lot of stuff to do before my showcase tonight, and I need to get some sleep."

"See, that's the problem, you were always thinking it was about me." Troy exhaled. He cocked his head to the side, trying to figure out my mood. "You know that I was always focused on us, baby."

"Mmmhmmm, so focused that you decided that having another chick sucking and fucking you in *my* car was for *our* benefit, right?" I shot a look at him that shut him down. "That's what I thought."

"Aight, look, Alexia, I ain't come to argue." Troy's demeanor changed up, switching to a more serious tone. He was never serious while we were together. "I know I fucked up, but we were good together, you know that."

"Yeah, you fucked up, that part you definitely got right." I huffed, pushing him out of my way to get to my door. "Now, if you will excuse me, I have to try and eat something before I crash."

"Yeah, I know, your *music career* comes first," he spat. "We all know you and your group are on the verge of superstardom any day now, right?"

The anger in his eyes was something new. His tone, it was never there before, even when things went bad between us. He never bad-mouthed my music or the group; he was an up-and-coming HipHop artist himself, trying to break out solo from the group he's been with since before we got together. His problem was that he wanted me to be a wannabe superstar's girlfriend who was cool with being behind the scenes.

Now that I thought about it, the whole issue with ol' girl

didn't bother me all that much. We were dating, so it wasn't like he locked me down with a ring or something like that. My ring fingers were as bare as naked daylight, and I didn't have papers on him, either.

If he was straight up, I might have been good with the program. As high as his sex drive was, I would have welcomed the break to let some other chick handle the sex marathons I wasn't willing to bother with anymore. It might not have been a popular opinion, but it would have been nice to have a break from his tiresome ass. Hell, maybe I would have had a piece or two on the side for myself.

Truth be told, he was becoming a bit boring in bed, pulling the same tired moves to get me aroused and the same tired strokes to keep my juices flowing. If he had the chance to learn something new from some other trick and bring it home to switch things up, I might have been able to roll with that. Still, he violated my car with a bitch who didn't hold a candle to me despite her belief that she was willing to do what I wouldn't do, and I still won't do: be a groupie and girlfriend to the "great" TramaDryl.

"Yeah, my career comes first, and the fact that you didn't bother supporting it, but you could support your need to keep your magic stick wet even though I was fucking you like a porn star is the reason you're stuck right now." I let him have it with both barrels, no longer in the mood for this conversation to continue.

"Alexia, I...okay, I caught you at a bad time, and you need some sleep, maybe that's why you're all hormonal right now." Troy backed off, heading toward the parking lot. "But we're not done talking about this. I know you're not over me yet, I can feel it on you, shawty."

"Go, Troy. I mean it, get the fuck away from me!" I slammed the door on him, irritated beyond words. Damn, he killed the buzz that I was on, but I hated the fact that he was right.

I wasn't over him, at least, not yet. It had been months since we called it quits, but he still had an effect on me, and that was something I wasn't comfortable with. I thought about the good times we had, the way he made me feel when we were in the throes of passion, the way he loved me in his own unique way.

It all came flooding back in an instant, whether I chose to remember it or not. It was so easy to ignore things, but it was times like this—when that temper and selfishness reared its ugly head—that made it easier to dismiss him from my life all over again without a second thought.

Still, I was tempted to reconsider my decision while he was still within shouting distance. I was in heat, held prisoner by unabashed fantasies about a man that I had yet to even have a full conversation with. My body wanted it, if only for the temporary release, but my mind made it crystal clear that I'd made that mistake once before, and I was not about to make that mistake again.

Considering that he caused me to have to microwave the chicken for my salad only gave me another good reason I didn't let him in. I wanted to beat his ass for causing my food to get cold, but that anger would have manifested itself into something else. It always did when it came to us.

No matter how feral I felt, I couldn't let him back inside. He'd been gone too long to ever get back in like that, too long to ever get back to where he thought he wanted to be.

As I waited for my chicken to warm up, my thoughts slipped back to the handsome stranger who I—for some strange reason—had me nervous about performing in front of for the first time in years. Why he had me like that would be the focus of my thoughts until I finished my salad and headed upstairs to unwind.

It had been such a long day that I needed to release and relieve the tension that I'd put my body through. The rehearsal, the two hours at the gym to keep my body thick and tight, my hormones in a frenzied state while flirting with Devin, and the final straw of the anger of going through bullshit with Troy. A hot bath—a good, long soak—was needed on levels I couldn't quite explain.

Filling the tub with water, I poured some vanilla-scented bath oils in to mix and lather while I slipped out of my clothes to prepare to slide in and indulge my senses. Thoughts of the encounter with this man wouldn't leave me alone. I caressed my skin, imagining my hands were his, slipping over my hips, my ass, moving over every inch of skin I was ready to make available to him.

Lexi, get a grip on yourself. It was harmless. You flirt with men all the time on stage.

My mind was convinced, but my body was on a whole other wavelength. The men I chose to flirt with during shows, I barely remembered once I got home. That was the first thing Laura schooled us on, to make sure that we didn't develop any stalkers, but that was hard to do in this social media crazed world we lived in.

Yet, in the span of fifteen minutes, this man made sure he was hard for me to forget him.

Before my body decided that it wanted to go from a slow

burn into a raging inferno, I turned off the lights, lit enough candles to give the room a warm glow, and slid my body through the coolness of the bubbles before my skin became intimate with the enveloping warmth of the water below.

No matter how soothing the bath was, those vivid images I thought I left at the vanity followed me, and I found my body writhing ever so slowly through the water, trying to find the fingers that wouldn't be there tonight.

God, what the hell had he done to me?

Taking hold of the loofah, I washed my body, sliding it over my legs and arms and across my shoulders and neck. The water dripped down my chest, teasing my nipples before returning to the pool's surface. My mind wandered as I washed arms and legs over and over again, the steam from the bath sending me into my misty, vanilla-scented world.

My skin felt alive again. I felt so sensual, so sexy, watching my caramel-hued skin shine against the radiance of the candlelight. My mind drifted further and further into the fantasy my mind created for me, not caring about the selfish nature of the fantasy itself. I closed my eyes, succumbing to the journey that I was so desperate to begin, and the destination that I couldn't wait to get to.

Although I was done with my bath, my body wasn't done with me. I turned on the faucet, pulling the plug to let the water drain from the basin at the same time. I was intent on not losing the heat that consumed me.

I was mesmerized by the flow of the water from the spout, splashing into the pool below. Within minutes, my sex soon replaced the porcelain being pounded by the water falling from the spout. My mind took me to him, imagining something long, strong, and chocolate, drilling into my wanton, succulent lips, taking in every inch he had to offer.

My hips gyrated and swayed, creating a dance all their own as my eyes fixated on the water, the intensity of the heat returning to my bath, much to my delight. My back arched and my hips thrust forward. So acute was the urge to feel my climax that I was willing to risk submerging my head underwater and the possibility of drowning, if for nothing else than to feel that little death consume my body and show no mercy in giving it what it wanted.

I lifted my butt and arched my back so that only my feet touched the floor of the basin and my arms propped against the side of the bathtub. Droplets cascaded like a waterfall while I held the position for those titillating moments. My clit felt hard and erect as I became aware of warm moistness forming inside. I was desperate for a long, hard fuck, and my mind was made up on who it was that I wanted to fuck me long and hard. I only wished that he could feel how much I wanted it from him.

The tips of my fingers found my clit and wandered across it as I submerged my body beneath the water again. A desperate ache surged and the pressure from my fingers only heightened it.

The water kept coming, working in tandem with my fingers like a liquid tongue, bringing me closer to the edge of orgasmic bliss. I didn't dare stop the flow, even though the rock and sway of my hips against the rhythm that I created with the water began to splash out of the tub and onto the floor.

Faster and faster, my fingers rubbed. Faster and faster, my fingers plunged in and out, my mind giving me images that I could no longer deny anymore. Tensing, as my body neared climax, I screamed out for him as the orgasmic waves washed over me, taking me to that destination that I'd longed to go.

I finally turned off the water, still throbbing and no one to put this fire out. I blushed at how horny I was, that I still needed another wave to crash so I could go to sleep and dream about those hands of his, taking possession of me in ways that I begged for.

By the time I got out of the tub, I finally felt the rush of exhaustion sweep me off my feet, knowing the Sandman would soon come to claim me. For the first time in a long time, I couldn't wait for him to come for me. He was in for one hell of a ride tonight.

Alexia

Chapter Seven: Say Yes

Saturday night was finally here. The three years of rehearsing, going through different showcases, talent shows, the promised studio time that never came to be, the sweat, tears, watching other groups that we felt didn't hold a candle to us signing a contract, only to not sell worth a damn. All of that pent-up emotion, talent, heart and soul would come out tonight.

I was so hyper that I felt that I could reach octaves that only Mariah could pitch. The way that rehearsal went a few hours ago, we all felt that way. This showcase would be the launching point. There was nowhere to go but up.

I imagined having that conversation with Mr. Richton and Mr. Parker that Monday morning, with Laura being all smiles, giving them the DVD of tonight's performance, having Mr. Parker asking for a live set right there in his office, if only to prove that we weren't a fluke. Then, an offer and a deal right there on the spot; the type of dollars that would take things to the next level.

No more working at the bank. No more trying to catch up on sleep before class at school, although I was a class or two shy of finishing my Bachelor's degree in Communications. And last but not least, no more playing showcases.

We would be so hot that the new Mercedes-Benz Stadium wouldn't be able to hold the crowds we would draw.

All of that would come to fruition, but first, we had to take care of business.

I went out to take a look at the crowd, scanning the front area where the VIPs were normally seated. Before I focused on the people that were sitting there, I said a quick prayer that the executives from RPK would be there. I didn't want to take anything to chances. Too much was riding on it. I didn't know if it was a relief to see the seats reserved for RPK were filled or if it was cause to put more pressure on us now that they were here.

My heart skipped a beat as I snuck a peek at Devin, sitting next to an older man. He wore a dark suit and banded collared shirt, not the shirt and tie that I would have expected a CEO to adorn. He was handsome, the type of handsome that made you do a double take, wondering if you could believe how gorgeous he was.

He and Devin were having a rather jovial conversation, an almost father-son type of conversation, so that's who I assumed it was. I saw Quinn and another dude that I didn't recognize, but I knew Camryn would be happy to be in the same company as DJ Infinity.

"I see you've peeped the RPK folk, huh, girl?" Camryn broke into my thoughts. "Who would have thought that sexy ass was rubbing elbows with some of the heavy hitters in the industry? Damn, now I know I should have laid it out for him to get it. One word in Mr. Richton's ear and it's a wrap."

I ignored her attempt at trying to sneak claim as I continued to observe Devin and Mr. Richton continue to entertain the masses surrounding their area. The thought of seeing Devin excited me like nothing else had, but it made me uneasy at the same time. *He* was the one Laura's sources were talking about, and I didn't know how to feel about the fact that he never said a word about it when we met.

I had to check myself. It wasn't like I'd made myself available to have that type of conversation. I didn't want to overthink it, but how could I not?

On the one hand, he would be one of the ones who would have influence over my career. On the other hand, that might cause a conflict of interest, and it might keep me from exploring what my body wanted. Being caught between a proverbial rock and hard place wasn't the best place to be in, but I wasn't assuming anything, either.

I wasn't sure if I wanted him to tell me upfront so I could deal with him in a different manner, or if I was happy to find out on my own. He'd picked the last two platinum-selling artists for RPK, which meant him being here might have big-time implications for our career. Maybe, if I could stop overanalyzing for a few seconds, I could have the best of both worlds.

Damn, he already had me second guessing myself. That was a feeling I hated more than anything. I wasn't ready to give my power to someone else, and I wasn't about to start— not until I was sure. One thing was for certain, he wasn't about to have that power over me the way that I allowed the other night. This night would be mine, and he would recognize the power I would have over him. He simply didn't know it yet.

"Laura, please, you and the ladies have a seat, be our guests."

We were on a high after the songs we'd belted out, harmonizing better than we'd ever been able to do before. The crowd was eating out of our hands, the men couldn't stop staring at the dresses that we wore for the night, reminiscent of En Vogue's ensemble in their *Hold On* video, complete with singing the actual song for the demo.

Keri took the lead on the first song as she wooed the men in the crowd, while the three of us flowed on the up-tempo jam Camryn and I collaborated on. It was so hot that we'd hoped to include it as the first single off the album, if we ever got to the point of making an album.

It was interesting to see the men in the crowd respond to Keri, who was an out-and-proud lesbian. I guessed that sex appeal was universal; it didn't matter how you identified when they thought they could have you.

I was intent on locking eyes with Devin during the entire set, playing a personal cat-and-mouse game with him. Watching his expressions during the songs, wanting him to want me now that he'd gotten a chance to see me sexed up and on display for his—and others'—entertainment and appreciation was intoxicating.

We weren't allowed to be in close proximity with the audience, at least not the way we wanted to, but if given the chance, a lap dance, even in that dress, would have been on the menu when it came to him. I wanted him off balance the way he'd had me off balance since we first met. The vibe between us was intense, and that scared me a little; I was playing with fire, and it would be a matter of time before that would consume me.

Neither one of us, through the glances that we gave each other, wanted to back down, which only heated things up. The more I tried to push, the more he pushed back, and I couldn't resist the urge to push further than he was comfortable with, realizing that he could push back harder and further than I was ready for him to go. I wanted him to take me there, even if it was against my will. *Damn, he's got me going again...I can't have him making me so naughty yet. I need to regain control, dammit.*

I sat in the chair next to Keri, a strategic positioning to create some space from Devin. It was all a part of the cat-and-mouse, and I could tell from the smirk on his face that he enjoyed the play, too. I wanted to keep it going until one of us gave in to the other. I didn't care what I had to do to not give in. He was going to earn this platinum between my thighs.

My better judgment did its best to offer some clarity, reminding me of the ultimate goal, and the fact that the light at the end of the tunnel was getting brighter by the minute. *Calm down, Lexi, remember your promise to yourself. He's not worth the trouble; your career comes first.*

I tried to clear my thoughts, admonishing myself for being so weak at the first sign of flesh of the masculine persuasion. I wasn't going to shy away from my self-imposed celibacy, but I wasn't about to be a born-again virgin forever, either. I had to resign myself to one simple truth: my resolve was melting away with each passing moment around him. The only way I would be able to get rid of temptation was to yield to it, or I would combust into a puddle on the floor.

Mr. Richton took out his cigar cutter, taking his time clipping the enclosed end before taking a match and lighting the stick. As he waived the flame out and pulled a couple of times, he looked at our manager with a satisfied smile on his face. "Laura, I think you've got a great group on your hands!"

That statement was music to my ears, but it always came with a "but" at the end of it. Not this time. Not the way that he was smiling.

"Here's what's going to happen: we're going to take a tape for tonight's event of the group's performance, I want Parker to hear you to make sure we're on the same page," Mr. Richton explained. "He's currently out of town dealing with one of our film projects, but I will personally send a copy by email to him so that, if he likes what he hears, he can be prepared for a meeting with you and the ladies in about three business days. Does that sound agreeable to you?"

"Mr. Richton, my girls might have other deals on the table by then." Laura's facial expression gave no indication that she wanted to say yes or no. She wanted to play hard ball by calling Mr. Richton's bluff. The way I figured it, he could have had Mr. Parker on FaceTime or Skype or something so he could listen in on the performance from where he was. We trusted her to handle the hard-nosed stuff; she was tough as nails. "I can't promise anything at this point, especially after tonight's performance. My girls will be on fire by Monday morning. The public is hot for girl groups, especially with Little Mix doing their thing overseas and Fifth Harmony still rocking Stateside, never mind all the K-Pop girl groups in Asia killing it, I may be calling you to counteroffer. You saw the other record companies that were here, do you honestly believe that we won't have at least three offers on the table to consider?"

Mr. Richton raised an eyebrow for a second or two, leaning back in the chair to ponder his next move. He looked at me before he turned his attention to Camryn, flashing a grin in Keri's direction, all while puffing on his cigar. I looked over at Devin, but his body language gave nothing away. My eyes pleaded with him to give me some sign. He slowly shook his head before he mouthed the words, *We're on the same page, Alexia. Play the game.*

I was almost sure we were sunk, and I waited for the hammer to come down on yet another potential album deal that would never happen. Mr. Richton instead gave a knowing wink toward Devin, acting like they'd been down this path before.

He flashed his eyes, meeting with Laura's stare, giving the impression that he would not be denied and that this would happen on his terms. I could have sworn I saw our manager turn beet red from blushing. I couldn't blame her; from the look that he gave her, it would have been enough to make me melt on the spot, too.

"I see my partner is in the midst of his usual hardline pitches to a prospective group." All eyes turned toward another gentleman who'd interrupted the stare-down between Laura and Mr. Richton. "Does anyone want to fill me in on the details? Rich wouldn't look like this unless things have taken an unexpected turn."

Camryn kept kicking my leg under the table, her eyes fixated on him, which seemed to irritate Quinn big time. I didn't care either way, I was still enjoying the energy between me and the object of my desires.

"Parker, I didn't think you would make it back in time for tonight's event, my friend." Mr. Richton didn't bother to hide the smile on his face upon seeing his business partner arrive at a rather opportune moment within the initial negotiations process. "I was just telling Laura that we would be very interested in signing her group, but we needed to hear them in person together so we could come to a consensus."

Mr. Parker nodded, getting the quick update to provide a seamless transition into the conversation. "Rich, I trust your judgment, but just to be on the safe side, let's go with the usual seventy-two hours to assess the group in our customary fashion, that way when the offer is made, there won't be any insults to their intelligence or their talent."

Laura shook her head, not swayed by the sudden show of solidarity. "Mr. Richton, Mr. Parker, as I said before, I understand your need to do your due diligence, and if you would like, we can square away any issues right here and now, if you have the time to do so. However, I expect competing offers by the time the video of the performance gets through the circuit, both here and across the country."

"Laura, Parker and I are ready to make your girls into a superstar group. They have the sound, they have the appeal, and they have the drive, thanks to you, to do what it takes to hit the next level," Mr. Richton stated with a matter-of-fact tone that turned the area about ten degrees cooler. "I'm sure you've heard this before, but our time is precious, and I don't like to waste it. Your girls weren't the only talent that my group was told about tonight, but they have told us that your group was *the* group to see. Now, if you know anything about us, and your sources probably do, then you know that once

I'm convinced, Parker is convinced, and vice versa. We're convinced."

I half expected Mr. Parker to be a bit more engaged in the conversation, but his constant glances in Camryn's direction were more interesting than the showdown happening around us. I turned to Camryn, and she was unabashed in her flirt-fest with Mr. Parker, like Quinn didn't exist. Now, Mr. Parker was a different kind of fine from Mr. Richton, and the fact that he had Camryn's attention was enough for me to take notice. She was smitten beyond all rational thought.

"Mr. Richton, I don't mean to sound ungrateful, but I have to protect my group." Laura's tone was apologetic, while trying to make it look like she wasn't about to back down.

Keri tapped my thigh under the table, grabbing my attention from the other scene playing out in front of me with Cam and Mr. Parker. "She's totally about to cave in, look at the way she's looking at him."

"She is not about to cave," I whispered. After all we'd been through, all the posturing she was doing to try and make it look like others were scoping us out, I was convinced Laura wasn't about to be swayed by a handsome devil of a man.

Sure enough, Mr. Richton leaned in, said something in Laura's ear that made her blush. That wasn't business, not from what I could tell, and there would be no way to find out if it was business or Mr. Richton being a silver-tongued devil, insistent on getting his way.

My eyes met Devin's again, searching for answers the best way I could. I suspected his smirk was from his experience in watching his boss in action in the past. I wondered to myself if Mr. Richton would still be able to be this smooth if our manager were male. I realized he had some influence, but I wasn't willing to believe that he could be this influential. Either way, he had his effect on her.

"So, we'll see you in three business days, then, yes?" Mr. Richton confirmed.

"We'll see you in three business days," Laura's replied, locking the date in her Note8. "Thursday, ten a.m. sharp, in your office. We'll be there, no problem."

Thursday. That felt like an eternity already.

"Devin, my boy, I want you to have the ladies over to the house for the pool party tomorrow night." He turned to Devin, grinning the whole time. "I'm sure they need to relax a little after putting in the work tonight, don't you think?"

"Yes, sir, consider it done." Devin cut his eyes at me, looking a little too pleased with himself. I made a mental note to give him a hard time if he tried to come on to me. "I'll make sure they are there."

We got up from the table and said our goodbyes to Mr. Richton, Mr. Parker and the rest of the group. Devin stood up to escort us out of the club. I wasn't sure I wanted him in my space so soon after a set, but I wanted to test my resolve around him, if only to see if I could resist his charms. With the way that the other men were gawking at us during the performance, it wasn't like we couldn't have a pick of the litter.

Walking with Devin and Mr. Richton's bodyguards felt like something out of a video sequence. He tried to watch how close he came to touching me; his indecision amused me. Turning the tables and having him on the defensive was a refreshing change, but I wasn't ready for this reversal of fortune to end.

He touched my arm to slow me down as we got to my car. He grinned as his eyes roamed everywhere he could to avoid eye contact. "Well, I guess this would be that moment where I ask you for your phone number, huh?"

"Well, that depends on the reason why you want my number, D?"

He tilted his head, trying to figure out what I was driving at. "How else am I going to be able to call you? The last thing I want to tell my boss is that I didn't have a way to contact you to get you to the estate."

I slipped in his space, capitalizing on his indecision, taking my role as the aggressor to the hilt. I placed my index finger against his chin, licking my lips as I felt him tremble. "Tell me the reason you want my number. Just say it."

He swallowed hard. I wouldn't let his eyes stray from mine until I got my answer. Whether he liked it or not, he was no longer the one in control. "Alexia, you know why I want your number."

"Stop teasing, sexy. I will make you tell me, one way or another." I wasn't about to make it easy on him, regardless of the heat I felt rising off my skin.

"I want you and the rest of the girls to come out tomorrow." He tried to resist, but I would not be denied tonight. "Happy?"

"You *want* me, Devin?"

His glare made me want to squeeze my thighs together. I challenged his words on purpose, wanting to get a rise out of him. I wanted to rattle his cage, tempt the beast that lay beneath the swagger. I didn't want to be the only one who felt something.

"I *know* what I said, Alexia." His tone came with a force

and depth that threatened to have me swoon on the spot. "I didn't stutter. I want you and the girls to be our guests."

I stared into his eyes, trying to find any reason to deny his request. He never once looked away, meeting my inquisitive gaze with one of his own. Everything else seemed to fade to black, leaving us in this space, wondering who would blink first. I almost dared anyone to try to separate us in that moment. There would be consequences.

I didn't care if anyone watched this dance. We could do this all night for all I cared. I was on top of the world after tonight's performance, and this would be the cherry on top of one of the sexiest nights of my life.

His eyes softened, almost begging me to say yes. *Maybe he isn't as bullet-proof as I thought.* "I don't know, D. I'm tempted, but I still don't know if I want to go. Persuade me."

His hands wrapped around my waist, pulling me into him. His fingers interlocked at the small of my back, teasing below the top of my panty line. His hands felt so good against my body that I didn't know whether I wanted him to take them off me or explore more intimate areas.

"Say yes, please? Say you'll be our guests. It would mean a lot to me if you say yes. Say yes."

I wanted to do more than say yes. I wanted to kiss him so badly my body trembled. I needed to purge, and he was the perfect outlet to exorcise some demons lurking deep within my core. The dam was ready to burst, but I had to do something to keep it together. The way his hands caressed me, resistance was futile.

He wouldn't release his hold on me, and I didn't want him to, either. Damn. Now I knew I was in trouble, only this time, I welcomed it with every fiber of my being.

"Come on, girl, you can play mack mama later!" I heard Keri yelling from the car. "Just give the man the digits so we can party, please?"

"Okay, my girls are a little impatient, they want to celebrate." I typed my number into his cell phone, trying to decide if I was more irritated over having my vibe being killed or grateful that they'd interrupted the spell he was casting over me. "And since they've answered your question for me, call me tomorrow so we can set up a time to be there."

As I put his phone in his hand, I moved in close to inhale his scent. It was different from the cologne he wore the other night, but it was as hypnotizing as what caught me then.

Devin smiled, his demeanor more easygoing now. He tucked his phone in his pocket before he moved in again. "I'll give you a call around noon. I don't want to ruin any beauty sleep that you may need in the morning."

That smartass remark earned him a pop on his shoulder. It gave me an excuse to touch him. I didn't need a lot of sleep, but I was exhausted from all the energy I gave on the stage tonight. Still, it was fun to tease him for a few more moments.

I moved closer to him, my eyes trained on his, watching his reaction. His breathing quickened as he licked his lips. *He thinks I'm going to kiss him*, I thought to myself. It wouldn't have been a bad idea, but with my girls watching, it wouldn't be a good look.

I did, however, leave a soft kiss on his cheek, taking my finger to trace a line from the spot I kissed to his lips. "You do realize I would have said yes the first time you asked, don't you, pretty boy?"

He smiled, shaking his head as I turned and walked away from him. "No, you wanted to see me sweat. You wanted to get me back for the way I made you tremble last night."

He was observant…way too observant. He was going to be trouble, but he was going to be even more fun to play with. I moved toward my car, but not before I stopped long enough to leave a parting thought. "I guess you'll never know if I was trying to get you back or not. If you play your cards right, you might be able to find out."

Deion

Chapter Eight: No Flex Zone

"I told you to be here an hour ago, D."

The tone in her voice was enough to make me want to put the bags down and head back to my truck. Okay, so I was a little late. She had every right to be upset, but I didn't mind it all that much. She was always so damn sexy when she was mad, almost to where I might have made the conscious decision to be late so I could see her scowl and pout at the same time.

Natalia Richton and I had been best friends since middle school. We dated a little bit in high school before we realized we were better off as very close best friends—or at least, that's what we thought was the best thing. Once we got older, our relationship had always blurred the lines between what friends should be and what lovers tended to be. She was my heart, and there weren't any women who held that distinction.

"Sorry, baby, I got home late last night. Your father had me at one of the showcases taking a look at talent again." I offered my excuse like I'd prepared for her onslaught. "Besides, we'll be able to get everything under control soon."

I hugged her the way I did when I wanted her to forgive me. She hugged me back the way she did when she didn't want to forgive me, but she forgave me anyway. "Do you still love me?"

"Yes, I still love you, and what trick do you have coming to the house?" Natalia cornered me after she broke from our embrace. She gave me the once over, leaning in like she was going to kiss me before raising her eyebrow and walking back to finish chopping up the cucumbers for the salad.

"I ain't got nobody coming to the house, baby." I tried to sidestep the issue, knowing good and well she would be able to see right through it. "You know you are the only woman I adore, so stop flexin'."

"You know, D, you're a lousy liar," Natalia pointed out, popping me across the back of my head. "I always know you got something up your sleeve because you always try to sweet-talk me, with your smooth-as-silk talking ass. You are also wearing my favorite cologne…you know, the one I bought for your birthday last year?"

Damn, she busted me, and the scent of the cologne lingering on my skin was a dead giveaway. I forgot about how much she paid attention to me, almost down to the smallest detail. "Damn, Natalia, okay. Her name is Alexia. Her group was one of the groups that your father is looking to sign in the next few days, and he wanted them to come to the party tonight. And for the record, she's not a trick."

Natalia stopped cutting the cucumbers, focusing her attention on me, trying to gauge the tone behind my response.

She wasn't used to me jumping to another woman's defense so soon after I'd met them. "I'll be the judge of that. Jenna couldn't fool me, and neither will this one. Just introduce me to her and I'll let you know at the end of the night if she's cool, all right?"

"Yes, wifey, and I'll even make sure I have protection when she gets ready to hop in bed with me later on tonight." I laughed, unable to keep my attempt at a comical response under control. I couldn't maintain a straight face as the words came out of my mouth. "I know the rules. I can't bring anything home to you."

Natalia popped me again, this time missing my head and landing across the back of my neck. "Forget you, D. Now, hurry up and get dressed, dammit. The guests will be showing up in the next hour."

"Why are you cooking anyway? You know your father always caters for these things."

"I like cooking, and you like my cooking. How do you think we've been together this long?" The smirk on her face gave away her implied sentiment. "Now, stop stalling and get dressed."

I headed upstairs to one of the spare bedrooms so I could change clothes and get prepared to perform my usual co-hosting duties with Natalia when my cell phone started ringing. "Speak your peace, I'm busy, yo."

"Are you telling Anton about the party tonight or what?" Quinn barked over my Bluetooth. The perturbed tone in his voice put me on the defensive. "This shit is becoming a pain in the ass, and sooner or later, something's gotta give. I mean, what the fuck, bruh? He's supposed to be *your* boy, not mine."

I shook my head, frustration creeping in with the quickness. This subject would come up sooner or later, even more so considering the nature of the party tonight. This was right up Anton's alley, but there was no way I could explain his presence, not with everything that had happened.

I rubbed my hands over my face as I buttoned my shirt, exhaling as my mind raced to figure out how to approach this conversation. Yeah, I told him not to tell Anton about the party, but I had one damn good reason. First, Natalia couldn't stand him, due to an incident with one of her girlfriends about a year ago. There was nothing else left to explain.

She always wondered why Quinn and I still hung out with Anton, and that incident strained my relationship with her for a few months, too. If I was honest with myself, I would have questions, too. It was hard to put my finger on it, but we'd been boys for a decade, through thick and thin.

"That's a negative, Q, you know that Natalia wouldn't go for it anyway," I told Quinn while tying my boots. "I'm gonna need you to keep this on the low, too, bruh. As a matter of fact, it's all on a need to know basis right now. That means no snapping, no going live on the 'book or on the 'gram, either"

"You know this shit is foul, D-Lo," Quinn stated. "We've been boys for too long with all this cloak-and-dagger shit whenever we go out without him."

"So, what do you suggest, Q?" I sat up on the bed, adding extra volume to my voice. "I should call Anton and say, 'Hey, bruh, we're doing a set out at Mr. Richton's estate, and we can't have you roll out with us because Natalia's gonna be there and you're still *persona non-grata* as far as she's concerned, so, we'll come by and scoop you another time?'"

Quinn cursed out loud, lending credence to my argument. "Yeah, I forgot about the shit that went down with him and Samantha. Do you think that Natalia's still hot about that?"

The incident that Quinn referred to surrounded a woman by the name of Samantha Burke. She and Anton hooked up at Natalia's birthday party and hit it off from the word go. To be honest, I thought she was good for him; she got him to cut down on the weed, got him cleaned up and presentable, the type of stuff that a girlfriend would do when she was trying to make her boyfriend into husband material. She even supported his adult film career, convincing him to get behind the camera and produce movies.

A pregnancy test changed all of that. Anton's actions after she told him and my loyalty to him in the aftermath almost ended my relationship with Natalia.

"You should know the answer to that question, bruh." The ice in my response should have given him the hint to drop the subject once and for all. "So, need to know, got it?"

"Yeah, I got it, bruh, but sooner or later, Anton's gonna feel like the third wheel and shit," Quinn cautioned. "If you don't find a way to let him down easy, this shit will snowball out of control, and even you don't have the skills to stop the flood once the dam's broken."

I took Quinn's words into account, and I realized that he did have a valid point. Sooner or later, the hammer's gotta come down, and it was better that he saw it coming than to get blindsided by it. I struggled with having to make that decision. Anton and I had been through a lot throughout our friendship, even more so than with Quinn. I hoped he would understand, but I didn't want to make him feel like I was turning my back on him.

Even though I was in the midst of my own crisis of conscience, I was upset that I was the one that had to do it. What pissed me off more than anything was that Quinn didn't want any parts of being the heavy hand, but he had no qualms about telling me what I should do about the situation. I wasn't cool with that at all. He was being a coward about this shit; that wasn't a good look at all. Quinn had always been a punk when it came to confrontations. It was almost to the point where he had to be pushed to the point of no return before he snapped.

I had my limits, too, but they weren't anywhere as high as his tolerance level. My problem had become the fact that I'd been enabling Anton's habit instead of being a real friend. I didn't abandon my boys, no matter how low things had gotten with them. If the roles were reversed, I wouldn't want them to abandon me when it counted the most.

There had to be a way to keep from losing Anton, and I hoped I could find it before it was too late.

Alexia

Chapter Nine: Anything You Wanna Do…

I didn't mind being awakened by a masculine voice. It had been so long since I'd had such a delicious pleasure that I wasn't sure how to react when Devin's voice pulled me from my slumber. He sounded so good that my body reacted in ways I wasn't ready for. I thought I was still dreaming about him, but it wasn't until I reached next to me and felt my body pillow that I realized I needed to be present and awake.

"Did I wake you, Alexia?"

I wasn't about to admit to being tired, even if I was up half the night trying to come down from the high that I was on. I clung to the covers like a jealous lover as I slept-walked through the conversation, trying to get final confirmation about the party later on today. I didn't care if he was irritated or not. I was serious about my beauty sleep, even if it was almost eight in the evening. "No, you didn't wake me…well, you kinda did, but I'm awake now."

"Well, I called to make sure that you and the ladies were going to make it out." Devin kept the conversation trite. He sounded like he was being rushed. "I really do hope that you all can make it."

I sat up in bed after hearing that tone in his voice. For a minute, I thought that he was nervous that we might not head out there. I changed my tone to reassure him that everything was okay. "No, we're still going to be there, I just need to know if it is going to be a pool party or something else. The girls might want to know so they can dress appropriately."

"Well, swimsuits are optional. The atmosphere is laid-back, so come in something sexy. I'm sure that won't be a problem for you or the other ladies." I felt the smirk spread across his face. I wanted to smack it off...before I thought about having to console him after I did it.

I looked at my phone, stuck in a place of wanting to shake him senseless and swooning over the energy I felt on him through the vibe of the conversation. He was teasing me, trying to bring me further inside his web.

"You are so silly, boy." I threw a seductive coo into my voice, determined to entice him as much as I could. Two could play the seduction game, and I was more than willing to make him my prey, even if I wasn't ready to do anything about it once he was caught. "If you want to see me half-naked, all you have to do is ask."

Devin laughed. "Okay, real talk; I want to see you completely naked. How's that for asking?"

Now we were getting somewhere. Hearing the authority in his voice as he told me what he wanted did things to my nether regions. Goodness. "And what makes you think I want you to see me naked just yet?"

"Your eyes give you away, Alexia, that's why." He paused for a moment before speaking again. "I didn't want to tell you that was how I figured it out, but it's only fair that I tell you, so you don't think I've been in your head the whole time."

"Whatever." I giggled along with him. My eyes always got me in trouble. "We'll see you at the party tonight."

After hanging up the phone with Devin, I called Camryn to make sure she was on her way over to my place to get dressed. The moment she answered the phone, I already knew it was going to be one of those days with the diva. Her attitude was on full tilt. "This party had better not be lame, Lexi. It really won't matter if Quinn's fine ass is gonna be there or not, if I'm bored, I'm leaving you there."

"The party won't be lame, Camryn. RPK is not some bullshit company. Have you forgotten that? And the party will be at the Richton estate. I'm sure Mr. Richton has enough swagger for the majority of us, girl. The guest list should be crazy."

"Speaking of swagger, it seems like you and that cutie, Devin, right? Looks like you two are getting a little cozy." Camryn switched the subject on me, trying to take the focus off of her. "So, when you gonna smash so we can get our record deal finished? I noticed how he was at the showcase last night; he has Mr. Richton's ear and influence. He could be the one to push things through and get us rolling in the right direction."

I looked at the phone, a flurry of profanities ready to fly at a moment's notice. When did I become the resident whore of the group? She had another thing coming if she thought she was gonna pimp me out over something that has already been taken care of. I was not for sale.

"You're a cold ass bitch, do you know that?" I was

annoyed that she would even think I would put myself out there like that. "I am not sleeping with Devin to seal a deal. *IF* I decide to sleep with him, it will be based on something a lot more important than a record deal."

"Aww, that's so sweet, but that shit only works in the movies, Lexi." Camryn tried to correct my romanticized thoughts. "You like him, I can tell that already, that's the only reason I'm not making the moves to smash so this can be done with."

"You won't do a goddamned thing, Cam."

"Look, you can fake-claim all you want. This 'playing hard to get when you already wanna smash,' cat-and-mouse shit is cute and all, but we got business to attend to, or have *you* forgotten that?" Camryn kept up her rant, ignoring my warning. "Truth be told, this really ain't about you, girl. Keri and I have a lot invested in this group, too. Don't sit here acting like you're the only one who has struggled and suffered. You need to handle that, for real."

"For the record, I am the only one who has struggled and suffered. You and Keri have had sponsors since the beginning, so stop frontin' like you've been eating syrup sandwiches and shit. But if I do smash—and I haven't decided yet—I know for a fact that you'll be the *last* to know. Besides, it looks like you have someone's attention yourself, don't you think?"

"I don't know what you're talking about, Lexi. I was too busy worrying about getting Quinn to keep his hands off my thighs during the whole damn meeting." Camryn sucked her teeth at my response. A few seconds later, she flipped the switch and started to sound more like she was in the partying mood. "Girl, why don't we just get all dolled up, head to this party, and get our freak on, please? All of the real ballers will be snatched up, and I'm no one's sloppy seconds."

"Then you need to get Keri and hurry up, for real." I was at the point to where I wanted to give her the business about the bullshit she wanted to trip about, but at the end of the day, we needed to get business handled. "The last thing I want to do is go through a sea of busters, either, and you know Keri's gonna want to have her pick of the femmes that will be in the house."

"I ain't trying to hear about all that, Lexi. Keri can do what she does, doesn't mean I want to see about it, though."

This wasn't the first time she'd been tripping about Keri's sexuality, but it was really working my nerves. Everything tended to be gender-fluid within the entertainment industry, and her conservative views would be enough to cause an issue with the LGBTQ+ community if she wasn't careful. Even more so, Keri would kick her ass if she ever let her lips loose over how she felt.

"Just get your ass over here so we can get up there at a decent hour, okay?" I needed her to get some action about her and stop running her mouth. "We'll rock with the other business when we get up there. I'll see you in thirty minutes."

Deion

Chapter Ten: Like a G6

"All right, D-Lo, where are your girls?"

Quinn was acting like a freakin' teenager wrapped up in his damn puppy crush or some shit when he walked up on me trying to find out when Alexia and the girls would show up. He had only seen the woman in person once and he was already at the point to where he was ready to show her the keys to the kingdom.

"They'll be here, Q, what are your panties in a bunch for?" I asked him, irritated that he'd been acting like such a damn buster.

"Look, D, these phony-ass, thirsty thots that are supposedly friends of Natalia's are starting to fuck up my vibe." Quinn came back at me, looking almost insulted that I even asked. "I just hope they hurry up, I'm bored as hell up in this camp, and I can't even blaze to take the edge off."

"Look, man, I said they'll be here, all right?" I felt like I was reassuring a little kid that the toy he wished for would be under the Christmas tree or something. I wasn't used to him sounding like this. "Maybe you need to find a spot in the front of the house so you can blaze one real quick before you have a coronary or something, damn."

It was becoming an absolute drain on my energy, and I needed to get away from him before he sucked the life out of me. I had enough nervous energy as it was, the last thing I needed was to take his issues and add to what I tried to suppress. He did have a point, though. The estate was crawling with gold diggers, all with dollar signs in their eyes, thinking the gold between their legs will translate into platinum and racks and stacks of green.

I saw Alexia coming through the back doors with Camryn and Keri in tow. I watched as everyone turned their heads to see the girls, including the wannabes who wanted a piece of them. That would have been enough to make most men sweat about the competition as they did their best to jockey for position. I wasn't most men. Never was, never would be.

"Any other questions, bruh?" I asked Quinn, watching him lose his mind once he got a glimpse of what Camryn had on. "You know how women like making an entrance."

"You got that right, bruh, and it's a hellified entrance, to say the least." Quinn couldn't take his eyes off Camryn, and her eyes met with his as soon as she saw us. "So, we're hosts, right? Let's make with the hosting and entertaining of the guests."

I grabbed his arm before he could break into a full sprint in their direction. I shook my head at his confused response, intent on reminding him that we're not the type of bulls to run down and get one heifer only. That's not how we rolled, and he needed to be reminded of that.

"Come on, playa, you know not to be all eager and shit,

right?" I wasn't sure if I was trying to remind him or remind myself of what needed not to happen. "Let the ladies breathe a little bit, let them come to us, and we'll rock from there. They need time to work the room. After all, they're supposed to be the center of attention as the potential new group being signed by RPK."

Quinn acted like he didn't hear me, salivating like a love-struck sixteen-year-old. As much as I tried to calm him down, my instincts and my body already betrayed me. Seeing Alexia in a lavender halter top and matching mini-skirt with a pair of open-toed stilettos with straps that wrapped all the way up to her calves was enough to inspire some aggression in me, too. Camryn didn't slouch either, wearing a strapless pink mini-dress with a pair of t-strapped sandals. Keri showed off a body I didn't know she had, wearing a bikini top and a skin-tight skirt that tried—and failed—to cover her assets.

I took a deep breath to compose myself. Alexia didn't wear this outfit for my benefit—that was my story and I was sticking to it. If they were trying to get the attention of every man in the place, regardless of marital status? Mission accomplished.

I would have kept them waiting a little bit longer, until I saw Natalia talking to them. *Damn, how did she get to Alexia first?* I sauntered over to get in on the conversation. Quinn followed suit, wondering what was going on.

Natalia saw us coming and waited until we were all together before she decided to blow up the spot. "Devin, baby, these ladies were wondering where you were. They must be VIP to get into my parties."

A little pop across Natalia's butt reminded her of a few

things, like not trying to put me on the spot like I didn't already invite them. Camryn's gave me this look like she wanted to say something to me about what I'd just done. I shot a look back at her to let her know to mind her damn business.

Natalia laughed at me, rubbing the spot that I slapped and turned her attention to the curious stares in her direction. "Don't mind D and me, ladies. I love him like a brother, but he's horrible at introductions. Enjoy the party, and if you need anything, come find me if D hasn't already handled it."

After Natalia left us, I turned my attention to Alexia and the girls and soon realized that someone was missing from the group. Or should I say *two* someones.

It didn't take long to figure out that Quinn had already taken Camryn and found a way to isolate and put the mack on. I caught a glimpse of them at a table by the pool, already wrapped up and into each other. I tried not to look too confused, but I failed. I couldn't get rid of the look on my face, and it soon became the source of amusement for the ladies. "Was there something I missed? There were two other people that were here for me to take on the tour of the house, right?"

"I'm sorry, Devin, I didn't mean to laugh, but your expression was priceless." Keri was still trying to stifle a giggle as she continued to muse. "You were so serious and calm last night, watching you cut loose is a different style for you. It's a good look, though."

Alexia chimed in. "Yeah, Devin, I would have sworn that you had this all planned out except for your boy throwing a curve ball in your game."

Keri tried and save me. "Come on, Lexi, I'm sure we can

still enjoy the tour that Devin had planned for us. He's trying to be a good host and all. We can cut him a little slack, right?"

Alexia slapped my shoulder and stepped a little closer to me. She felt good; I was a little surprised by that move, though, considering she wanted to act like she didn't want to give up much rhythm even though there was an obvious vibe between us. "Okay, Mr. Lowery, lead the way, we would love to see the house, and then perhaps maybe we can get a little dancing in afterwards?"

If she was trying her best to take me off my game and make me pay attention to her?

It almost worked.

Almost.

Deion

Chapter Eleven: Red Light Special

"Okay, I have to warn you, I can't dance all that well."

"You seem to be doing okay to me, but I'm sure we can find a way to improve on it."

Alexia couldn't stop laughing at some of the moves I tried to pull off during different songs, but I could thank Natalia for teaching me the few moves I had. It gave me a chance to see how Alexia moved those hips of hers and appreciating the view at the same time.

The girls decided to get together and decided to do their thing as a group, so I tipped off the deejay to let him know to come up with something for them to take it up a notch. My dude didn't disappoint, poppin' off a few up-tempo tracks first to let the ladies get loose and get loose was what they did! Nothing like letting Cardi B's latest songs set things off in the proper fashion.

The bruhs at the bar broke their necks to turn their attention toward the choreographed routine that Alexia and the girls came up with. All I did was hang and relax, enjoying the view and keeping eye contact with Alexia the entire time she was dancing. The song switched to the Migos' 'Stir Fry,' and the girls really let go. Yeah, I know, but the song was fire! Alexia avoided eye contact at first, but when she did look up and saw me staring, a slick grin spread across her face. She even managed to blow a few kisses before letting the rhythm take over again.

Yeah, this was the side of her I couldn't wait to see, and I liked what I saw. The sensual energy that exuded from her was on full display. Hell, all of the girls were enticing the crowd so much that even the women were feeling the vibe. When a few of the fellas tried to step in to break the group up, all they did was point in my direction, letting them know that this was their moment to entertain.

Quinn was on pins and needles at his table, caught in that zone of whether to stake his claim or play it cool and let Camryn come back to the table after they were done. I wasn't sure how I felt about that. I was the same way when Jenna and I were together, so I couldn't be a hypocrite about it.

The night soon went from high energy to more of a seductive mood as midnight began to creep up. Most of the crowd had begun to make their way home, leaving the rest that had coupled up to get to know each other a little better to enjoy the ambiance that the back yard and pool area had to offer.

I waited for Alexia to come off the dance floor, but she took my hand and led me back instead. Damn it, why'd she have to go and do that? "I told you I can't dance all that well, Alexia, what do you want to do, embarrass me some more?"

"No, but I do wanna slow dance with you, if that's okay?" She winked as she led me further into the sea of couples already getting their groove on. "If you're a good boy, I might let you feel my booty."

Feeling her arms around my neck as I clasped my hands around her waist as we danced, I forgot how intoxicating it was to be this close. Her body was warm and it felt so damn good it was scary, but I didn't hear any warning bells sounding off in my head.

"Are you having a good time?" I asked, trying to break the silence between us. "We can go sit down and talk for a while. We haven't had a chance to do that with all the excitement going on."

Alexia's eyes held me prisoner, and I didn't know if I wanted that to happen or if I needed to relax and quit over-thinking things. We danced to a few more songs, inhaling each other's essence, the mix of songs kept putting ideas in my mind that I wasn't ready to act on yet. After about three or four songs, we left the dance floor, with her following my lead to one of the tables by the pool so we could talk.

"To answer your question, Devin, I am having a really good time." Alexia answered once we sat down. She looked a little tipsy, and I pretty much figured I needed to find either Camryn or Keri to make sure she didn't drive home in her condition.

"That's good, I hoped you would. So, what would you like to know, I know you've been curious about a bruh." I blinked for a moment, trying hard to avoid getting caught in her stare again.

Alexia grinned, almost giddy that she knew the effect she had on me. "I want to know a lot, D, but I didn't want to seem too personal. After all, we haven't known each other long."

"I know it's been less than a week, but I have nothing to hide, ask me anything." I managed to blurt out. "I'm kinda interested in finding out what's in that pretty head of yours."

"There is something I would like to know, but I think I want to wait until later on tonight." Alexia licked her lips as she spoke.

She's holding back, I thought to myself. *She wants to find out, but she's playing hard to get.*

I felt her foot stroking the inside of my leg, causing the heat to rise off my skin. Her body language confused me, as the quiet and demure demeanor she put on conflicted with the sensual aggression in her actions. She was driving me crazy, but in light of the #MeToo movement that had been trending as of late, I didn't want to read the signals wrong.

I was about to find out what Alexia had in mind as I felt her foot move to my thigh when Keri walked over to where we sat with a worried look on her face. "Lexi, have you seen Camryn?"

"No, I thought she was with you," Alexia mentioned, doing a quick scan of the area to see if she could locate her. "I'll try calling her on her cell. She and Quinn might have tried to sneak off somewhere."

I hoped that they hadn't left the grounds, but knowing Quinn, Camryn was probably in his car, halfway to Buckhead by now.

"I'll tell you what, I'll search the grounds and see if they're anywhere close, you try her on her cell and I'll try Quinn and we'll go from there." I slid my cell open and called Quinn once I was outside of their earshot. I already knew the answer I was going to get, but I needed confirmation.

"Yo, D, sorry I split on you back there, but Camryn wanted to see the studio and all." Quinn didn't miss a beat the minute he picked up the phone. He was expecting me to call.

"You could have given me the head's up, bruh." I snapped.

"Are you rolling back here so Camryn can take Alexia home?"

The answer to my question came in the form of inaudible moans and screams coming from Camryn. He was still in his car, I could tell from the background noise, so that answered my other question. "All right, bruh, this shit ain't fly. You better hope that I can calm her group mates down."

"I got faith in you, playa. Now, if you'll excuse me, I need to blow this girl's back out and get it all on tape at the studio. Peace." Quinn cut the call before I could say another word.

I shook my head and started back toward where I left the girls, trying to figure out what type of spin to put on this bullshit.

Natalia found me before she went off with the dude that she was spending time with. I forgot his name, but it didn't matter, though. If dude lasted until morning, he might last another week before he got tossed to the side. Natalia's only twenty-five, and she really didn't need to settle down. We did our thing back in high school, even did the relationship thing for a minute when she graduated, but she was my best friend now. Sometimes, things worked out for the better in ways that you never really imagined.

"Can you cover for me for the rest of the night?" Natalia asked me, giving me a kiss on the cheek. "I've gotta fly down to Miami for a film shoot this week, and I need to get some sleep."

I figured I was good to go to do that. I assumed that Keri or Camryn took a separate car, so Alexia could leave with either of them and they could make sure she got home safely. Mr. Richton was always cool with me spending the night after the parties were over. He didn't want to have me drive home after putting in work. I loved that old man like my father sometimes.

"Go get some rest, baby girl. I'll get rid of the crowd in a little while." I got my hug in before she headed into the house, not giving a damn about the dude mean-mugging me. He might have gotten some in a few, but it would be the last time he would get a whiff of her essence. I felt the heat on her earlier, and I hoped he had it in him to wear her out.

I turned my attention to figuring out what to do about Camryn and smoothing things over with the girls. I figured that playing dumb might be the best move, so I walked over to where they were sitting and asked, "Any luck getting in touch with Camryn?"

Keri shook her head. "She and Quinn left almost thirty minutes ago, Devin."

"Yeah, and the trick took my keys, so I can't even drive home tonight." Alexia's eyes conveyed the irritation evident on her face. They also told me that she'd been drinking more than she should have been.

This put a crimp in my plans. I cursed Quinn for putting me in this position, and all for an easy lay. Damn. Alexia wasn't going to leave her car in a strange place. Hell, I wouldn't leave my baby, either.

Keri taking Alexia home complicated things; she rode her motorcycle to the house, which I found a bit odd considering the outfit she wore. Even more interesting was the fact that she didn't bring her extra helmet, so I made a judgment call that would at least provide a temporary solution until morning.

"Keri, you can go home. I'll make sure that Alexia is taken care of, okay?" I offered. It was a long shot, but it was the only way that I could cover all my bases. "She can take the spare bedroom that I usually crash in."

Keri gave me a look like she thought I was a serial killer.

She looked at Alexia, who nodded that she would be okay with me. Her eyes met mine again, the tone of her voice lending to the protective nature she exerted over Alexia. "All right, Devin, I'm gonna trust you with my girl. But you better not try nothing, understood?"

"No worries, Keri. I don't think I ever want to be on your bad side," I joked, which got a smile from Keri before she left. "Besides, once this all goes down, we will be working together, so I gotta make sure we are able to work together."

"We're cool, Devin; I get good vibes from you, but I still have my eye on you." She walked toward her bike to head home, which left me with a woman who felt like she was abandoned and left for dead.

"I hope I haven't put you out too much, Devin." Alexia stumbled as she closed the distance between us. The truth was, I didn't want the night to end, at least not yet. It was crazy to sound like that, but there was a vibe between us, I could feel it.

Her body language gave her away, and in her inebriated state, there was nowhere to hide. "I didn't expect my girls to leave me stranded, but I guess that's on me for letting Cam keep my keys."

"It's okay, Alexia, I have a run of the house. Like I told Keri, you can have the room that I normally crash in and I'll sleep in one of the spare bedrooms downstairs." I wanted to keep myself honest, but as close as she was, my body had a few ideas of what it wanted to do.

"But, what if I don't want you to leave?" The suggestive tone in Alexia's voice threw me off balance. She moved even closer, enough to feel the heat on her skin. "I want you to stay with me, D. I don't want to be alone tonight."

The way she begged made my manhood twitch. My mind's eye flashed forward to an image of her, in nothing but her heels, motioning her finger for me to come inside and feel the full measure of her femininity. It was an image that was hard as hell to shake, and the fact that Alexia suggested that I stay in the room with her seemed almost too good to believe.

Then I remembered she had been drinking a lot throughout the evening. There was no way in hell I was going to take advantage, only to have her not remember a thing in the morning. That's not how a real man behaved, and I had to maintain my discipline.

I was about to answer her question when she stumbled again, which sealed the deal. She needed to hit the sheets and sleep the buzz off. There was no further doubt in my mind.

"Okay, Alexia, we're going to the bedroom, you're definitely not yourself right now." I ordered, wrapping my arm around her waist to walk her to the bedroom in the house. The further we tried to walk, the heavier her legs became, so I lifted her into my arms and carried her to the bedroom before she passed out.

Her moans and coos in my ear were the death of me, my body betraying me with each moan that escaped from her lips. If I was being tested or this was supposed to prove my virtue, I wasn't sure if I would fail miserably or not.

I got her in the bedroom that I normally slept in, laying her down before pulling the covers back on the other side of the king size bed so that I could get her under the covers. She pawed at me, trying to unbutton my shirt, sounding out of her rational mind. "Mmmm…stay with me, Devin. I don't want to sleep by myself."

"Alexia, I'm going to sleep in one of the other bedrooms."

"Why, don't you want me? You know I want you. Please, stay with me." Alexia poured it on thick, and I was at the point to where I wanted to break my promise that I wouldn't touch her. "I know what I'm doing, and I need to feel you. Please, don't make me beg, but I ain't too proud to beg. I really need you tonight, please."

I shook off my haze and repeated my original statement. "Alexia, go to sleep, I'll be here in the morning."

I leaned to hug her. I don't know why I did it; she was in my arms the whole way to the room. The way she felt in my arms now was nothing short of bliss. The kind of feeling that you never wanted to break free of, and you would fight tooth and nail to keep no matter what. I wanted to let go, but my body had stronger intentions for its own selfish intentions.

Alexia fell asleep while I was at war with myself. She was snoring, removing any lingering temptation I may have had. I slipped the covers over her and walked out of the room, making my way back to the spare bedroom after clearing out the last of the partygoers. I was in desperate need to calm down, willing my body to not betray me, but the storm was coming, and there was no stopping it once the thunder clapped.

By the time I made it to the guest bedroom on the main level, all I wanted was to hit the shower, work out in the home gym, anything to calm down. I saw the bed and felt it was best to crash. I had a photo shoot to do in the morning, so whatever my body wanted, it was going to have to wait until tomorrow.

I cursed out loud, bemoaning my sudden and unexpected desperation. I wasn't used to being in this space, and it irritated me. A host of bad decisions resided in my cell phone, and any of them would be more than happy to help me relieve some tension. It didn't matter; I wanted who I wanted, and I was used to getting who and what I wanted. But I couldn't have who I wanted in this moment, thanks to a few too many drinks at the bar and trying to avoid contributing to the rampant rape culture that still pervaded the entertainment industry on the whole.

Under normal circumstances, I would be in Natalia's room right now, waking her up to wear her out so that I could get some sleep, but I didn't want to complicate matters by taking my frustrations out on her. Besides, she wasn't a possibility, either; the dude that she was with might have still been with her. God, I was off my game, but there wasn't much I could do about it.

I stripped off my clothes, resigning myself to my accursed fate for the evening, moving toward the bed before I changed my mind and acted on my impulses. It would have assuaged my physical tension, but it would have put me in a bad spot later, I could feel it. The pillow met me before I knew it, and as I crashed, I prayed for a dreamless sleep.

Alexia

Chapter Twelve: No Sleeep

It took me a couple of minutes to realize that I was not at home in my own bed. The shock of that realization had me in a state of confusion that bordered on the possibility of a panic attack. I hadn't yet had a chance to wake up so I could focus, but I was certain I didn't go anywhere last night.

The luxurious feel of the sheets was a dead giveaway of the foreign atmosphere I found myself in. I didn't keep satin sheets on my bed, but a girl could get used to it when they felt like this, though. Once I tried to sit up in the bed, a slight headache reminded me that I had a little too much to drink last night.

Oh my God, what did I do last night?

I took quick notice of my strange surroundings. I didn't even remember walking into this room, much less how I got in this bed. I slid the covers off me, noticing that my dress was still on my body.

I tried to backtrack as best as I could, and the last thing I remembered was being pissed at Camryn for taking my keys and splitting to get broke off with a dude that she didn't know much longer than a New York minute. Once I got that out of the way, I still had yet to solve the question of how I got up here last night. After seeing the RPK Entertainment plaques on the wall, the answer became obvious—Devin must have managed to get me up here last night.

While I was relieved that I hadn't done anything out of the norm, it did cause other questions to pop up in my head. Did I sleep with him last night? And if I did, why didn't he at least have the decency to stay until morning, or wake me out of the haze I was in to let me know he had a good time, or something?

The answer to my question had already presented itself, if I had bothered to pay closer attention. In my attempts to try not to assume too much, the questions kept coming. *Okay, Lexi, think. What the hell happened—or didn't happen—last night?*

I reached for my cell phone to call Keri when I noticed a text message on my phone. When I saw it was from Devin, I almost didn't want to read it, but I opened it anyway to satisfy my curiosity:

Alexia, I am sorry about leaving you last night. I slept in another bedroom instead. I arranged for a car to take you home if you like, and Natalia knows about your car still being here, and she's cool with it until you get your keys back from Camryn.

I looked up from my phone with some relief. At least I hadn't screwed everything up. I looked back down at the text to finish what Devin had written:

We never got a chance to sit and talk to get to know each other better, so, give me a call later on today so we can get together. Natalia should still be around the house before her flight later this evening, so you're not alone in the house.

I was speechless, dropping my phone in my lap to process things. If I hadn't known any better, I'd have sworn that Devin was trying to impress me. He succeeded.

I managed to pick my cell phone back up to get an idea of what time it was so I could figure out how to plan my day before I called him back to get together. Natalia found me trying to get my bearings in this house. I almost wanted to ask for directions the way I felt.

She gave me a curious look, but her smile put me at ease. "Did you have fun at the party?"

"Yes, I had a lot of fun, thank you for having me and the rest of the group." I returned the smile that she greeted me with. "I was trying to figure out where the kitchen was. Devin left me a text message saying he left breakfast for me."

"Yeah, that sounds like D, alright." Natalia grinned. "There must be something about you for him to go to all this trouble."

What's that supposed to mean? I thought to myself as she led me to the kitchen and took out the breakfast platter that Devin had left for me. As I took a look at what lay out on the kitchen island, it didn't take long to understand why she said what she said.

Fresh fruit and crepes…

Bacon and eggs…

Pancakes and coffee…

For a minute there, I thought he was trying to give me a hint. It's not like I was skinny or anything; I had enough thickness in these hips of mine to give him a run for his money.

Natalia leaned against the island in the middle of the kitchen, studying my reaction to everything. "I can only imagine what's going through that pretty head of yours."

"Let me guess, he does this with every woman that he brings to the house?" I assumed based on her expression that she'd seen this before.

The look on her face told me different. Natalia took a bite from the croissant she'd warmed up as she thought about her answer. "Actually, I haven't seen him go all out for a woman like this in quite a long time. Not since his last girlfriend, and that was some time ago when he did that."

So, that's why she's wondering what's going on. I figured it might have been to my advantage to get a little closer to Ms. Natalia Richton. She could be my "plug" into what made Devin tick. Sure, I was cheating a little bit, but in my experience, most men had one person who knew the real. She was that person.

I didn't want to forget my manners as we sat down in the breakfast nook to enjoy the view of the backyard. "I hope you don't mind me being such an imposition in your home. I am a guest, even though my date had to leave me in your hands."

Natalia waved me off. "Devin is like a big brother to me, and he's had run of the house since high school, so it's fine. Besides, it gives us girls a bit of time to get to know each other, considering your group may be finalizing things in a little less than a week."

God, I hadn't thought about it in at least a few hours, so for Natalia to bring it up again had my mind floating. I didn't worry about the comfort level that she seemed to have developed with me in such rapid fashion, instead focusing on the small bomb she dropped in my lap. I couldn't resist. She opened the door for the conversation. "Do you really think things are that certain? We've come so close in the past, just for it to slip away."

"I know my daddy," Natalia replied, looking straight at me with the most arresting pair of light brown eyes I'd ever seen on a woman. "He and Mr. Parker work like yin and yang, and I know for a fact that once they get a chance to really take a look at the video from that night, you guys are as good as part of the RPK family."

I didn't know whether to stop breathing or hyperventilate. How was I supposed to take her word for it? Yes, she's the daughter of one of the owners, but still… "We've been so close in the past, Natalia, I can't take the chance to believe that it's just that simple."

"I'm not wrong too often, and even though D is one of the best videographers in the business—yeah, I'm a little biased— he's had a hand in the last two groups that the label has signed. One went Double Platinum, and the other went Platinum."

"Oh, wow, I didn't know Devin had an ear like that." I took another bite of the pancakes in front of me, taking every bit of information in. But there was something I needed to know. "So, were you and D an item? You seem to have a real feel for him."

Natalia regarded my expression for a moment. I didn't want her to think I was asking out of jealousy or anything like that. He didn't belong to me, so there was no need in claiming territory that I hadn't declared as mine.

The way she looked at me, though, it triggered something that I wasn't sure I wanted to ask about quite yet. I gave up a half-smile, licking my lips as my subconscious swirled in so many directions it threatened to make me dizzy. I might have aroused her curiosity, noticing as she slowed her enjoyment of the croissant in her hand for a moment. There was something else that I couldn't quite put my finger on, but I wasn't about to read too much into it unless something else happened to make me want to ask questions.

"Yeah, we kicked it for a minute, but that was when we were younger and enjoying life," Natalia remarked, a smirk spreading across her face. She winked at me, causing flutters in my stomach. She took another sip of her tea as she continued to dish. "He's one of the good ones, Alexia, but he's been burned bad, so he might slip a bit here and there. Don't tell him I told you, though. In time, he'll probably tell you everything you need to know."

I tried to keep my affection for Devin from showing too much, but Natalia saw right through me. The fact that she didn't flinch when I asked about her relationship with Devin was enough to stoke my curiosity. With all the non-monogamy talk going around in the industry as of late, it wouldn't surprise me if there was more between them than what she wanted to let on until she felt she could trust me.

My mind drifted back to Devin. I couldn't stop thinking about him. That was dangerous, but I dismissed it as my body rebelling against my vow of celibacy. He had me to the point to where I was willing to break my rules, but I wasn't ready to, not until I knew how he felt.

The things that went through my mind were enough to throw me into a frenzy. Did I want him? Yes, I did, but I still thought that he was a player. A man that *fine* usually was. But I was willing to give him the benefit of the doubt.

For now.

Deion

Chapter Thirteen: Touch Me, Tease Me

I was in the midst of an outdoor photo shoot at the home of Terry Blanchard, one half of the producer duo of Blanchard and Barnett. It was an album cover shoot and promotional stuff with one of their newest male artists, X2C. I didn't keep up with the dudes all that much, that's not my flow, but from the way the women were swooning on social media, it was obvious he was the hot ticket right now.

They wanted to do the photo shoot with some of the models that I usually work with and some new girls that the singer had a vibe with. I was fine with that, it didn't matter to me what they wanted, I was in a flow this morning, coming up with some outside the box type of stuff to match with what the cover concept was discussed with the artist.

From the glances that I got from the models that I shot and the questions that one of them asked me while I was switching out the zip drive cartridges in my digital camera, it was safe to say I was not all that pleasant to deal with when that shit went down with Jenna. That's the last time that I let a woman kill my flow, I didn't care who I was with.

The new girls tried to flirt with me through the camera lens, giving me all the pouts and kisses that I wanted to make things even hotter for the artist that they were draped all over. I guess dude didn't realize that they were only doing the job that they were paid for. He found that out the hard way when one of my regulars, Lita, had to take him down a notch or two when he thought that she was giving up the vibe during a couple's segment of the shoot for the inside of the cover.

When would these male artists learn that the women who were in the industry had seen them all? Save that shit for the regular women and girls that were ready and willing to sex you for breathing in their direction.

Sarai, one of my regulars, tried to corner me once the shoot was over so she could get a more in-depth answer from me. "Okay, D-Lo, who is she, and what did she do to get you out of your funk? Come on, baby, you can tell me who she is, your secret will be safe with me. I wanna know who it was that helped you get your swagger back."

She either had to be a glutton for punishment or she didn't care where my mind was. I was in business mode, the one where I could stay professional and not let feminine distractions compromise my position. I was on loan from RPK and I wasn't about to mess up outside money.

I winked at her, staring at the curves that I'd managed to run my hands over before I got into my last relationship. The memories came flooding back to a particular shoot in Barbados, where she damn near turned me out with another model that wanted to have me, too.

My body betrayed me, and Sarai sensed my weakening defenses against her wiles. I tried to shake off what my body wanted, but I was losing that fight with each passing second. "My swagger has always been there, Sarai. I know I've been off my game a little bit, but I had some stuff to go through, and now I'm out of it and I can get back to what I do best."

"I remember what you did best, Devin." She slid closer to me, giving me an up close and personal whiff of the combination of the perfume that she wore and the pheromones that begged me to take her right there in the open, regardless of who was watching. "I was hoping that we could get back to doing that again now that you're back on the market. You sure you don't have room for one more?"

"Or two more?" Lita cooed as she walked from around the front of my truck, catching me and Sarai in the compromising position we were in. A slick smile spread across her face as she approached us. "Is he game or what, baby? I wanna know what it is about D-Lo, too."

I closed my eyes, willing my body to calm down as best I could. *This cannot be happening right now; I should have taken care of business last night if I was going to deal with this shit today.* I did my best to make it look like they didn't have the upper hand, but these two women had a desire to have me and didn't care if the other one watched or participated or both. I was only a yes away from making a quick phone call to the nearest hotel to get this off my chest, literally and figuratively.

Through all of the carnage and debauchery going through my mind, another image flashed, lending a bit of clarity to the situation. Alexia. I had lunch plans with her in a little over an hour. I even planned my day around it.

By the time that I'd regained control of my senses, Sarai's lips were already searching for my tongue, while Lita had managed to get my shirt unbuttoned. I wanted this…badly. I wasn't going to lie about that. Even though it was a mild day today, the heat that these two created made it feel like it was the middle of June already. I could smell their scents, and the exotic mix of the two had me ready to succumb to the beauty that surrounded me.

I had more visions of doing some major damage to a hotel room, not giving a shit about who might hear the screams and moans that came from the room. I had planned to leave a generous tip for the housekeeping staff, once they walked in and saw the mess that those two would create.

My phone singing in my pocket was the only thing that kept me from following my thoughts to their conclusion. I tried to sound like I wasn't distracted, but the truth was far from that. "Lowery."

"Yo, D, I need to holla at you, man." I heard Anton's voice over the phone, sounding hyperactive. "I know you're at the gig right now, but I need to get at you ASAP."

"Ant...make it quick...I'm in the middle of...shooting now, just had to...reload smartcards." I struggled to hear what he was saying because Sarai was on my spots, triggering all kind of defensive lapses.

"Nah, bruh, I need to holla at you *now*. I think you're going to want to hear about this from me."

"Ant, quit trippin', you know I can't blaze the set unless it's life or death," I snapped. "And from the sound of it, you're still breathing if you're trying to cuss me out."

"Man, whatever," I heard him spit out. "Go handle your business and I'll be at you later on in the week. We're going to settle this one way or another."

Click.

Talk about a buzz completely gone. *Damn it, Anton. You*

can fuck up a wet dream, I swear.

"Okay, ladies, that's enough fun for now." I slipped Lita's hands off my chest and managed to get Sarai to calm her advances down, despite not wanting either to take their hands off me. "I have another appointment that I have to make, and I don't want to be late for it, okay?"

Sarai looked over at Lita before they focused on me, trying to assess what to make of my attempt at blocking their advances. Sarai moved in close again, this time to gauge the look in my eyes, daring me to change my mind. I felt every word she wanted to say with her intense stare into the windows of my soul. "You know you want it, Devin. All you have to do is say you want it, baby."

Lita pressed her breasts against my back, kissing my neck. I cursed Sarai for giving away my weak spots, and my body was a nibble on the ear away from telling me that this was what it was going to have, regardless of what I said I had to do. She whispered in my ear, "We won't take long, promise. She's had you, but I want you."

I didn't know where I found the strength, but I stared back into Sarai's light grey eyes with conviction, determined to find the best way to end this interlude. "I can't do this, no matter how much my body wants it. I don't know how to explain it, but she's on my mind right now. I need to stop."

I took a chance by turning them down. Women could be worse than men when it came to rejection sometimes, and I still wanted to keep our professional relationship intact. Sarai was one of the best in the business; being on her good side was always good for business.

Her eyes widened for a moment, like she couldn't believe I was spurning her advances, but her lips widened into a warm smile, a knowing wink giving me the chance to relax a bit. I might have upset her, but not enough for it to affect how she felt about me. Our business relationship—despite the blurred lines—was more important than a few moments of bliss.

"I hope she's worth it, D-Lo." She kissed my lips a final time before she took Lita's hand and disappeared around the front of my truck. "But if she isn't, you know where to find me. Oh, and in case you were wondering, Lita's game, too, for real."

I banged my head against the glass window on the side of my truck, trying hard to calm the revolt my body waged against my mind. Whether I wanted to believe it or not, I'd found myself caught up in the rapture. I managed to rebuff the attack, despite what my body wanted. I blew out air, collecting my faculties, looking to the sky before lifting from my truck. *Yeah, I hope she is, too.*

Deion

Chapter Fourteen: Brown Sugar…

I had Alexia meet me at Chops Lobster Bar in Buckhead. I was in the mood for steak, and I remembered that she had a weakness for seafood, so it felt like a good spot to do a lunch date. It was a bit more expensive than the average locale, but I wanted to impress her. Considering I was coming from Alpharetta, she would beat me to the restaurant and already be at a table by the time I got there. I did that on purpose; I wanted to see what she was wearing while she was seated. It sounded a little mannish, but I wanted to get a peek at those pretty legs again, and on my terms this time.

"I'm sorry if I kept you waiting too long." I kissed her on the cheek before sitting down at the table. "The shoot that I told you about was in North Fulton at the B&B estate."

"That's fine, D, I was just getting something to drink, so you're not too late." Alexia let me off the hook as she winked at me. "Maybe I should order something really tasty and expensive to make you pay for making me wait an extra ten minutes on you."

"Oh, now you're just being mean." I teased, enjoying the banter between us. I also enjoyed the smoothness of the exchanges between us, like there was nothing in the way of things taking their natural course.

"So, are you ready for the questions in my mind?" Alexia had this cute little inquisitive look in her eyes that made me want to tell her anything. It scared me a little; I didn't want to divulge too much information so soon after meeting a woman. I wanted to retain some level of mystery.

"What do you want to know? I'm twenty-eight, born and raised in the A, anything else you will have to ask me." I leaned in to drop my voice a couple octaves to get my last statement across. So much for wanting to be mysterious. "And I do mean *anything*."

I observed her as the wheels began turning in her head after I clarified. The minute that she realized that I was serious, a mischievous smirk spread across her lips. I was worried that maybe I'd allowed her to go as far as she wanted in her line of questioning. "The answer to your question is yes, it is true."

I grinned after making that statement, thinking I had her off guard. Her eyes widened for a moment like she was trying to adjust her line of thinking. I waited a few moments for her to figure out what she wanted to say, leaning back in my chair as I continued to peruse the menu.

"How did you know if I would ask that? I could have been thinking about anything." Alexia blushed, giving away the secret to the depths of her thoughts. Yeah, I had her off guard.

"No, I didn't know anything, I'm just guessing here, Alexia," I admitted to her, trying to calm her a little. "So, what's really on your mind, cuteness?"

I took her hand and stared into her eyes, feeling her hands tremble the minute our eyes connected. I used the effect my eyes had on the women I was interested in to my advantage, and they didn't fail me. Alexia let out a slow exhale, trying to regain some sort of balance and control, licking her lips before I snapped her back from whatever world she traveled to.

"Alexia?"

"Mmmhhmmmm?"

"The question you were gonna ask me?"

She shook out of her trance, refocused on my face, studied it a little more before the next question popped out of her mouth. "I would have figured that you have a girlfriend or someone special in your life. You've got things together, not like the other brothas I've dealt with."

Damn. She went for the jugular. That question hit me hard; I hadn't thought about *her* in at least two months or so. The feelings started to rush from the protective wall I thought was strong enough to hold them at bay. To say I was wrong was an understatement, but it's all out there in the front of my consciousness now. Since she wanted to talk about it, I guessed there was no other choice but to talk about it.

"I had someone—" I uttered as my voice trailed off. I really wasn't sure that I was ready to talk about it yet, but there was no turning back once I started the sentence. "Yeah, I had someone, but that feels more like a former lifetime at this point."

"Devin, it's okay, you don't have to talk about it if you don't want to." Alexia squeezed my hand to get my eyes in her direction again. The look of concern on her face, her eyes told me that I might be okay if I got that ghost out of the darkness. "I'm sorry if I brought it up, I didn't want to put a damper on how things were going between us."

"Her name was Jenna. I spent my last year doing everything in my power to try to please her. Out of the blue, she started talking about marriage and kids, and I wasn't ready for all that," I replied. "In the end, I found out that I wasn't her ideal anymore, at least not like the next man that she's probably getting to know and wanting to marry."

The confession coming off my lips felt like I'd vomited pure acid. I wasn't willing to admit that I was wrong or that I might have had some hand in the demise of my previous relationship until I looked someone else in the eyes to tell them what happened.

"Before I met her, yeah, you were right. I was a player on levels that most couldn't even touch. Young, dumb and full of come and didn't give a fuck who I hurt or how badly I did." I continued swallowing dagger after dagger in front of a woman that I wasn't sure would even want to bother with me by the time I got done baring my soul. "I guess this was Karma letting me know that all of that shit was gonna come back to haunt me."

"Devin, from what I know of you now, and what Natalia told me about you this morning when we talked, you're not as horrible as you're making yourself out to be." The conviction in her voice seemed to center me. I couldn't help but pay attention to what she had to say. "You could have taken advantage of me last night when I drank too much wine and probably offered myself to you on a silver platter."

"Yeah, but I did think about it." I exhaled. At that point, I didn't want to be made out to be a saint or some dude that would have never taken an easy out. "You made me weak, and I could have and acted like I didn't."

"D, you didn't, and that counts in my book." Alexia was insistent, regardless of my protestations. "Sooner or later, you're gonna have to stop thinking you're some bad guy. You're not allowed to. Not this time."

I felt hands moving across the back of my shoulders and a pair of lips brush across the side of my neck. I jerked, turning around to figure out the source of the unexpected presence. I looked up, but the delicate hands that were on me disappeared as quickly as they'd appeared. The look on Alexia's face was a mix of confusion and irritation.

"Hi, daddy, miss me? Don't tell me you forgot to call me after the party last night?" The sound of her voice felt like hot needles piercing my ears, a constant reminder of one of those bad decisions I regretted.

Being in the same space as Tina Parker, Mr. Parker's youngest daughter, was the last thing I wanted or needed right now. The tension in my shoulders ratcheted up a few notches, and I hoped that my knee-jerk negative reaction to her invasion of my personal space would have tipped Alexia off that this was not wanted. After pouring my heart out, the timing couldn't have been worse.

I could tell that she wanted to show off in front of her clique. I nicknamed them the "Brat Pack" because they were all spoiled daughters of powerful and affluent families here in Atlanta. Even though they were all over eighteen, their maturity level would have led to a different assumption.

Alexia picked up on the tension, but if it was bothering her, she never let on. Instead, she smiled and extended her hand in Tina's direction. "Excuse me, I'm sorry but we haven't met. I'm Alexia Anthony, a friend of Devin's."

"That's nice, I'm Tina Parker. I'm sure that my daddy has told you that I am his baby girl, haven't you, daddy?" She looked down at me, ignoring the disgusted look on my face. She was laying it on thick, no doubt putting on for the crowd looking on with interest. Some were in the midst of pulling out their cell phones in anticipation of a video-worthy moment, others were whispering loud enough for me to figure out that a few of them knew who I was. Hindsight had me wishing I'd requested a private dining area, but it was too late for that now.

Alexia had this look on her face, causing me to wonder if she was about to say something to take Tina down a notch. She gave up this evil smile, like I'd had her in every way imaginable. "Well, honey, I am sure that your *daddy* has told you that he and I were together all night last night…*all night*. Maybe that's why he didn't get a chance to call you, since he was otherwise, shall we say, tied up with a few things."

To say I was shocked would be a gross understatement.

Tina's eyes widened, showing a storm on the horizon. She popped on the water works, looking like she wanted to rip Alexia apart. The other girls pulled her away as Tina continued yelling obscenities at her. *"Devin is mine!! I'll beat your ass first!!"*

Alexia grinned like she was the cat that swallowed a canary. She looked unbothered as she waved Tina off, knowing that the rest of the group was unwilling to let her go to keep a scene from occurring. "I'll make sure to save you some later today, if he has the strength to see you later."

I sat there, at a complete loss for words as I watched Tina and crew disappear out of the area. "Why did you…you could have busted me big time, Alexia."

She smirked, shrugging off my concerns like they were as trivial as Tina was. "Please, I read your body language the moment she caught you by surprise. It was obvious you were uncomfortable with her being draped all over you, and not in an 'oh shit, my girlfriend showed up' kinda way."

"But we never slept together last night." I protested. I wanted her to know that, now that I was in my right mind. "Believe me, I wanted to—God, I wanted to—but I didn't want to have to refresh your memory."

Alexia slapped my hand, her eyes piercing through me as she regarded me with curiosity. "Why are you so sure of yourself when you're at work, like you were at the showcase, but now you're so insecure around me?"

"Alexia," I hesitated, trying to find the right words to say. "Real talk, I'm not sure of myself around you. I'm completely vulnerable and it's driving me insane. Hell, I think Quinn had something to do with that last night at the party."

"What do you mean by that?" Her curiosity was full tilt now.

"That fool damn near lost his mind the minute that you and the girls showed up." I was still shaking my head at my inability to control my emotions. "Next thing I know, I'm doing everything that I can not to look like I was happy and relieved to see that you showed up. I haven't felt like that since—"

"Jenna." Alexia completed my thought.

"I refuse to get you wrapped up in my bullshit, Alexia, no matter how bad I want you," I told her, breaking yet another one of my rules. *Never let them know how you feel until you know how they feel.*

Yeah, real smooth, D-Lo.

Her eyes narrowed, and it confirmed that I played my hand too damned soon. "Do you want me, D?"

I swallowed hard, realizing there was no turning back now that the proverbial cat was out of the bag. "Yes."

"I want you, too," Alexia replied in seconds, putting me in complete shock. "I wanted you last night, even before I got so lit. I wasn't sure whether to let you take me or not. I'm still not sure I'm ready to, but you turn me on in ways I haven't felt in a long time."

If looks could kill, we'd both have been dead right there on the spot.

The look on my face told her we needed to go *now*.

The look on her face told me to find the shortest route to get there.

Like I needed to ask? There was nothing else that I needed to say. Alexia mouthed the words "let's go" before I could say anything further.

The only thing left was to get the check.

Alexia

Chapter Fifteen: Lose My Breath…

I was pinned against the wall before the door shut. God, I wanted him so much I was dripping wet before I knew what was happening. I wrapped my leg around his waist, my tongue finding his with an urgency that scared me as I felt his long fingers gripping my hips.

He whipped me around, picking me up and setting me on top of the island in the kitchen, spreading my legs and sliding his fingers inside me, confirming what I already knew. I didn't want to stop him; I didn't try to, either. He slipped his fingers in and out of me, pulling them out and licking his fingers one by one. He pulled me in for a kiss before I could push him away or slow him down.

That shit was so nasty and so damn sexy I could have exploded right there on the spot. I didn't want him to wait. He could have me right there for all I cared. I needed to be taken. I grabbed at him, clawing at his shirt as he tried to take it off.

Devin grunted and growled, his urges causing him to take

leave of his senses. I felt the heat oozing from our bodies, the sweat beads rolling down my chest.

"*Oh...God, D...give it to me,*" I whispered, trying hard not to disturb the zone that we were both in, threatening to consume us both for at least the next few hours. If I had my way, it would be the rest of the night.

I would have gotten my wish...until I heard Cardi B's voice cutting through the air, spitting fire about her love for the finer things in life.

Damn it...I didn't want to leave him. I was about to get into something long and strong, despite my apprehension of not having been physical in months. The ringtone meant Keri was calling me. She and Cam picked out their ringtones for their numbers, and this was Keri all day long.

I squeezed my eyes tighter, losing myself in his touch again, raking my nails down his back, pulling him deeper into me, trying my best to make him one with me.

Cardi wouldn't stop rhyming. Fuck.

"Maybe...you should...get that, Lexi." Devin tried to kiss and talk at the same time, and I could feel him. He was so close...so damn close.

"They...can...wait, damn it." I protested, my body getting even hotter at the thought of him slipping deep inside me. "Give it to me, please."

Oh my God, quit teasing me, I screamed in my head. I squeezed my legs tighter around him, not daring to let him leave my space. I couldn't believe how needy I was, but I didn't care anymore. I wanted this release. I needed this release.

But Cardi was relentless in her anthem:

Your chick wanna party with Cardi
Cartier Bardi in a 'Rari
Diamonds all over my body
Shining all over my body

She wouldn't stop blowing up my phone until I answered it. Devin realized it, too. He broke from me, giving me room to hop down and grab my phone.

I was ready to light her up, I was not in the mood to show an ounce of mercy. "Oh my God, this better be life or death, Keri."

"Not quite, but it's close, baby." Keri's voice piped through the earpiece. "Laura wants us to do a fresh demo for the meeting with RPK in the morning."

"In the morning??" I was stunned. This couldn't be real. "I thought we had at least another couple of days?"

"Yeah, babe, it threw us off, too, but Mr. Parker loved the demo once he got a chance to sit down and listen to it, so he called Laura and pushed the date up. The meeting has been reset for tomorrow instead of Thursday," Keri told me. She was trying to sound all business-like, but she couldn't resist giggling. "I can tell from the sound of your voice that I caught you in the midst of getting some, but—"

"I'll be there," I shot back, cutting her off. "As long as we're not in there all night."

I clicked my phone off, feeling like I wanted to cry. I thought my drought was over. I turned around to face Devin, but he already had his shirt on, reading my body language almost to perfection. I tried to explain myself, but my heart sank with each word coming from my lips. "Mr. Parker wants to meet earlier than scheduled, so Laura wants us to cut another demo for the meeting. They've scheduled the meeting for the morning."

Devin, to my shock and surprise, was calm about it all. "Don't worry about it, Lexi, I do work for the man. I should have known he would drop everything once he heard you guys. It's how this industry works."

Devin moved closer to me, sending more chills down my spine. What he did to me should be declared illegal. His eyes were all over me, making me feel naked, so delicious in front of him. He kissed me so softly my body melted. His voice sounded as silky smooth as my skin felt under his touch. "Go take care of business, sexy, there will be another time."

As I felt his hand move down to my ass to let me know that we would finish what we started, I made it clear the feeling was very mutual. "I promise, it will be soon. I'm still irritated we had to stop, but I don't have a choice."

Devin smiled, putting me at ease in moments. "There's a time and place for everything. This wasn't the time, and I'm good with that for now. My head was a little clouded from the mess with Tina earlier, and you deserve better than that. I'll catch up with you in the morning when you're done in the studio, okay?"

"I'm looking forward to it. I miss you already."

"All right, Lexi, what's the info on the meeting in the morning?"

We were in the final stages of finishing the other demo that we needed, and while Laura spoke to the engineers in the booth, the three of us chatted in the lounge area before we headed home for the night. After four hours of taping, plus the fact that it was creeping up on midnight, the last thing I was in the mood for was a damn fishing expedition from Camryn.

I narrowed my eyes, wondering what she was getting at. "You tell me? Keri was the one who called me to cut this CD on less than a moment's notice."

"Come on, Lexi, Keri told me you were with Devin." Camryn cut to the chase, but she wasn't about to get anything out of me. "Did he tell you anything before you left him?"

"D never told me anything." I lied. Some things did not need to be divulged. "Can't y'all wait a few more hours? Damn."

"Maybe if we had waited another thirty minutes or so and let her take care of him like she was in the midst of doing, we wouldn't have to grill her so damn hard." Camryn countered, folding her arms across her chest. "Or maybe if you hadn't taken your sweet time waiting for the 'proper moment' and handled him the way I handled his boy last night, maybe you wouldn't be in such a sour mood."

"Oh my God, Cam, the word is loose, chick," I snapped back, causing the temperature in the room to drop a few degrees from the tension. "I am not out to get at every high-profile name that I run into. So, you had DJ Infinity? Some other bitch is probably laying claim to that while we've been handling business in the studio."

Camryn huffed, unfazed by my onslaught. "Are you jealous because I got stroked and you didn't, Lexi? What's the matter, did your little photographer friend get a little camera shy on you?"

"Okay, you two, enough with the cat-fighting bullshit," Keri finally chimed in, doing her best to shut us down. "If

Lexi says she doesn't know anything, then she doesn't know anything. We'll find out tomorrow, got it?"

Laura walked into the room, noticing that something was off between me and Camryn, but instead of saying something to either of us, she issued a blank directive. "Whatever business that needs to be handled before morning...make sure it's handled. If you don't, I will."

Camryn backed off, but not before she whispered in my ear as we walked out of the studio, "Yeah, this is a business, and you use who you need to use and what you need to use to get to the top. Remember that."

Deion

Chapter Sixteen: If You Don't Give a Damn…

I was already fighting sleep, so why I decided to answer the phone was anybody's guess. Hearing Tina's voice on the other end should have been enough to make me hang up the phone, but I was convinced I was in a dream state the whole time.

I guess she was insistent on letting me know it wasn't a dream. "Why did you let that trick call me out like that? I should have beat her ass."

Was my cell phone wired with explosives or something? I was trying my best to figure out what possessed this child to call me at damn near midnight and she didn't have girlfriend privileges like that. "Tina, did you really think there was anything going on between us? What do you want from me? I have told you several times that you are too young for me."

"But you need a girl who lives to please you, daddy." Tina insisted. "I can do all of the things you want, and then some."

"Stop calling me daddy, I never told you that it was okay

to do that," I responded, trying to figure out the first possible exit from this conversation. "There's nothing you can do for me, Tina. You need to experience life first. You're barely out of high school."

"Yes, there is something I can do for you, D. I can convince my father to invest the capital you need for your new film studio, and you know I have girlfriends and their friends that can supply you with all the actors and actresses you'll ever need," Tina sweetly cooed in my ear. "I bet that woman you were with earlier today can't do that for you."

I blew air over the mouthpiece, wishing that this conversation was over before it even got started. "God, I'm sorry I ever told you that."

"Well, you did, sexy, and the choice is up to you now. I get what I want, and you get what you've always dreamed of," she proposed. I felt the smile wash over her face through the phone. "Be my first lover, make me a woman, and I'll get you the money and the space you need to make me and every girl I send to you Hollywood ready."

I felt a migraine coming on. Whenever I got stressed beyond all recognition, those things would kick in and it was a wrap. I didn't know what made me confide in her, but it was only a matter of time before that indecent proposal would find itself out in the open, regardless of the fact that I flat out told her I wouldn't do it. I could never do that to old man Parker, and Natalia would kill me.

Tina Parker was fifteen when we met. I was getting started at RPK as a staff photographer and Mr. Parker hired me to take pictures at her sweet sixteen birthday party. I convinced him that I could make her daughter look mature but not overly sexual, which seemed to be the rage for teenage girls.

I was good friends with Tina's older sister, Nicole, at the time, which is how I managed to get on at RPK in the first place. Nicole set everything up.

Her friends took one look at her finished head shots and photo spread and beat a path to my makeshift studio in the spare room of my old apartment in College Park. Next thing I knew, I had more business than I could shake a stick at. In fact, her old high school is still one of my biggest clients away from RPK.

I had a good thing going, except my flirtatious nature combined with her friends at school making comments about what they would let me do to them if they had a chance, and it became the recipe for a crush that hadn't waned three years later. It's not like Tina wasn't gorgeous, that's beside the point. She's not even nineteen yet. But she's the daughter of one of the men that I respect above any other on this planet. I'd already went down that road with Natalia, and I was lucky I didn't catch heat from that.

The only reason that Mr. Richton didn't blow a gasket was that he took a liking to me and had always thought of me as a son, so when Natalia and I started hanging out, it didn't faze him all that much. The fact that we were close in age might have had something to do with it, too. But I didn't get it twisted. I kept the sexual adventures that Natalia and I had a secret. So secret, in fact, that even the FBI wouldn't know the details of what happened. If I had the proper connections, they wouldn't be able to find out shit, either...at least, not without special interrogation methods.

At the end of the day, Tina was like a little sister in my eyes, despite the fact that her hips and curves had developed into something that Shakira must have been referring to in one of her songs back in the day. Now, she'd put an indecent proposal out, laid down a gauntlet that any man would probably kill for: seed money in exchange for a zipless affair. All thanks to trusting my "little sister" with a dream that no one else on the planet knew about—except Natalia. But she never used that information against me, not like Tina was doing to me right now.

God, I hated myself for giving her the power over me like this.

Something's gotta change, and soon, or I may do something I may regret, I thought to myself as I got up from my bed, with Alexia on my mind and what would've happened if she hadn't been called to the studio.

I needed to get out of the house before something else happened, and I knew just the person I needed to see.

"Since when did you have time to come see your boy in the studio?"

Quinn was right, I never had time to make pop visits, but I needed to holla at my boy about a few things, and I needed the time away from the house. Anton was on my mind. He'd been avoiding me since the night we were at the club. I needed answers, and I figured Quinn could have an idea of what might be the problem.

"I had two things I needed to get at you about. First, are you jumping on producer credits for the girls' first album?" I asked that question to butter him up before asking the second question. "Second, have you seen Ant? He's not returning my calls. I tried him on the 'book, on the 'gram, nothing."

"Damn, Camryn got to you, too, D? Was it good to you?" Quinn snapped. He gave me this look like I'd taken a knife and cut his heart out. "Oh well, it's not like I had feelings for her. Rumors are all over the place about her, cats hitting me up on the 'gram and the 'book and shit. I should have known better than to get caught up in the mix."

I put my hands up in protest, confused over what just happened. "Hold up, Q, I don't know where your mind was, but you know I don't roll like that. How you gonna believe that I smashed Camryn because I asked about you producing a few tracks?"

Quinn's eyes widened after he'd realized what came out of his mouth. "Devin, damn, my bad, that shouldn't have come out like that, for real. That woman has me trippin'."

"Yeah, she's got you twisted all right." I looked at him, trying to figure out what in the world had gotten into him. It wasn't like Quinn to let some female rule him like this.

"Bro, if you knew what I knew, you'd be a little twisted, too. I'm almost tempted to let you see the video I took the other night. She even let me snap that shit for the folk." Quinn shot back. He gave me a quizzical look, wondering if he wasn't the only one getting the "treatment." "I'm surprised that Alexia hadn't already tried to grease the wheels a little. You know, to push the date up to get this deal done? I mean, Cam's been popping off all over social media about the pending deal, yo."

When I didn't answer to that comment, Quinn looked disgusted, jumping to conclusions without a second thought. "Damn, is this gonna be Jenna all over again?"

"Low blow, Q."

He laughed, thinking he'd struck a nerve. He kept

digging, stoking my anger even more by the second.

"Nah, it's gravy, my dawg. You're getting soft and sweet on her, and that's cool, you're built like that. I'm not ever turning in my player's membership, unless I get old and can't do what I used to do anymore."

I wanted to slap him silly for that comment about comparing Jenna to Alexia, but I slowed that down. All that would do was confirm what he'd suspected. Still, if Camryn was all but confirming that the deal was a wrap, there was no telling what the other two might have been up to. I'd been so busy trying to keep things flowing at RPK that I hadn't had a chance to see what was going on in the social media world.

Quinn was still on his rant, oblivious to anything I might have said. "I know Camryn's got gold in her eyes, and if you're honest with yourself, Alexia and Keri can't be too far from the mark. I'm hoping the rumors aren't true about Cam and one of the execs at RPK, because if they are, I'm gonna have to drop her quick. Just do me a favor, keep Alexia around until she wears out her welcome; they always do. Besides, the group already got what they wanted anyway and—"

"All right, Q, *that's enough.*" I cut in, shutting him down quickly. "You got one more time to—"

"I'm just sayin', D-Lo—"

"Feel where I'm at *right now*," I raged, jumping in his face. "One, according to Alexia, Mr. Parker pushed the meeting up to tomorrow morning after he got a chance to listen to the live performance for himself. Two, I did everything I could to stay out of the mix with regard to what their group has to go through, because, conflict of interest, hello? And three, I'll drop you where you stand if you ever mention Jenna in the same breath as Lexi again. Are we clear?"

"All right, bruh, chill, no need to get your chest all puffed up, shawty." Quinn switched gears, remembering the other question I asked. "Anyway, Ant's been off the grid for a while, man. I'm surprised you hadn't noticed it yourself. Now that I think about it, you've been knee-deep in distractions of the fairer sex for the past few, getting dropped by one and picking up a few more on the back end."

"What do you mean by that? We hung out a couple of weeks ago." I countered, a little irritated that the conversation was taking this tone. Damn, I was trying to take my mind off things, not weigh more shit down on it.

Quinn shook his head like I was on the outside of a really bad inside joke. "Ant's been salty about some stuff, bruh, especially when we side-stepped him about the party at Mr. Richton's house. When I called to check on him the other day, he was talking stupid, said we chose women over him."

Here we go, Anton being his melodramatic self again. The weed got him straight paranoid. Still, the way Quinn looked at me, something wasn't adding up, and I needed to know what the fuck he was holding back. "What aren't you telling me, Q? You know Ant, he usually comes off his high and it's squashed."

Quinn rubbed his hands over his face, and his body language gave me the impression that he really didn't want to be the messenger on this one. "I know he's your boy and all, D, and I wish it was just the weed talking, but he's graduated."

Graduated? To what? "Spill it, bruh."

"I caught him doing lines at the club with the female he

was messing around with after you left with that woman you were with that night."

What the?!?!?!

I speed-dialed his cell phone and it went straight to voicemail. I got a bad feeling something was wrong. I didn't panic, but it was coming close to that.

"I would have told you sooner, but he swore it was his first time doing the shit, and he didn't want you giving him a lecture about it." Quinn's eyes were about as unyielding as they could be in that moment, like he couldn't have cared less about how this was going to go down. "Besides, it's not like you've been home team lately anyway."

Lecture? I'd give him more than a damn lecture, right after I ripped Quinn a new one for coming off smug like I didn't care about my friends. "I've been home team a lot longer than you, bruh, or do you have a bit of revisionist history going on?"

"You're doing too much, D-Lo, for real. Just let the man be. Damn. Last I heard, he'd been rocking with some new chick anyway. I'm sure he doesn't want to be disturbed."

"I'm going over there now to check on him, and if I disturb him, then I disturb him." I stared Quinn down before I left the studio, daring him to say another word. "You better hope that he's still in one piece, bruh, or you and I are gonna have words."

"Look, Devin, let it go, I'm telling you, you don't want the work that he's been wanting to give out." Quinn tried to grab my arm, but I shook loose, coming close to knuckling up.

"And you don't want the work I'm gonna give you if this has gotten so far out of hand that I can't get him right." I glared at Quinn like he was a complete stranger to me in that moment. "The fact that you didn't even want to bother telling me is enough of a problem in and of itself. I'll holla at you later, though, you can bet that."

Deion

Chapter Seventeen: U Don't Know Me

I was on my way to my truck before Quinn could stop me. His last words of warning were to let sleeping dogs lie and to not go looking for ghosts in a graveyard. He was still in the doorway leading into the studio, shaking his head as he watched me peel out of the parking lot like the situation was a matter of life and death.

This was my boy, I couldn't let him go downhill like that. We'd been tight for too long, since middle school. No way was I going to let him be. He would have never left me in such dire straits, why would I leave him?

On the way up I-285 to Vinings, my mind flashed back to the last few months before I broke up with Jenna. Anton was there, in my face the whole time, trying to tell me that I needed to get over it, not letting me sink deeper, that she wasn't worth keeping. Quinn couldn't understand that; he was on the West Coast producing another album when I was going through that.

If Anton was in trouble, I wouldn't let him sink. That was

not how we rolled. The problem that kept nagging at me were the thoughts that kept flowing through my mind, trying to figure out where things could have gone wrong. I didn't want to believe that things had gotten so bad that he had to resort to cocaine.

While were playing basketball in high school, I sort of turned a blind eye to the marijuana usage, even though it would ruin his prospects with colleges that were recruiting him if he got caught. I should have told his parents back then, but the way that his mother was, I didn't want him kicked off the team. If I was honest, I was more concerned with winning a state title than I was getting into family business. I even tried to get the girls that he was with to sweet talk him into not doing it so much, and for a while it worked.

But when we signed at different schools, even though we never lost touch, calling after games and things like that, I guessed in hindsight I couldn't have known if he'd graduated to the harder stuff or not. I loved him like a brother, but he was a grown man now, and I was not his babysitter. Quinn made sure to make that point. Still, I felt a twinge of guilt that maybe I could have steered him away from the shit if I really wanted to, especially when he got kicked out of school over the weed use.

I should have taken the clue back then, but I didn't. I continued to turn a blind eye to it, not realizing that he was going down a road that I couldn't turn him away from. I wasn't strong enough for him; I couldn't be strong for him. He had to want it for himself. That was the way I began to look at the situation.

Natalia was done with him after an incident happened last year with one of her girlfriends, Samantha Tyler. It felt like that night happened last week. That night, we were all invited to a baby shower in the couple's honor. Samantha was in her final trimester, but it was a difficult pregnancy. Anton knew about it, but the proud father we thought he would be wasn't as proud as we thought by that point.

At first, he was happy about it, even told his parents that they would be welcoming their first grandchild into the world, but all that changed when he received a text message out of the blue. We didn't know who it was from at the time, but it was a screen shot of a conversation between the mystery person and Samantha, telling her to come clean about who the father was.

Right there at the party, Anton confronted her about the paternity of the child. Samantha explained that it was an ex-boyfriend who was still trying to get back at her for breaking up with him. Natalia told him that Samantha had been staying with her at the estate, and no one ever came there to visit after she found out she was pregnant. No matter what was said, it wasn't enough for Anton. He was convinced that Samantha had slept with another man and wouldn't let the issue go. The screen shot was enough of a smoking gun to keep things confusing.

They argued the rest of the night, going back and forth, screaming at each other, when Samantha screamed out in pain, saying something was wrong with the baby. The blood trickling down her legs was the telltale clue, and we did our best to rush her to the nearest hospital, but it was too late. The doctors did everything they could, and the baby girl they should have been having was in an incubator for all of ten minutes before she died.

But that wasn't the straw that broke the camel's back.

Anton barged into the room after the baby was pronounced dead and demanded a blood test be done to determine if he was the father or not. The scene was something out of a freaking Lifetime drama, complete with security officers escorting him from the hospital against his will. A few weeks later, they were in front of a judge, getting the final determination on public record. The baby was Anton's after all.

That incident nearly ended things between Natalia and me. She wanted him gone from all of our lives, but I told her I couldn't do it. Even in the wake of the incident that was clearly his fault, I couldn't do it. I was brought up to believe that you didn't leave your friends when they were at their lowest. You couldn't get any lower than what he did.

That was then, this was now. I made up my mind that once I got to the spot that it would be a make or break conversation between him and me. Either check in to rehab, or he was on his own.

I got to Anton's condo and I recognized his car sitting in its usual spot in the driveway. I walked up to the door and noticed that it was slightly ajar, which tripped my senses. I ran back to my truck to get my Glock. I'd be damned if I was gonna get caught up, and I was worried about my boy, too.

I debated whether to keep the safety on as I slipped inside the door, not knowing what to expect. Once I got into the living room, though, my anxiety level kicked up a notch. The room looked like a disaster area. The flat screen was gone, leaving a gaping hole in the wall in its place, and the windows were shattered. The only thing that was missing was a dead or dying body. I feared the worst.

"Ant! It's D, man, you in here?!?!" I shouted. I realized I

might give myself away, but I needed to know if Anton was in the house or not.

The next thing I heard was a pop. The next thing I felt was a burning sensation and an intense pain shooting through my left shoulder. Grabbing the source of my pain, I turned around, coming face to face with Anton, who stood in the hallway between the living room and kitchen.

"You shouldn't have come here, D-Lo." The calmness in his voice worried me. Anton faced me, gun pointed, eyes wild and looking right through me. "I thought Quinn told you to leave me alone. I guess you didn't heed the message. You never were good at taking orders, but you damn sure were good at giving them, weren't you? Oh well, no worries, I won't miss with my next shot."

"Ant, what the hell, bruh?!?!" I tried to take the fear out of my voice, but considering I'd already had my shoulder plugged by a bullet with his first shot, I was failing miserably at that task. "What are you doing, dawg?"

"What do you think I'm doing, *brother*?" Anton sneered. The way his eyes looked as we stared each other down, it was like I was another dude on the street. "I'm about to take care of two problems today. This was something I should have done a long time ago."

"Anton, you ain't gotta do this, man." I tried to reason with him, but I'd seen that look in his eyes before, and if I didn't have a reason to fear for my life, I had one now. "Just put the gun down and tell me what the problem is."

"You're my freaking problem, Devin!!!" Anton screamed, cocking the hammer back on his gun. "No matter where I turn, what I do, your shadow keeps popping up!"

"What is wrong with you?!?!" I yelled at him. "I haven't

done anything to you! I've been like family for over fifteen years!!!"

Anton's eyes were glazed over, and I noticed white powder under his nose, confirming Quinn's accusations. He kept his gun trained on me, watching my every move. "We used to be friends, bruh. You abandoned me, but I guess I can't blame you for it, not after what I've done."

"You're not thinking straight, bruh." I tried to stay calm, stay in the moment with him, but that was slipping away. "What do you mean by what you've done? There's nothing you could have possibly done that would have had me turn my back on you."

"That's what you think." Anton narrowed his eyes, throwing some papers in my face. "Once this gets out, it's going to change a lot of things. Too bad I won't be around to see it all go down."

I could have choked the hell out of Quinn for letting me walk into this buzz saw. I read the details on the papers while keeping one eye on him. "Is this what I think this is?"

"You really are slow tonight, huh? I guess a bullet in your shoulder will do that."

The paperwork was Ant's STD results. Among the results, it showed that he had tested positive for HSV type 2 and gonorrhea. In an instant, it hit me: this must have been what he was trying his best to get my attention about.

"Damn, Ant, I'm sorry—"

"It's too late for all that, my dude. My career—my life— is over once that gets out. I can't hide from it, and there's no life for me once I'm out of the industry." The tears flowed as Ant did his best to keep his hands on his gun. "A lot of this I can lay at your feet. If you hadn't been fucking around with my life, I would be married to Sam with kids by now. But you had to try to take her, too."

"Are you serious right now? She was only into you, bruh. No one had her heart but you!"

"Nah, yo, I saw how Sam looked at you, how she flirted with you when you both thought I wasn't looking." Anton sniffled, taking a free hand to stuff the coke inside his nostrils. "No one wanted to believe that you would ever do anything like that to me, but we both know better, don't we?"

I blinked at the absurdity of his accusations. He was making stuff up now. None of that happened, and if he wasn't so far gone he would realize that, too.

"Look, Ant, put the gun down, let's talk this out. I love you like a brother, doesn't that matter to you?" I held back tears as I tried to find any way to get to him. My uncle was a cop, and he used to warn me about people who were coked out of their minds. Reality was twisted into some convoluted mess, and they used it against you to make themselves look better. I swear I never thought I would see it happen…not to one of mine.

I watched his face. He was struggling, but there was no way I was going to figure out what was in his head. His eyes moved all over the place, finding me every few seconds, waiting for me to make a move.

I kept my gun drawn, but the safety was off now. I couldn't let him get the drop on me, regardless of whether he was high or not. I grimaced in pain every time I tried to raise my arm, and my grip on my gun was shaky. I was losing blood, and it was only a matter of time before I passed out from shock. It killed me inside that this had reached this point, but the point of no return was reached when he shot me the first time. There was no turning back, no matter how much either one of us wanted to.

"Put the gun down, Ant! It doesn't have to end this way!" I yelled at him, placing my left hand around my right, trying to hold my gun steady, not sure what would happen next. The pain was intense, but I gritted my teeth through it. I didn't want to shoot him, but it was either going to be me or him, and it wasn't going to be me. "Think about your mom, what will she think?"

Mentioning his mother seemed to snap him into reality, if only for a brief moment. He stared at me, and I saw my shotgun partner again. He lowered the gun, wiping the tears from his face. I wanted to move toward him, to get the gun out of his hand so I could help him out of this nightmare that he found himself in. I needed to get him out of this somehow, but I was running out of options.

Against my better judgment, I took a step toward him, putting the safety on my gun and tucking it away in my back. I moved slow, trying not to trip his fight-or-flight mechanism. He stayed in place, not moving a muscle, his eyes on me the entire time. I wasn't sure whether to say anything or to keep quiet, but I was in desperate need to get to him before he did anything stupid.

I was within striking distance, ready to lunge and get the gun out of his hand, when he raised the gun in my direction again. I was at near point-blank range, and one squeeze of the trigger would be the end of me. He had me dead to rights, but he hesitated. If he was going to put me out of my misery, I almost wished he would get it over with.

Anton wiped the remnants of the tears from his eyes, his lips trembling as he scowled at me, remembering his contempt for everything that had anything to do with me. His eyes were cold; I knew then that there was nothing left for us as friends. "It has to end this way, D-Lo. You're going to suffer for everything you've done to me. It's over. I'm done."

Alexia

Chapter Eighteen: See You at the Crossroads…

Seeing Natalia's number on my cell phone's caller ID was an odd thing at this time of night. I couldn't figure out what she could have wanted as such a weird hour, but I didn't want to be rude and not answer her call, either. As I reached for my phone, an ominous sensation came over me, sending chills down my spine. Something didn't feel right, and I did my best to brace myself for whatever it was that she had to say.

"Hello?" I tried to not sound too groggy, but I failed in every way possible.

"Alexia, I'm sorry to call you at such a late hour, but something bad has happened and Devin's been hurt." Natalia didn't waste time explaining, the urgency in her voice all but confirmed the chills I felt. "I don't know all the details, but one of the officers found his phone and they found my number as an ICE contact."

An ICE contact was the emergency services code for "in case of emergency." I remembered my mother begging me to input it into my phone when she heard about it on a news broadcast. The only reason they would call was if the owner of the phone was incapacitated. If I wasn't worried before, I was terrified now. I screamed at the phone, not realizing that my concern for Devin's safety was deeper than what I wanted to let on. "Oh my God, where are you now, are you on the way there now?"

"Yeah, I'm heading to Anton's condo now." Her speech patterns were erratic and she was speaking at such a rapid pace that it was hard to keep up. "I can come get you on the way. Where do you live?"

"In Dunwoody, outside of Perimeter Mall," I told her, my hands shaking more by the minute. "I'll be ready in fifteen minutes."

"Thanks for picking me up, Natalia."

"No problem, I needed the company. My nerves are shot." Natalia pulled off before I could shut the door. I knew she was concerned, but she was scaring me. "The officer sounded so damn cryptic, I didn't know what to think."

My mind raced faster than the Corvette she drove. No other thoughts were in my head except for getting to the condo. I did my best to figure out how to keep her calm, but she was rolling at break-neck speeds, putting us both at risk. "Let's just hope that the officer was just doing his job and not telling you anything over the phone. We'll know more once we get there."

We sped across the top end of I-285, heading toward Marietta, and I couldn't help but wonder where we were going. "You said we were heading to Anton's condo? Who is Anton? I know Quinn already."

Natalia took a deep breath and exhaled like she was

preparing for a long story in a short amount of time. "Anton is the bad seed of the three of them, Lexi," she started, alternating her glances between me and the road. "He's not an evil person, but he has done some really fucked up things in our collective past."

I sat in the passenger seat, trying to get the gist of things. I got the feeling that Anton was someone that I didn't want to be in contact with. I continued to watch her body language, taking note of how tense she was at the mere mention of his name.

"Anton is a weed head, not that there's anything wrong with that. Don't tell D, but I unwind a little from time to time with Mary Jane. He thinks I don't rock with using it." Natalia kept going as we got off at the Paces Ferry Road exit. "But he's always tried to compete with Devin, like he always had to be better than him at everything."

I couldn't put my finger on it, but she was holding something back. "So, why haven't I met him? If they are that tight, wouldn't he have been at the party at your house?"

"Well, he's not welcome in my house, nor is he allowed within shouting distance of me," Natalia quipped. "The things he did to my best friend…fuck it, long story short, he did some things in light of a miscarriage, things that I can't forgive, and nearly drew a wedge between me and Devin because of it."

My eyes grew wide at that last comment, my silent plea to her that I needed to hear it all, and Natalia decided to finish the story as quickly as she could.

"When everything went down, I lost it, told D that it was either Anton or me; he couldn't have both of us in his life." Natalia recalled, trying to blink away the tears. She gave me the short version, getting into the alleged cheating, the huge fight that caused the miscarriage, the whole nine. "Devin is a stubborn man, and loyal to a fault, so he said that he wouldn't do it, that he would just keep Anton away from me instead. They'd been boys since middle school and he couldn't abandon him because of a bad decision."

I didn't know what to think at that point. I didn't want to share Natalia's disdain for what happened since I wasn't there, and I didn't want to come off like I was taking Devin's side since I understood where he was coming from. If it happened to Keri or Camryn, it was a good bet I would have cut Anton, too.

"It took us a while to build back to where we are now, and the fact that something's happened at Anton's house and D might be hurt because of something that jackass has done—" Natalia's voice trailed off as we approached the chaotic scene that surrounded Anton's condo. "What in the name of all that is holy?"

There were police cars all over the place, and an ambulance was parked across the front lawn. The neighbors were out trying to figure out what was going on, talking to the news crews on scene, which took me by surprise considering it was almost two in the morning.

One of the officers saw us getting out of the car and walked toward us to stop us from heading toward the house. "I'm sorry, ladies, this is a restricted area. There's been an incident."

"We know; we were called regarding the incident." Natalia explained to the officer. "This is Devin Lowery's girlfriend, and I'm the ICE contact who was called, officer."

I knew I wasn't his girlfriend, and I wasn't put off by the reference. It was the only way that the officers would let me in to see him. I stood my ground, willing the tears from falling, staring at the officer as I nodded in agreement with her. My voice was almost gone; I was trying to save it until I saw Devin was okay with my own eyes.

The officer spoke into his radio to let someone inside the house know that we were there. After a few seconds, the voice on the radio told him to escort us to where he was. "Follow me, ladies."

We walked toward the house, noticing the front door had blood streaks on it. I looked over at Natalia, almost mirroring the same worried expression on her face as we continued to follow the officer to the stairs. The place was a mess. It looked like someone did a number and wrecked it beyond any recognition. I almost wanted to back out as we made it up the stairs toward the bedroom.

"Are you okay, Lexi?" Natalia could sense my hesitation. "I'm scared, too, these officers haven't said much of anything, and it's got me on edge. I'm here with you, okay?"

I exhaled, taking her hand as she led the way. "Okay, let's do this."

Walking into the bedroom and seeing that Devin was in one piece, I didn't know whether to scream or cry. Natalia wasted no time sitting down on one side of where he was being attended to by the EMTs, while I found space on the other side of him.

The medic was wrapping and placing a sling on his shoulder while we were doting on him. I didn't care that the medic looked irritated over the two of us being in the way of what he was trying to do, I was glad he was okay, regardless of the wound they were attending to. I spotted a gurney being wheeled across the doorway. I got a quick glance at a dark-skinned man lying on it. I only saw his arm, but from the skin complexion, I assumed that it was Anton, but I'd never seen him before.

I refocused my attention to Devin, and while he could hear us, he looked at us like we weren't there. He had this blank expression on his face, looking exhausted. "Did you call Natalia and Alexia, detective? I know they would be here by now."

"Baby, we're here, both of us." Natalia took hold of his shoulder, trying to get him to snap out of the fog he was in. "Lexi's sitting right next to you, D."

He turned his head toward me, and it seemed like he was looking through me instead of at me. "God, I hope I'm not hallucinating, the medic said I'd lost a lot of blood. This whole thing still feels so surreal. I can't believe he did it. I tried to stop him, I promise I tried, but he—"

"He what, Devin?" I asked him, a gentle nudge to try to pull him out of wherever his mind was and get him to focus on the here and now. "It's okay, sweetheart, tell us what happened? What did he do?"

"Maybe he might open up with you here, this is the most that he's spoken outside of asking for you two," the detective expressed to us. "He's been through a lot, and he's probably still in shock from the gunshot wound, but we need to get a statement from him before we leave."

"D, baby, do you think you can tell the detective what happened?" I tried to coax him by whispering in his ear. "Go ahead and tell him so we can get you home, okay?"

That seemed to do the trick. He straightened up, closed his eyes, and began to recount how he got to where we were. At that moment, Quinn showed up with another officer and saw us there with him. Natalia motioned for him to not say a word until Devin finished making his statement.

"I left Quinn's studio to head up this way after he told me that Anton had been popping cocaine lines and that he might have graduated from smoking marijuana. I wanted to find out from Anton and maybe try to get him some help." Devin sort of talked to the air around him; he wasn't looking around at anyone. "I got here and headed for the door. When I went to reach for the doorbell, I noticed the door was unlocked and cracked open."

The detective scribbled away on his notepad in a furious attempt to keep up. He wasn't prepared for the words to come in such rapid and large bunches. "Continue, Mr. Lowery."

"I went back to get my gun before heading into the house, and I saw that the inside of the house was trashed." He still wasn't focused on anyone; his eyes were closed now. He grabbed for Natalia's hand, as he continued to let the words flow. "I shouted for Anton to let me know he was in the house, and when I didn't hear him, I headed toward the kitchen to continue to look for him. I heard a shot before I got there and grabbed my arm when I realized I was hit. I turned around to see what happened with my gun pointed and saw Anton standing there with his gun pointed at me."

I saw the tears well up in his eyes. I continued to massage his shoulder to try and keep him calm, and Natalia kept a grip of his hand.

"He kept blaming me for all the stuff that was happened in his life, and no matter what I said, it didn't sway him." His voice cracked while he spoke. I wanted to hold him closer, but it wasn't the time or place to do that. He needed to be at home first. "I told him that he was being unreasonable, that I didn't do anything but be there for him, even when it meant it would be heat for me if I did. Then he said it was over and turned the gun on himself."

"Oh shit, he committed suicide?!?!" Quinn couldn't hold his outburst. "I didn't think he would take it that far."

"I tried to stop the bleeding while I had nine-one-one on speaker." His voice continued to fade in and out, prompting the EMT to ask for the detective to coax Devin into finishing his account. He mouthed that Devin was dehydrated and needed fluids. "I thought I had it stopped, but he fought me to let him go."

"We found a note as we were going through the house, and we found a suicide note," the detective stated. "He said that he couldn't live with the guilt of infecting a lot of his co-stars and that his life would be ruined once the truth of his test results came out."

The officer that escorted me and Natalia walked in to whisper something to the detective before he walked back out. The detective dropped his head for a moment and repeated what he'd just been told. "I'm sorry, Mr. Lowery, but your friend died before they could get him to the hospital."

Quinn shook his head when he heard that statement. "Damn, D-Lo, I'm sorry about Ant—"

"You should be sorry!" Devin yelled, breaking free from us and getting in Quinn's face before anyone could react. "I could have done something before it got to this point, don't you understand that?! He could have killed me!"

The detective whipped Devin away from where Quinn stood, trying to get him to calm down. Devin jerked away from him, causing the detective to grab his wrist in an attempt to restrain him. "Sir, I understand your frustration, but don't complicate matters."

Devin's eyes were wild with anger, and he continued to advance toward Quinn, yelling out that it was his fault that Anton died and a host of other colorful words that I didn't know existed. The detective tried to keep him at bay without hurting him, and another officer jumped in, realizing that Devin was overpowering the detective, despite his shoulder being injured and immobilized. A third officer had his hand on his taser, and it was only a matter of time before things got out of hand and Devin would be hurt worse than he already was.

Natalia got in his face soon after, waving the officers off as best she could. "D, listen to me, there was nothing anyone could have done about Anton. He did what he wanted to do."

"He would have listened to me, Talia, and you know it!" He tore into Natalia, this time the tears were flowing freely. "You're probably glad he punked out and took his life! This was what you wanted, are you happy now?!"

I'd never seen Devin this irate before, and I would have been scared to move into his line of sight after what he said to Natalia, but someone had to stop him before he got too far out of control. I didn't want him to risk arrest or worse.

I focused his eyes to meet with mine. He was still huffing and grunting, but I didn't shy away from him. "D, look at me…I mean it, *look at me*. You're hurting, I know it hurts like hell right now, but we're here to help you get through it, do you understand me? Stop what you're doing before you do something you'll regret."

To everyone's surprise, Devin softened up, and he closed his eyes when I caressed his cheek. "Lexi, I…I just want to go home. Can we go home, please?"

He looked over at Natalia, his body slumped like he'd been

beaten down. "Talia, baby…I didn't mean…I mean, that's not what I wanted to say."

Natalia walked toward us, grabbing his hand again. "You don't scare me. You never did, baby. Let's get you home."

"Mr. Lowery, we have to have you observed and get that gunshot wound taken care of. We still have more questions for you to answer, too."

"Detective, he's been through enough for one night. Can we set up an appointment with you in the morning when he's not in so much shock?" I didn't want to sound like I was being belligerent, but he was becoming a pain in the neck. "We will get him over to the hospital to get him cleared and stitched up, but he needs to be home so we can look after him. Once he's had some rest and is strong enough, we'll come to the precinct to finish the questioning. Is that fair, sir?"

The detective nodded, leaving the room so we could get him settled and ready to get on the stretcher and get him to the hospital. Devin seemed to have other things on his mind as we continued to coax him toward the ambulance. "I still have to call his parents. They need to know what—"

"Shhh, baby, listen, we can take care of that in the morning." I settled him down before he got hyper again. "Right now, we need to get you home as soon as we get your shoulder looked at."

Alexia

Chapter Nineteen: Cater to You…

He was asleep before I had the chance to make the transition from I-285 to the entrance ramp to head down I-75 South. We'd just left Northside Hospital to have his shoulder taken care of, and it took everything within me to keep from throttling the nurses fawning all over him while he continued to resist any real treatment and insist that he was okay. One of them gave me this glance like I had no business being there, and she was about to catch these hands until D called out for me. The cold stare I returned told her that I was not the one to play with when he needed to be taken care of—and I was the one who was going to take care of him. I was going to make sure she saw that before we left up out of there.

He was so peaceful compared to the raging storm that I witnessed over an hour ago. It was almost adorable. He looked so cute and so sexy it was hard to keep my eyes on the road. I steered the truck onto the expressway, trying to find a lane where I could ride down to Devin's exit without changing lanes too much and hit the cruise control so I could be alone with my thoughts. There was a lot to think about, considering where I was in at the moment, and what I was doing while in that moment.

For starters, the fact that I was even driving his Cadillac Escalade was a moment for pause in and of itself. The way that Natalia explained it before I got in the driver's seat, no one, not even she, had *ever* driven his truck. It was bad enough I'd already thought he was a control freak, all this did was confirm why everyone was in shock. I did my best to wave off the alarm bells; this was no ordinary night, so I didn't make it out to be more than what it was.

I felt needed when the officers said that he had been calling for me. It had been so long since a man let himself be that vulnerable around me, but I wasn't sure how to feel about that since we'd only known each other for such a short period of time. I didn't want to question it, but my defenses were on high alert, doing my best to protect myself against wanting to melt and be whatever he needed me to be tonight.

The other side of me couldn't resist being warm and moist and wanting to show him how much I wanted to be with him. The sensation threatened to override my ability to apply the common sense that was needed to do nothing more than help him get through tonight in one piece.

Watching him stretched out in the passenger seat, I got to appreciate how tall he was, and that only fueled the thoughts in my head. I tried to take my mind off of my lustful thoughts to concentrate on the road, but my mind kept moving toward finishing what we'd started yesterday before we were interrupted.

Damn, the intensity of that moment was hard not to think about. I wanted him to take me as hard and rough as he could.

My body wanted to feel the abuse that I'd deprived it over the past year, and my battery-operated boyfriend wasn't doing it for me anymore. While I drove, I kept hearing him moaning and saying my name over and over while he was sleeping, which only fueled sensual state that I was trying my hardest to avoid. He sounded so good, placing me in the unenviable position of giving in to the visuals in my head. I needed him to do unspeakable things to me, and I was coming to the point to where I didn't care about keeping my promise to myself.

I closed my eyes as I came to a stop at the traffic light at his exit, shaking my head, willing my body to calm down and remember that this wasn't the right time to indulge in its selfish desires. It wasn't easy, but the quick meditative stasis I placed myself into seemed to do the trick. I was almost able to regain some of my faculties, until I heard Devin slur in his sleep like he was having a live conversation with me. "I don't want to be alone, Lexi. Don't leave me, please?"

I squeezed the steering wheel with a death grip that conveyed my need to not be pulled into the abyss of my own wantonness. The only thoughts in my head in that moment led to a cliché that seemed to fit this situation: the only way to beat temptation was to yield to it. I needed to yield to it, be consumed by it, to no longer be afraid to let go. The last relationship I was in taught me the consequences of not taking care of the needs that came to light in that moment.

The only problem was, while I'd thought I'd handled that part of the equation, the other part of the equation handled that part with someone else. An unknown variable that I wasn't aware was helping me balance the equation without my consent. I promised myself that things would be different once the group was signed. Now that that was becoming a reality within the next day or so, I needed to keep that promise.

We got to Devin's house, and the moment that I decelerated to activate the garage door, he stirred awake, trying to get his bearings as best he could, asking questions in a rapid-fire manner. "Lexi? Damn, where am I? What happened? What's going on?"

"D, baby, we're heading to your house. Don't you remember?"

"On the way home? I just left Quinn's studio an hour ago," he protested before he opened his eyes wider, realizing he was in the passenger seat. "Wait a minute, why are you driving my truck?"

"D, listen, you've had a traumatic night. Your friend died." I told him, trying to be as delicate as I could.

"Who died? What the hell are you—" he tried to get up in the seat before he clutched his shoulder in pain. "Damn, my shoulder…oh yeah, now it's coming back to me; Ant shot me and then punked out on me."

"Baby, don't get upset, I promise we'll get you out of those clothes and get you to sleep as soon as we get in the house." I vowed as I eased the truck into the garage. "You don't have to worry about anything. Tonight, I'm taking care of you."

Deion

Chapter Twenty: Don't Let Go

I was still in a fog, feeling like I was in a bad dream I couldn't wake up from. A million thoughts flowed through me, but only one question continued to pop through my mind: what in the bloody hell was Anton thinking? I kept rewinding the conversation over and over, trying to find some reason he would say the things he spat at me before he took himself out. I thanked God he wasn't a good shot, but damn, why did he shoot me?

Even though the officers said that they would visit his parents, I still felt I owed it to them to let them know I was there, that he wasn't alone. I still wasn't in any shape to physically visit them so soon after the incident, but I still needed to reach out. That was the hardest call I'd ever had to make.

His mom did not take things well and was raging at me by the time her husband picked up the phone. He wasn't Ant's biological, but he was the closest thing to a father that he had. All he could do was express his appreciation that I was able to do what I could for his stepson in the final moments. I wasn't sure if I wanted to offer the detail that had Ant been sharper, I wouldn't be here to make the call. I made the executive decision to leave things be; there was no need in pouring salt in the wounds.

I took solace and comfort in the hot bath that Alexia ran for me while helping me out of my clothes, and even that small gesture I didn't have a complete recollection of at this point. I kept trying to figure out how she and Natalia got there together, but I was grateful that they were both there. I rationalized that the officers found my cell phone and found the ICE number, which got the ball rolling. I knew I could count on Natalia if I ever got jammed up.

Watching Alexia moving in and out of the bathroom in nothing but my personalized Falcons jersey was a sight to enjoy, but my mind kept trying to convince me that this was still a dream. I didn't want to be alone tonight, so I wished against my mind with my emotions and hoped that this was all real, bad images included. My muscles ached, and the sting from the wound made itself known, so being able to relax was a welcome feeling. The minute she touched my shoulder to dress my bandage, I knew I wasn't dreaming anymore.

She moved about her business with the skill of a nurse, and I caught her staring, but it wasn't at my injured shoulder. She stared at the brand on my chest with a smirk on her face. "And what's that look about?"

"You're a Que?"

"Yeah, and your point is?"

"I should have known, you move like a Que-dawg," she pointed out. "That explains the swagger, like you own everything."

I laughed it off. "I'm no different than any other man, and Alphas and Kappas and Sigmas and Iotas think they own everything, too. I'm just saying."

"Yeah, right, Mr. 'Everyman'," she winked at me while finishing the wrap. "Don't think that I didn't notice the women trying to get your attention at the showcase."

I raised my eyebrow when she said that. I looked up at her, watching her blush once she realized she'd let that tidbit of information slip from her subconscious mind. This whole time, she'd been trying to act like she wasn't paying any mind, and now she wanted to clock like she already had papers on me?

Two could play that game. I stared into her eyes, realizing I was taking a chance of getting caught up in the spell she cast over me. "Oh, like I didn't see all the drinks that the ballers were trying to shoot in your direction, trying to get your attention? And don't try to front like they were going to Camryn or Keri, either."

Alexia blushed when she realized that I had her dead to rights. She leaned next to the tub, studying my face to figure out my thoughts. "All right, so I was keeping an eye on you and you were keeping an eye on me. So, now what, D?"

I sat up with that question, wincing in pain the entire time I tried to move. My eyes turned serious; there were questions in my mind that needed answers. "What do you want, Alexia? We've been hinting around whatever this is between us ever since we met. What do you want most?"

Alexia knelt down and kissed me. The force behind it caught me by complete surprise. Her eyes were as serious as mine; that kiss held all types of purpose. "I want you. I want you to want me, too. Do you want me? I wanna hear you say it, please."

"I want…ouch, it still hurts to move…I want you." I adjusted to her next kiss as I took my hands to explore under the jersey. A sneaky grin spread across her face, watching my reaction to her bold move, hoping I'd like her surprise.

"Do you know what you're doing?" she managed between moans.

"Not yet, but I am trying to feel my way around, if you don't mind?" I joked, still working up her back, feeling around her hips and slightly parting her thighs. "We were interrupted last time, remember?"

"Mmmmm, I know, baby." Her voice dripped with orgasmic bliss and we hadn't gotten warmed up yet. She looked at me, the concern showing on her face, but she wanted to succumb to what I wanted to do to her. "I know your shoulder is hurting, baby, and I don't want you to stop, but maybe we need to wait until you're not in so much pain before we try this again."

I wanted to ignore her suggestion, willing the pain away and failing at every turn. I fought the painkillers as best I could, but they were winning this battle tonight, whether I wanted them to or not. "Maybe you're right, Lexi, but know that I want you, period. I don't want to make the same mistakes twice, you're important to me, more than you know."

"I know, baby. Let's get you out of the tub and get you in bed so you can rest. There will be plenty of time for…well, you know." She winked as she headed to the sink to grab a towel. "I'm not going anywhere."

Alexia

Chapter Twenty-One: What About Your Friends?

I felt so comfortable attached to his hip as we slept the rest of the morning away, I almost didn't want to check the clock to see how late it was. Last night was more than I'd thought was possible, regardless of what I thought I needed. It was a wonderful feeling, one that I didn't want to go away anytime soon—until I realized I wasn't attached to his hip.

I looked up, checking the sheets and the body pillow I'd somehow ended up grabbing on to while I was in deep slumber. I caught him moving around in the bathroom like he was getting ready to leave, but I didn't want him to go yet. I wasn't ready for the fantasy to end, and he wasn't in any condition to be up and about. I reached out to him as he sat down on the edge of the bed. "Where are you going, baby? Come back to bed, sexy, please?"

"As much as I would love to, Lexi, I have shoots all day long." Devin continued dressing, slipping on his shirt. "And you laying like that in my bed isn't making it any easier."

I pulled the covers back, exposing my naked body to him,

trying to convince him that he was better off with me this morning. I know I was teasing a man who was still in a weakened state, but it was fun to be a little sexy. "I don't want you to go, you're not going to go. I'll make you breakfast and feed it to you if you stay."

Devin stopped in mid-motion, making me think that I might have worked my magic. He angled his body toward me, his eyes taking mental inventory of my body as I laid there, doing my best to take his mind off leaving. He moved further up the bed, getting a closer look at me. I wanted him to feel instead of look, so I inched closer to him, wrapping my legs around his waist. I felt a low rumble and heard a grunt escape his lips as I kept grinding against him, kissing his neck, cooing in his ear, anything to take his mind off leaving for work.

"Lexi—" I grinned at his inability to get the words out of his mouth. "I need to go, baby."

"Don't go." I insisted, sliding around to his waist, straddling him and kissing him some more. Yes, I wanted him to stay, but it was more out of concern now. What he went through last night would have—it should have—shaken anyone up, and he was acting like nothing had happened.

"Devin, listen to me. Last night was wonderful, but you didn't sleep well." I had to let him know that he tossed and turned last night after we settled down. "Did you expect to act like nothing happened?"

He tensed up for a moment before I felt him calm down. He rubbed across his shoulder and still felt the pain course through where he'd been hit, a frown washing over his face. I hoped that he realized that I wasn't simply babying him. After watching him unleash his anger on Quinn last night, I didn't want him in that headspace again.

"I wasn't trying to think about it, but I gotta do something, baby." He shook his head, staring at me a few times before he closed his eyes. "Why he chose me to do that shit to, I don't know. If I sit here and do nothing, it's going to gnaw at me, drive me crazy."

"Baby, stay here with me, let me help you take your mind off things, if only for a little while." I didn't budge an inch from where I sat. "You're not going to be any good to anyone, including me, if you push your way through this without trying to rest, okay?"

"Lexi, I don't take the day off, I have too much to do." He lifted me off his lap with surprising ease, despite his injury. He was insistent on doing what he set his mind to do. "I know you're trying to take my mind somewhere else, and I love that you can do that with such ease, but the best thing for me is to go to work."

I pouted a little, and he must have seen the expression on my face. He kissed my lips again, giving me his keys. "Take me to work and pick me up for lunch, that way you can get some errands run before I take you home later."

The smile on my face spread like I was the Cheshire cat that had a large bowl of catnip. "Promise me that you won't overdo things while you're there, and we've got a deal."

"Okay, I promise. Happy now?" He smirked as he got back up to head back to the bathroom. "I need to freshen up before we head out."

I slipped back under the sheets for a few minutes of stolen luxury when I heard his phone vibrate in the bed. I picked it up with the intent to take it to him, when I noticed the text sitting on the top of the lock screen. *Remember our agreement, sexy. It will benefit the both of us, I promise.*

Seeing the text was from Tina, I almost regretted picking the phone up to begin with. All these questions flooded my mind, but I did my best to push them away. He wasn't mine, at least not yet, but it didn't help having that cloud of doubt messing things up when it was such a wonderful morning.

I was in the midst of taking his phone into the bathroom when my own phone vibrated. I blew air when I saw the number on my screen. "What is it, Camryn?"

"Damn, what's with the attitude, trick?" Camryn snapped back. "What are you doing, and where are you? I tried to come by last night."

I side-stepped the question. I didn't want her in my business like that. "Something came up last night. I had someone drop me off somewhere to take care of it."

"Why you have to do all that when you have your car?" Camryn wouldn't let up in her inquisition. "Or did lover boy come by to finally smash?"

"You're really a nosey heifer, aren't you?" I scoffed. "You're with Quinn now, so why does my life have to become so important to you? It's not like I call you out of the blue to keep up with you."

"Just answer the question, Lexi." Camryn wouldn't back down, and it was starting to piss me off. "If you got some, just say you got some, I wouldn't blame you if you did. He's fine! I wouldn't be wasting all that sexiness, I'll tell you that much!"

"Mind your business, Camryn, I'm warning you."

"You wouldn't be this damn defensive unless you got your back blown out." Camryn observed. "Look, if you think I'm trying to be in your shit, I'm not. I'm just trying to look out for you. He's a player, and you need to protect yourself, darling. There aren't too many happy endings when it comes to dealing with them."

"Listen, Camryn, the last time I checked, I was a grown-ass woman." I had reached my boiling point, and I let her know it. "Worry about your own madness, I'm good over here."

"Look, keep your blinders on, I don't care in the slightest," Camryn lashed back at me. "I'm doing this for the good of the group. You're getting too wrapped up in this dude, and we got a job to do."

Enough was enough, and I dropped the hammer quick. "We can roll for the good of the group, as you say, but we have nothing more to say to each other. You and I are no longer tight like that, since you insist on disrupting my flow."

Devin walked back into the bedroom while I was conversing with Camryn. He saw the look on my face and kept about his business, thinking that I was discussing group-related issues. My potential relationship was not a group-related issue, regardless of what Camryn thought.

"Lexi, I...alright, damn, I'm sorry." Camryn softened, trying to find a way to continue the conversation. "I didn't realize you felt this strongly about your personal—"

I hung up the phone before she could finish that sentence. I turned to get dressed, slipping on my jean skirt and top quickly before Devin turned around and got any ideas. Not that I would refuse him, but after last night's intimacy, I didn't want to ruin it with a quickie as our first time.

"Ready to go, baby?" he asked, snapping me out of the funk that I was in. It was amazing how he could do that to me, among the other things that he did to me. I was getting tingly thinking about it.

I slipped my hand inside of his, watching his long fingers swallow my hand whole, in complete awe at how warm he was to the touch. I did my best to ignore the text messages I saw, and Camryn was not about to ruin the feelings that I was enjoying right now. For the good of the group? Whatever. "Yeah, I'm ready. Lead the way."

Deion

Chapter Twenty-Two: Nothing Like Loving You

"Just a few more, baby, and we'll be done." I was putting the last touches on a photo shoot with Natalia, trying to freshen up the images for my website so I could attract some new clientele. I wasn't hurting for it; RPK was generous about taking care of a brother.

She nodded between the flashes, giving these looks and expressions that let me know she wanted to talk afterwards. After watching Alexia drive off with my truck this morning, I figured she would want to have that talk.

As I slid the flash drive into the PC to start looking at the shots, Natalia took that time to begin her questioning. She slid behind me while glimpsing over my shoulder at the images. "I really like your new girlfriend, D. I can tell that she's into you. So, did she end your misery last night and give you some?"

"She's not my girlfriend yet, Natalia." I tried to correct her, but she rolled her eyes and tried to set me straight.

"D, I love you to death, but you're ignoring the facts," she started. "Anytime a woman comes out in the middle of the night to be with you in a time of crisis, it's safe to say that she's into you and cares for you."

I tried to open my mouth to rebut, but she moved in closer to me and stared into my eyes. "She's acting like your girlfriend, Devin. I can feel it on you now."

She always had a way of making me weak whenever we made eye contact. It was something I would never admit to her, but she had a hold on me. I wanted to tear away from her stare, but I couldn't escape it. To be honest, I never wanted to. "Well, you saw that she dropped me off earlier, and for the record, we didn't exactly do anything last night. I wanted to, but I was in so much pain last night. Is that why you've been giving me curious looks all day?"

"Now I know she's your girl; you don't let anyone caress your baby," Natalia smirked, sliding across my lap. Her eyes probed mine, trying to find something, but I couldn't figure out what she was looking for. "You never let me drive your truck. Should I be jealous?"

"As much as we've been through, and you want to ask that question?" I needed to break the connection between us before I did something that I wouldn't regret. "If you're making fun of me, we can finish the Q&A now so I can get back to work, baby."

"Am I still your baby?" Natalia brushed her lips against mine. I wasn't sure if she was testing me or if she was being serious, but she had me hypnotized and willing to succumb to whatever she wanted. My mind told me that this was not something we should have been doing, but my body had other ideas. I took hold of her hips as she grinded against me.

"Talia—" Resistance was futile, all she would have to do was beg me to take her and it would have been over. "You know how I feel about you. Do you really need me to say it?"

She stopped in the middle of the flow, kissing me on the cheek and placing her fingers to my lips to stop me from asking why she stopped. "I would never make fun of you, you mean too much to me for that. I only wanted to make sure that I was still where I was supposed to be."

Whether it was wrong of me or not, I really didn't care all that much; she was right where she was supposed to be. Number one...with an asterisk.

Natalia stared at me again, this time with a concerned look on her face as she raised herself from my lap. "How are you holding up, baby? You looked really out of it last night."

"I don't feel anything, to be honest," I deadpanned. "He tried to kill me last night, and if he wasn't so hopped up on cocaine, he might have succeeded."

"I needed to be sure that you were okay," she answered, rubbing my shoulders, taking care not to cause any more pain to the damaged one. She always had a way of changing my mood for the better. "Do you want me to go with you to the funeral on Saturday?"

"No, that won't be necessary, but we would love to have you with us anyway," I heard Alexia jump into the conversation. Her arrival caught me off guard, to say the least. "I hope he hasn't been working too hard."

"No, he's actually behaved, for once in his life," Natalia responded, giving her a hug and kiss in greeting. That surprised me; I didn't know they were so familiar. "We were just talking about you."

"I hope it was all good, I haven't done anything naughty...at least, not yet." Alexia winked at me as she broke from her embrace with Natalia.

"A woman after my own heart." Natalia smiled and winked at her, tipping me off to something that was going on between them. I wished I knew what it was, though, but I didn't complain. Having them getting along like pseudo-best friends ensured that both could co-exist in my world. What more could a man ask for?

"Well, I was just about to take this sexy ass man to lunch, would you care to join us?" Alexia offered, but Natalia held her hand up in protest.

"No thanks, I have another appointment that I have to make," she replied. "But I want to get together later in the week—just us girls—to celebrate your signing."

There was this pregnant pause between the three of us, almost like one of us was waiting for the others to say something after Natalia's bold prediction. It was hard to call it a prediction, though; can it be called that if the person making it has a bit of direct influence over the persons who can make said prediction come true?

"Umm, I'm going to head in the back to get these images logged into my system while you two get some plans out of the way without my interference," I mentioned, knowing good and well I was going to eavesdrop on the conversation anyway.

I popped in the flash drives to let them load, tuning my ear to the girl talk that I was "missing." I kept myself busy so I wouldn't sound so obvious, but I had to admit, I was curious to find out a few things without having to ask the questions for a change.

"For someone who has a glow on her after spending the night at Devin's, you look distracted." I heard Natalia get down to it. "Don't worry, some things are between us."

"Natalia, I—" Alexia hesitated for a moment. She shrugged and spoke on what was troubling her. "There is this girl who I ran into while Devin and I were out, Tina Parker. I didn't tell him, and I feel awful about it, but while he was getting ready for work, his text messages went off. She has been leaving these weird messages all morning about keeping their agreement."

"Lord, she's at it again." Natalia sighed, echoing my own private thoughts. "Look, girl, Devin blew her off a long time ago; she's a child for goodness sake."

"I know, but she tried to make a scene in front of me like he was with it," Alexia explained.

"Tina unfortunately eavesdropped on a conversation that Devin and I had a long time ago that she's taken advantage of ever since." Natalia recalled. "Just ask him what his deepest dream is…the one thing that he wants more than anything. Once he tells you that, you have power over Tina's threats."

This was my cue to jump back into the conversation before Natalia sold me out. I put on my best poker face so that I couldn't let on that I didn't hear their conversation. I'm sure one, or both, of them will tell me something sooner or later. "Are you ready to go? I'm starving."

"Yes, I am, baby. We'll talk later, Natalia." Alexia winked at Natalia as she took my hand and headed out of the studio.

"What were you and Natalia talking about, Lexi?" I couldn't resist asking.

"D, try not to be nosey, it's just girl talk." She kissed me on the cheek as we walked to the elevator. She seemed to be more at ease than before, and I was relieved over that, but it also meant that I needed to come clean about it sooner than later. "If you need to know, I'll tell you."

Alexia

Chapter Twenty-Three: If It's Love

All throughout lunch at the Atlanta Fish Market, I kept prodding Devin to tell me what the fuss was all about. The way Natalia spoke about it and watching her face light up when she mentioned it, it seemed like a big deal. Every time I asked, he side-stepped the question. It was getting to the point to where I was ready to let him suffer on his own and deal with the mess that Tina put him in.

His demeanor changed in an instant and he was subdued as he measured the words that he wanted to say to me. He flexed his fingers, closing his eyes and speaking under his breath. I took it as something that he really didn't want to talk about, or he was uncomfortable, to say the least. "Lexi?"

"Yes, baby?"

"I assume that Talia told you that I have a special secret, a dream of mine that I've kept for a long time now."

"She said something about it, but she didn't say what it was exactly. She would only say that it would take some of the power away from Tina once you told me." To be honest, I had no idea what he was about to tell me. The only thing I could do was listen and brace for whatever it was.

"I'm not gonna lie, Lexi, I'm taking a big risk even talking about this with you, but I feel like I can trust you." He looked like a teenager about to reveal his first crush. "I don't like feeling vulnerable, and telling you this feels like I'm letting you further than I think I'm ready to let you in."

"D, you can trust me, tell me what it is. I am here with you, aren't I?" I stared at him, trying to get him to understand. I took his hand in mine, hoping to make my point clear that I was not going anywhere. I'd never seen him so nervous about anything. It was sexy-cute to know that I was being let inside of such an intimate and vulnerable side to him.

I understood his hesitation, though. We'd known each other for only a matter of days. While I'd not yet given my body to him, it was only a matter of time before my heart and body would belong to him, and a gesture like what he was in the midst of doing was a sure-fire way to expedite that process.

"Okay, here goes." Devin sat up in his chair to get himself together. "I want my own studio, state-of-the-art equipment, and not what RPK gives me. I want to be able to do work for RPK and other clients without having to worry about being on loan. I love RPK, I don't want to leave them, but I also want to make my own money. I even want to get into producing and directing movies one day."

"What's so silly about that? It sounds like a wonderful idea!" I lit up. I was relieved that it wasn't something else that would have thrown me for a loop. I narrowed my eyes and whispered low enough for him to hear, "And when you do, you can do a special set for me...you know, some nude and lingerie modeling for you? Maybe even make a few movies for our own personal enjoyment?"

The devilish grin that spread across his face was enough to make me blush, but he gave me this look like he wasn't finished purging. "But here's the thing; Tina overheard me telling Talia one day while we were in the studio and she's been using it as leverage to get me to consent to being her first sexual experience ever since."

So that's what the messages were all about. My mind clicked as that final piece of the puzzle revealed itself. No wonder Tina had been such a relentless little trick. Did she think that she was the only one who can come up with the money to back his dreams? "Devin?"

"What is it, Lexi?"

"Is that one of the reasons why Jenna broke things off with you? Did she think that you wanted to sleep with Tina?"

"Yes, to both questions." His eyes searched mine for any wavering. "No matter what I said, I can't help but think someone else had her ear, saying something different."

I'd been there before, so I could understand where he was coming from. Troy thought I was having sex with one of the would-be producers before the group's last album deal went sour.

"I don't know, but she believed who she wanted to believe, and there was nothing I could do to change her mind." Devin kept shaking his head, trying to figure it out all over again. "Tina won't let up, and she's using my penchant to flirt with women against me, and since women are always around me due to the nature of my job, I only have myself to blame. That's why I'm telling you everything now, so I don't have to deal with this madness. I wouldn't blame you if you washed your hands of me now."

"Why are you blaming yourself?" I wasn't used to this side of him. He was beating himself up a little more than I thought he should, but all this had happened before we met, too. "Tina may be a child, but she's not innocent in all this."

"It is my fault, if I'm honest with myself. There's so much that wouldn't have gotten this far if I stood firm instead of trying to spare her feelings." The look in his eyes melted me on the spot, even though he wasn't trying to seduce me. "It's not like I don't deserve it. I don't even like what I'm feeling right now."

"What are you feeling, D?" I asked, forcing him to look at me. "I'm serious, cuteness, what's going on in your head?"

"Alexia...after all the bullshit that I went through with Jenna, I'm afraid to fall in love," Devin confessed. I'd never seen him so vulnerable. He struggled to maintain eye contact. "I don't want to feel like this, not yet. I don't deserve to feel this way, not after the things I've done in my past."

"It can be wonderful, baby, especially if you're with the right woman," I tried to explain to him. "I'm willing to close that chapter with you, but you have to be willing to let me help you close it. I have my own past to deal with, too, you know?"

"I know what you're talking about, baby, but I don't like the loss of control of my emotions." He steeled himself, watching him as he tried to regain control. "I fall in love easily, and I've done this too many times before. My heart can only take so much. I'm sitting here sounding weak because another woman ripped me to shreds."

He moved his hands from mine, putting his head in his hands. He didn't move for several minutes, looking at me for a moment before looking down again, his silence saying more than whatever words were in his mind.

I refused to let him slip away from me. "I need to know, am I the one you want to be with? Is that why you're sounding like this?"

He tried to avoid my glance, but I wouldn't be deterred. After a few seconds, his eyes focused and locked with mine. "Yes, Lexi, I want to be with you. It's scaring me to death to say it, but, yes I want to be with you."

"How are you so sure?" It was my turn to be a little scared. I wanted to know, but now that I knew, what was I going to do about it? "It's not like we've known each other that long."

I saw the familiar smirk that made me warm inside and put me at ease. "Lexi, I turned down a lot of women when I was at a club earlier with my boys the night that I saw you and Camryn. I even ended up sleeping with a woman who lied to me and told me she was married after I fucked her. That night was a mixed bag of drama and fate. If she hadn't have put me through all of that, who's to say we would have met when we did?"

My eyes widened. He was blunt, no sugar coating whatsoever. I wasn't sure how to handle what he was dishing out. His candor was refreshing, there were no two ways about it, but I guess dealing with my ex and his lack of honesty sort of took me off balance. Sometimes you have to be careful what you ask for.

"I've done a lot of things that I'm not proud of, but the one thing that I've never done is lie to the women that I date," he continued. "If I say that you're the only one I'm dating, then you're the only one I'm with. If I'm with another woman when I meet you, then I'm telling you straight up so you can make up your mind to deal with me or not."

"Damn, you're laying it all out there, Devin." I was

overwhelmed by what I was hearing. Still, the one question that needed to be asked was out there, so I took the opportunity. "So, is there someone else?"

"There is no one else right now." Devin leveled with me. "If I get too low between women, Talia and I usually kick it a lot."

"Speaking of Talia." I had questions in my mind regarding her that I wanted to ask her when we got together later in the day. "I get the feeling that you two are close...I mean, *really* close."

"Yeah, we are really close," Devin answered. "In fact, you're probably the second woman that she's ever really approved of."

Now, that was interesting. My mind went back to the conversation that she and I had while we were still in the studio. I'm sure that he heard a lot of it, but what he didn't suspect was that Natalia and I were in close proximity to each other.

It's not like I wasn't bisexual or anything like that; I had a few girlfriends in college, so I could feel when another woman was into me, and vice versa. Being in the music industry, sometimes I had those women that tried me, considering that it was the new hotness to be into women as much as men. It wouldn't be a shock if Natalia was feeling me; I was feeling her. How could I not? She exuded her own sensuality that I wouldn't mind getting a taste of. In my wildest dreams...never mind, I didn't want to think about it right now.

"Well, I'm glad that I held up to her standards," I grinned, throwing him off. I changed the subject to something he could concentrate on. "So, you know I'm feeling you, and I know you're feeling me, so what do we do now?"

"I want us to keep going the way we are. You're right, I'm feeling you…I'm *really* feeling you." He leaned in close, placing his hands over mine, squeezing them. "We can let things flow from there, but I don't want you to go anywhere. It feels…it's exquisite…every time I'm around you."

As we walked out to his truck, I felt his demeanor change. He felt more relaxed, more comfortable around me. I slipped my arm inside of his, enjoying the closeness and the hint of the cologne he wore at the RPK party. The scent took me hostage the way it did that night, and I couldn't get enough of what it was doing to me.

"So, can I take your truck to go see Talia after I drop you off? I promise I'll be gentle with her." I teased him while getting in the driver's seat. A girl could get used to this.

"You better be, or I may have to put you over my knee." He winked, kissing me on the neck. "I have a shoot to do with a crew a little later today, but I'm taking one of the company cars down and back. Oh, and tell Talia I said hello."

Deion

Chapter Twenty-Four: Bitch, Don't Kill My Vibe

"Devin, this is TramaDryl. Dryl, this is your photographer for the shoot today."

From the minute that we shook hands, I had a feel this would be an interesting day.

TramaDryl, the stage name for Troy Ingram, was a part of a rap group called *MFPL*, which meant *Money First, Play Later*. The "P" meant something else, but their label wanted to try and market them mainstream. They were up-and-comers, which meant they were trying to find a wider audience so the label could take them out of Atlanta. From my vantage point and experience being around other groups that were looking to take the next step, these dudes weren't even half the group that they thought they were. But these wannabe trophy wives-in-training seemed to be feeling the group, so it was my job to make them look presentable.

Too bad you couldn't take the hood out of these dudes. This fool was busy acting like he was the one running the show. "Aye, my dude, you the one tryn'a put the stuff together for our social media pages, right? Aye, look, make sure you get me solo with a lotta hoes, bruh. I gotta rock for the 'gram!"

"I'm going with the format that your label wants to rock with, bruh." I made it clear to him I was listening to the client…the one who was paying me. "Just look for my cues on what you need to do, and I'll make you famous."

He looked at me sideways, acting like he didn't want to hear what I was telling him, but he's not the one signing the check, so, it's whatever for him. He responded to my answer by trying to clown me in front of the rest of the group. "Hey, look, folk, this corporate nigga tryn'a act all cornball and shit. How about you do what *we* tell you to do and we'll get along just fine, you feel me, yo?"

Yeah, my girls were not going to enjoy working with this dude. The thing that worked my nerves was him calling me a nigga. In order to get through this shoot, I would have to get on his level, since there was no way in hell he would be able to get on mine. It wasn't my preferred method, but the client had taken care of me with more polished talent in the past, so I could slum it for a day.

I got my dig in while the iron was hot. "Yeah, and unless you follow my cues during this shoot, this "corporate nigga" is gonna have to work miracles making your tatted-up, Rich the Kid-reject-sounding-ass look anything close to what your label needs to even market you to sell to the public. Who's the cornball now, huh?"

I had to get him, he didn't leave me any choice. My face concealed the disdain that was growing for the low-level idiocy he was on. He started flexing his muscles like he wanted to shoot a fade or something, but all I did was wag my index finger to remind him that we weren't on the streets. "Remember, money first, pussy later, right? You got either one, nigga, or are you hurting for both?"

The reaction to that play on words was the laughter of the rest of the group. They sat back and waited for Troy to come back for me. I was a little curious to see what he had for me, too, but I had a lot more where that came from. I didn't think he quite knew what he was ready to roll with.

The confrontation would be put on pause, though. He got a glimpse of Sarai, Lita and the rest of the girls getting out of their cars and forgot about me snapping on him. I saw the look in his eyes and figured he would be the one that would have to check his libido at the door. Why did it always have to be the ugly ones that thought they could play above their pay grade?

What a disappointment; I was looking forward to the challenge of matching wits with the witless. It had been a minute since I had someone dislike me at a shoot. I wanted to milk it some more before we got to business.

Lita got to me first, kissing my neck and pressing into me as I hugged her. "Did you miss me?"

"Yes, I did, baby." I gave a quick kiss on her cheek before we broke from our embrace. Out of the corner of my eye, I saw salivating, wannabe ballers thinking that these women were going to be easy. They had another thing coming.

Sarai followed suit with her greeting, leading me to believe that they'd been having some rather extensive conversations about me. I didn't know whether to be scared or flattered. I voted for a combination of both.

She sized up one of the group members standing next to Troy. I think his stage name was G-Style or something. "So, are these the guys we're working with today? He's sexy, D. I think I wanna work with him."

That put a frown on Troy's face. He must have figured he was supposed to have first dibs on the women that come around them since he was supposed to be the lead in the group.

Lita picked up on the negativity on Troy and walked over to the other member of the group, L-Dove. Dude looked like he'd won the lottery with the way she'd draped herself all over him. He did his best to keep from looking too happy; this was business.

I tried to stifle a laugh when I saw Troy's expression, but to say I failed would be an understatement. My models picked up on my cues well, and they picked up on a bad vibe as well as anyone on a shoot. I almost wanted to put ol' boy out of his misery, to tell his label that I couldn't shoot with him today and I could reschedule for a time the next week with just him, but I didn't feel like dealing with him next week, either. This dude had trouble written all over him, and the sooner I could get him off my vibe and away from the models, the better.

So, to keep the client happy and to keep the big baby from feeling left out, I whispered into Lita's ear, "Do any of your girls feel like doing charity work today? I'm sure I can make it worth the trouble."

She smirked at me, licking her lips at the suggestion I'd left. "Yeah, I think I can convince one of the girls to help ol' boy out. But I wanna watch whatever you do to the poor girl."

"I'm supposed to be a good boy now, remember? I can't rock like that anymore." I tried to stick to my guns, but Lita wasn't having it.

She slipped her fingers around my ear and stared into my eyes, making sure she had my attention. I couldn't resist the urge to kiss her, but that wouldn't be the move to make. The other models would take exception, thinking they would have run of me, too. I hated how weak she made me, but I couldn't help but love the way it made me feel. I figured this was going to be a trying day, but damn, I didn't expect all this to happen.

Lita could sense the effect she had on me, but she didn't take advantage of it. I was willing to let her do what she wanted to do, if for no other reason than to keep the flow casual and flirty. She pulled away from me, holding my gaze the entire time. I winked at her, letting her know that I still kept her on speed dial…in case of an emergency. "Okay, good boy, make sure that the shoot you do for free is worth every penny, okay? With the attitude on this dude has on his face because Sarai and I didn't choose him first, it's gonna cost you a long session."

Alexia

Chapter Twenty-Five: Cold Sweat

I needed some girl on girl bonding time, but my options were a bit limited. Sometimes, being around the group could be a drain, especially since things weren't so hot between Camryn and me. I mean, I could have kicked it with Keri, but it wouldn't have felt the same. It was hard to explain, but I wanted to be around Natalia.

Even though Devin was the commonality that bonded us, she was a welcome distraction from all the madness that we were dealing with. The signing was in a matter of hours—to let Natalia tell it—and it had most of us on edge counting down the clock. Still, there was something else between us. I couldn't put my finger on what it was, but I figured that we needed to work out what drew us to each other in such a short period of time.

I stepped through the door, giving her a hug and kiss on the cheek before she led me into the kitchen. "Hey, girl, I figured we needed to get together sooner instead of later. I'm still a little on edge considering everything that's happening the next few days."

"You sound like I do right now." Natalia walked out to the pool area in the backyard. It was a particularly warm day today, and she had a sarong on, leaving so little to the imagination that I couldn't resist staring at her. "Between the funeral and your signing, it's going to be a crazy few days."

Damn, I didn't want to think about the funeral, but there was no choice but to deal with it. It sounded selfish of me, but I was glad that the signing was going to happen before the funeral. Mr. Parker and Mr. Richton pushed the meeting up so that they could support Devin. Anton's parents wanted to have the funeral as soon as possible, and it threw the whole schedule off for Devin, but they didn't want to do this signing without him. It made me feel good to know that the owners of the label were so in tune with their employees, and it made me feel more comfortable to sign with RPK.

Natalia led me out to the backyard to where she was sunbathing, and the minute that she took off the sarong to show off the bikini that she wore underneath, I'd all but lost my composure. Her mocha-rich hue made her look like she was shimmering against the afternoon sun. If I wasn't crazy, I could have sworn it was sparkling, like diamonds were embedded in her flesh.

She kept staring at me, winking as we did nothing more but exchange glances at each other for the better part of five minutes. It felt like she was showing off for my benefit, but I didn't want to delude myself. Her body was so stunning, it defied all logic. I didn't care if I thought I was imagining things or not, I enjoying every minute of whatever this was between us.

"So, what's on your mind, Lexi? I could feel something

on you the minute I saw you at the door," Natalia asked. Her question put me in a different frame of mind from the more decadent thoughts racing through it.

"I feel like I'll be out of place at the funeral, Natalia. I mean, it's not like I knew Anton or anything," I confessed, feeling like I wanted to avoid the conversation altogether. "I mean, what do I do? I'm not even sure that I should do anything more than to be a friend to support right now."

Natalia sat me down in one of the chairs by the bar, sitting across from me. She studied my expressions, causing me to blush. I didn't want her to be able to read me, but I was so open, I didn't make it difficult for her.

She gave me this look like she wanted to choke me, but the sing-song cadence in her voice only served to hypnotize me. "I think D will back me up when I say this, so I'm gonna cut to the chase: *you are going to be with Devin at the funeral.* You can act like you're not more than what you are to him, but I know differently. I know my baby, and he's as into you as I am."

"I know, Natalia, but I just didn't want to…what did you just say???" I wasn't drinking, and I wanted to believe that she might have been having a few while the sun made love to her body. Needless to say, my mind swirled and I prayed that this wasn't really happening…at least not yet.

"Lexi, don't flex like you haven't been feeling the vibe between us." Natalia got up from her lounge chair, slipping closer into my personal space, causing my heart to race. "I wanted to say something at the party, but I wasn't sure how you flowed until now."

My mind was still swimming. I still couldn't believe what I was hearing. Natalia moved close enough to kiss me, her scent invading my senses and claiming me before I could put up a fight. "But, what about Devin, Natalia?"

Natalia blew past that small attempt at a roadblock like it was paper-thin. To tell the truth, it was even thinner than that. "What about D? Look, Lexi, I like you, and I think there's a chance there could be more than that, and there are things that he knows that you might not be in the know about yet."

She kissed me, igniting my body. The way she touched me gave me a sensation that was so much different than when Devin touched me; that only another woman could send through me.

"Do you want me, Lexi?" Natalia asked between kisses. "Do you like the way this feels?"

"Yes…I do." I couldn't catch my breath, trying hard to find my balance. "God, you feel so good, Natalia."

My cell phone went off, but Natalia stopped me from looking at who it was from before she continued her assault on my senses. "It's only your baby trying to figure out if you're with me. Don't worry, I sent a text before you pulled up in the driveway to let him know you were in good hands."

I ached for release, but I felt guilty, too. Devin and I hadn't been able to get to this point yet, and I didn't want to betray that. A flood of lustful thoughts crashed through, leaving me nowhere to turn, but I was intent on fighting what my body wanted to succumb to. Natalia was relentless in her pursuit, trying her best to push me beyond the point of no return.

I was weak for any type of attention as I fought with my own sense of loyalty to Devin against the obvious sexual attraction—and God knows what else I was feeling—that I had for Natalia. As weird as it sounded, I was willing to do whatever it took to have her—and him—and I was coming close to the point of no longer caring which one I would give into first.

Acting on my desires was something that I wasn't ready to do yet. It was the downfall of my relationship with Troy. In hindsight, I did it because he had already burned me over the course of the relationship. Two wrongs didn't make it right, but it felt damn good when I got my revenge. This, however, was different on levels I couldn't quite grasp. This felt…delicious… salacious…and I liked it.

My phone sang as Natalia moved to caress and kiss me deeper. I looked at the image on the phone and saw Devin's face staring at me. I answered it, even though Natalia worked her tongue over my neck.

"Hi, baby," I tried to take as much of the sex out of my voice as I could, but Natalia wasn't having it. "How was the shoot?"

"It was good, except for this one dude that fucked with the vibe of the shoot, but it's all gravy, I had him humbled before it was all done," Devin answered as I stifled a moan. "Put me on speaker, I know you're still with Natalia."

"How did you…know I was…still here?" I struggled to ask, feeling the tip of Natalia's tongue against my ear.

"GPS on my truck, baby girl, now put me on speaker," he demanded, which only turned me on more with the mood I was in.

After I switched the phone to speaker, Devin said, "Hi, baby, enjoying your girl time?"

"Yes, daddy, we are, thank you for letting us bond some more," Natalia cooed over the phone, locking eyes with me to convince me that he wasn't pissed about what was happening. "Can I have her, too?"

Wait a minute…too? I felt like I was being captured, possessed, and I wasn't sure I liked the feeling at that moment.

"D, baby, you're not upset about this?" I asked him, a mixture of trepidation and pleasure swirling around me, trying to keep from screaming because Natalia was back at it, making me weaker by the second. "Please tell me you're okay?"

"I guess Natalia never got the chance to tell you she texted me to tell me she was planning on seducing you when you came over?" I felt his voice drop a few octaves, adding to the lust that already washed over me. "Just let it go, baby, it's okay—"

I finally succumbed to what I wanted…with every fiber of my being.

"Alexia, are you okay?" Natalia stared at me, trying to figure out the expression on my face.

I was flushed and my skin was white-hot. I couldn't recover from whatever my mind put me through, and I was sure Natalia read it all over me. I tried to recover from my daydream, but my body had already left subtle clues that whatever was on my mind, it was as hot as I was. "Yeah, Natalia, I think I'm fine. What were you saying?"

"I was telling you that you were going to the funeral to be the support that Devin needs," Natalia re-iterated, her eyes as intense as they were before my mind went elsewhere. "He's really into you, Lexi. I've been around him longer than anyone, and I know when he's falling."

I didn't know how to respond to that. I was into him, I was feeling him deeper than I wanted to go, but I wasn't sure if I was ready to say I was in love with him yet. But it wasn't like I wasn't heading in that direction fast. "I can't argue with that. I'll be there, Talia."

"Good, I didn't want to have to kill you for trying to come up with some crazy excuse to explain why you're not there." She laughed, taking some of the sting out of the seriousness I thought she was trying to be.

Natalia looked at me again, this time with a quizzical look on her face. "Are you sure you're okay? You have this look like you were trying to shake something off that crossed your mind."

I blushed, realizing that my facial expressions and my body gave me away big time. I wanted to come up with a reasonable explanation, but I had a pitiful Poker face when it came to what I wanted. Natalia sort of smirked, almost like she'd read my thoughts and drew her own conclusions.

I smiled as the battle between my mind and body continued, deciding between telling her what my body wanted or my mind overriding the decision because it was not the time to give in to the things that I wanted her to do to me. She winked at me, and I wanted to believe that I wasn't dreaming this time, but after my last fantasy got to me, I didn't want to take the chance. If she wanted me as much as I thought she did, she was going to have to make the first move.

Natalia walked over to take my glass from my hand, and in that instant, we were close enough to kiss. She grinned at me, glancing over my face. I felt naked, wanting to open everything to her. I hadn't felt that way in a long time when it came to a woman. It scared me to wonder what might happen next.

She brushed her lips against mine, daring me to take things further. My body trembled as the urge to kiss her became too much to bear. Before I could make up my mind to follow through on my impulse, Natalia kissed my cheek and whispered in my ear, "I know you do, and I do, too. There will be another time soon, I promise."

My ability to speak was robbed from me as I struggled to find my voice. She walked behind the bar and started making another drink, acting as though the last few seconds didn't happen. "Now, let's enjoy the rest of this beautiful day, shall we? We can talk about some more pleasant things…like your signing in the morning."

Alexia

Chapter Twenty-Six: Feeling Myself

Signing day was here, and I didn't know how I would react to what would happen over the next few hours. We'd been waiting for this moment for the past three years. I was so hyper I thought I would have an anxiety attack. Having Devin in the room during the meeting was even sweeter than I thought it would be. I needed him there, if for no other reason than to settle my nerves and keep from saying anything off the cuff.

The meeting that we had before heading over to the RPK Entertainment building was high energy, with Keri leading the way, keeping things positive, no matter what. Camryn and I managed to keep things on the professional side, but I still didn't trust her with as far as I could throw her. As long as she stayed out of my personal business and I stayed out of hers, things would stay solid between us.

Laura couldn't stop smiling the whole morning. "I want to tell you ladies that I am extremely proud of what you have accomplished. I'm looking forward to you doing some big things over the next few years."

"Yeah, we can get to the mushy stuff after we sign on the dotted line, Laura." I was dead serious about what I said, but it still caused the other girls to laugh.

"Yeah, Lexi, but you can let me have my moment, too." The tone in her voice was the cue for us to settle down so she could talk. "You girls are like daughters to me, and watching you grow as a group has been fun to watch. Now, when we get to RPK, let's make sure that we stay professional, regardless of what we may think will go down."

"Come on, Laura, the way Lexi's been acting, this deal is a no-brainer," Camryn mentioned, cutting her eyes at me. I rolled my eyes in silent response, not giving her a second thought. She didn't know half the shit that she thought she knew. "All we have to do is rock the live cut, and we're good for at least a multi-album deal."

"Look, I know you know you still have to sing for Mr. Parker, since this will be his first time hearing you live." Laura continued. "Just make sure that you're on your game, and we can start doing some real damage, okay? I don't want you falling into that one-hit-and-done category, you three are too talented for that."

Camryn, as bold as ever, looked at me before turning her attention to Keri. The grin on her face said it all. "We got this, Mr. Parker is feeling the vibe, and that's all I'm gonna say about that. All I want to know is what are y'all gonna do with your signing bonus?"

We were sitting in the reception area of RPK waiting for

our appointment, and as nervous as I felt, the last thing I wanted was to have any conversations whatsoever. All I wanted to do was focus on making sure my voice was at the right pitch and we could sign on the dotted line and get ready to move forward.

Camryn seemed to have something else in mind, whether I liked it or not. "Lexi, can we talk? I mean, we need to get this handled before we go in there, please?"

At first, I didn't want to have the conversation with Camryn, but after a quick second thought, I figured that we needed to clear the air between us so that things could be at least cordial between us. "Okay, you want to talk, so, talk."

"Look, I know I stepped over the line concerning Devin, but I didn't want you getting hurt again." Camryn got straight to the point, not wanting to get too wordy. "I remember how bad things got when you split with Troy, and I couldn't let you go down that road again."

Hearing her bringing up Troy's name brought back painful memories. I almost pulled a disappearing act during that relationship, no matter how I tried to avoid it. But what I didn't consider was what happened to me within the group when I was going through that, too.

Singing flat during rehearsals, missing steps that I'd known for years, and the worst part was letting myself go and wrecking my body in ways that I felt ashamed of. If it wasn't for my girls, I didn't know what I would be doing or where I would be, and I couldn't discount that, no matter how much I wanted to keep them out of my business. Laura could have easily replaced me with the things I was doing, but they stuck with me. No matter how mad I was with Camryn, there was no way I could forget what she did during that time.

"Cam, you and Keri were there for me when that bullshit went down with Troy. Hell, you kept me going when I didn't want to keep moving." I admitted, a tear sliding down my cheek. "But you, nor anyone else, can be mother hen to me when I get involved with a man. I need you to understand that I still know how to handle myself, okay?"

"I can't promise I won't smother you, girl. I may not always have the best ways of showing it, but you're like a sister to me, we all are to each other." Camryn explained further, wiping a few small tears streaking down her face. "But I will try to respect your privacy unless I feel it's starting to affect our performances. If that happens, all bets are off, babe."

"Okay, fair enough, Cam. But that road rides both ways, girl. If Quinn starts to affect you, we're gonna be all over you as much as you've been rolling on us." I made sure my stance was as clear as she'd made hers.

"Fair enough. I can live with that."

Keri walked by in the middle of the conversation that we were having and she almost jumped the gun. "Okay, can you two please squash whatever madness is going on between you? I love you like sisters, but you're going to be the death of me one day."

Camryn gave up a half-smile, nodding toward Keri while patting my arm. "We're good, girl, we had to get some things handled between us. I think we see where the other is coming from right now."

"Yeah, we're good, or at least we're going to be, in due time," I said to Keri. "She was worried about Devin hurting me, but I think she realizes that things are different, and they will be different, even if something goes wrong."

"Well, I'll be honest. Cam and I were a little concerned about you, especially after that last jackass nearly fucked everything up for us," Keri mentioned. "We'll all have men in our lives one way or another; well, y'all do, but you get where I'm coming from. We cannot let it affect our work. We're on the verge of making something big happen today, and everything we do from here on out will either make or break us."

"Okay, we're in agreement, then: work first, and we can play later." I stated.

"That's what I like to hear." Keri smiled as we saw Laura heading out of the office. "Now, let's go handle business so we can party."

$\mathcal{D}eion$

Chapter Twenty-Seven: C.R.E.A.M.

"Devin, my boy, are you busy?"

Hearing Mr. Richton's thick Bajan accent over the phone wasn't a shock to the system, at least, not today it wasn't. I'd been waiting for his call all morning. "Mr. Richton? No, sir, I'm not busy until later this afternoon, what's on your mind?"

His voice was as even as I'd heard it. I wasn't sure what that meant, but I prepared for whatever he was about to say. "I figured that you needed to come on up for the meeting with the group that you wanted me and Parker to sign."

I'd halfway expected him to let me know that *Envyye* had been signed and I was on the laundry list of folks that needed to be privy to that information. Being in on the meeting was not in my original plans. I protested, insistent upon making my point clear. It wouldn't work, but I was going to try anyway. No one could simply say no to either of them. "Sir, I don't want to be a distraction. I'm sure you and Mr. Parker can handle this without me."

"I already spoke with Parker, and he agrees you should be

there. Besides, you can make the transition smoother with the introductions with Parker and the group." Mr. Richton explained. He didn't have to, but he made it a point to be clear that I needed to be there, whether I wanted to or not. "This is your group, and you should see this through, son."

Dammit. The trump card has been dropped. No backing out of this now. "When do you want me there, sir?"

"The meeting is in forty-five minutes. See you then."

I walked out of the elevator, my mind in a hundred different places other than the destination I was scheduled to arrive at in ten minutes. I wasn't sure if I was supposed to be there or not, but what I thought no longer mattered. The bosses were the bosses, and no matter how deep their affinity was for me, I was no different than anyone else in the company not related to either of them.

What made the morning all the more difficult to deal with became even more contentious the moment I walked into Mr. Parker's reception area. "Hello, Laura, it is nice to see you again."

Laura's demeanor was edgy, almost like she wanted to be confrontational. "It's nice to see you, too, Devin. I left the girls downstairs so that we could talk privately. There's some things we need to clarify before they're escorted up for their meeting."

I was taken aback by that, and I wasn't sure where she was coming from by the intent behind it. "May I ask what needs to be clarified and why that is the case?"

"I want a straight answer from you, Devin. Did Mr. Parker listen to the demo?" Laura was stone-faced as she blurted out the questions in her head.

"Yes, he has, and he was impressed. He doesn't short cut anything for trivial reasons, if that's what you're thinking." I perturbed by the insinuation. No, scratch that, I was pissed. "If they sound as good to him live as they did on demo and on the video from that night, they are prepared to offer the drafts of the contract for your legal team to review."

"Off the record." Laura moved in close enough for the conversation to be heard only by the two of us. "I hear it from the girls that you and Lexi are seeing each other."

"Yes, that's true."

"Is that why we're here?"

My eyes narrowed, causing Laura to take a step back from me, noticing my posture had changed. I wasn't in the best of moods, I didn't want to be in the room while all this went down, and now I had to deal with baseless innuendo. "Laura, your group is good, damn good. I was at the showcase that night, if you remember. I'm not biased, nor do I let my personal affairs get in the way of anything. This is business, and I don't waste either of the big men's time or energy when it comes to making them money."

"Devin, please understand—"

"I'm not done." I cut her off, shutting her down. I didn't know who she thought she was talking to, but she was about to get a first-class lesson in how things were done around here. "I'm not even an A&R rep, but my bosses think that I have an ear for talent based on the last three acts that RPK has signed. Two went Platinum within the first week, the other went Gold in three weeks. I didn't even want to be at this meeting to begin with, but I was coerced into attending, despite my reservations that it might be uncomfortable for Lexi."

Laura tried to find a word in edge-wise, but I held my hand up as a silent cue that if she was going to interrupt me again, I would find a way to cut her deeper. "If you don't want them to be here because you think I greased the wheels, that's fine, no sweat off my back. I have two other groups on speed dial that can be here within the next half-hour, and I can grease the wheels and get Lexi a solo deal and leave the other girls out of it, if you really want me to play favorites. Now, how do you want this to go?"

"All right, I had to make sure that you were on the level, Devin. There is no need for this to get any more intense than it has gotten." Laura sighed. The business could be cutthroat, and I had no issues with her in that. This wasn't personal, but I took exception to the implication that I somehow did this to get Lexi in bed. She extended her hand to me. "I apologize if I offended you. You know how this business can be."

"Actually, no I don't know." I was still a bit irritated that I'd been compromised. "It's one of the reasons I stay insulated in my photography studio, it keeps me out of the bullshit. The music industry is heartless and cruel, and I'm not in the mood for the politics of it. My private affairs are exactly that, *private*. The bottom line is simple: Alexia did nothing to persuade me to do anything, despite your thoughts to the contrary."

"If that is the case, please accept my apology for jumping to conclusions, Devin," Laura said. "My girls deserve the shot."

"Then let's get it done. I will see you and the girls in the conference room in about ten minutes." I headed inside the conference room to try and clear my head. This day was already turning crazy, and I wasn't trying to have it go any weirder than it already was.

Mr. Parker met me before I could adjust and re-focus. *Fuck, I'm here, what else do you want?* He eased into one of the chairs in the room, leaning back to make himself more comfortable before he spoke. "Devin, I wanted to talk to you about something before the group comes in for this meeting."

I wasn't sure I was in the mood for any more talks, but I jumped into it anyway. "Yes, sir, what did you want to talk to me about?"

"It's about the meeting that you helped to bring about, actually," Mr. Parker began. My nerves were on edge all over again. This was not the conversation I wanted to have right now. "Rich and I talked it over, and even though you're not exactly chomping at the bit to be a part of the A&R Department, we need to discuss compensation for the past three groups that you helped with and negotiate the compensation for this group that we're planning to sign if all goes well today."

"Mr. Parker, I don't think that would be—"

"I don't want to hear one of your legendary speeches about being part of the team, D-Lo." Mr. Parker cut me off. "We've already established that you don't want to be in A&R, which is why I didn't want to hear your spiel. But there are some things we need to discuss regardless. But we'll talk about that after we get things settled after the meeting, do we understand each other?"

"Yes, sir, you know I wouldn't argue with the boss." I held up my hands in mock surrender. "But I am perfectly fine where I am in the studio. I would like to try my hand at producing the videos and films in the near future, though, since you're in the talking mood."

"This I know, son, and we'll be talking about that, too." Mr.

Parker smiled, leaving me clueless as to what he was alluding to. "There are some things that are long overdue, but we will rectify that as soon as possible."

I took my seat at the table as one of the executive assistants escorted Laura and the group into the room. Seeing Alexia's face made this meeting all the more bearable. I watched Camryn's face as she walked in, while observing Keri's demeanor as she slipped into the chair at the table. Laura's demeanor was back to all business, never once letting anyone know of the brief talk we'd had a few minutes earlier.

"So, ladies and gentlemen, shall we begin?" Mr. Richton sat down in his chair at the other end of the table. "Give me something we can feel."

Alexia

Chapter Twenty-Eight: Get This Party Started

"I'm impressed. Very impressed. I think we can put *Envyye* on the map."

Hearing those words made the past ten minutes after we finished performing surreal. The fun part was watching Devin sitting with Mr. Parker and Mr. Richton, acting like it was just another meeting in the course of his day. I saw the smile on his face. He was as excited to see how things worked out as I was. He gave up a smile here and there, nodding to the flow of the performance, but I chalked it up to him trying to conduct business so that everything would be on the up and up.

Worked for me, as long as the end result was what we had hoped for.

The way Mr. Parker smiled? We were in for a whole lot more. He beamed as he scribbled down something to pass to Mr. Richton. "Ladies, I really must say your voices are incredible, and we need to get you squared away and ready to record immediately."

After Mr. Richton nodded at whatever Mr. Parker gave to him, he texted someone before he continued. "The legal team is sending the drafts of the contracts as we speak, and the signing advances are also being cut in accounting. Ladies, I think you'll be very happy with the package we're offering."

I wasn't sure of what he was referring to until the doors opened and a couple of people—I assumed from the legal department—walked into the room to show Laura the drafts. A smile spread across her face as she flipped through the pages. "Yes, I believe this is a fair offer, but I want my girls to make the final call on it, to be certain."

As my copy of the contract was placed in front of me, I took a look at the most important part of it: the compensation package. I thought I would faint when I saw the number that was set in front of me for the advance alone. *One million dollars???*

Thank God I was sitting down, or I would have needed a chair.

Keri cursed and slapped her hand over her mouth a few seconds later, apologizing for her outburst two or three times over. Camryn screamed like she'd caught the holy ghost in church or something. I couldn't do much of anything but sit there in total shock. I didn't scream, I didn't curse, I only managed to lock eyes with Devin and mouth the words, "Is this for real?"

I felt the excitement building in the room as Mr. Richton cleared his throat. "Well, that settles it, I think. Ladies, welcome to the RPK family."

Laura had to speak for us because I didn't think any of us could really speak right now. "Mr. Parker, Mr. Richton, thank you for believing in my girls, I know they will live up to the billing."

"I have no doubts that they will, once we get them packaged and ready to roll." Mr. Richton agreed. "Devin, do you still have the contact of yours out in Cali, the one that owns the beach house?"

"Yes, sir, I have it."

"Very good, please let them know that we will need to occupy it for about a week."

Devin had a puzzled look on his face. "May I ask why, sir?"

"First, we're going to need to do some digital prints so we can get the buzz going on the Internet sites. We'll need poster shots for the girls to help with promotions in the stores, and they will be doing some recording out in L.A. also."

Laura got a text message on her smartphone, and after a brief moment, she replied, "My legal team has received the formal contract. Once everything is in order, we should be able to get back here to sign the originals so we can move forward."

"Wonderful! Ladies, I can't wait to see how everything turns out, and enjoy the start of your new journey," Mr. Richton said, standing to shake our hands. "I think Platinum may be just around the corner for you."

I had a feeling I knew where Devin had gone while we were still in the conference room taking selfies and posting on social media over the biggest moment in our professional lives. He'd managed to slip out of the room in the midst of all the excitement, and while no one else seemed to notice his absence, he could have left from a crowded club and I would have known in a heartbeat.

I fumbled my way through the building since I didn't know how to get there from where we were on the top floor offices, but I managed to walk through the door to his studio without too much incident. He was busy at work, flipping through pictures of another group he was working on. I did my best to tiptoe behind him so I could wrap my arms around him.

He flinched for a moment before he realized it was me. "What are you doing down here, baby?"

I kissed his lips, grinning the whole time. The surprised look on his face was what I wanted to see. "I wanted to see you first. I hope you don't mind."

"I thought you would be out celebrating with Camryn and Keri and Laura by now." He gave me the onceover like he hadn't seen me in months. "It was a bit crazy in there, so I figured I'd leave you all to it so I could get back to work myself."

"I know, and I will, but I needed to see you." I sat on his desk and crossed my legs. "I wanted to say thank you for helping to put all of this together."

"Baby, I didn't do anything, I put the word in. You and the girls did the rest," Devin told me, moving closer to where I was on the desk. He stood in front of where I was perched, licking his lips as he eyed the outfit I wore. "Between you and the big men, I'm being given a little bit too much credit."

I kissed him deep and slow, spreading my legs to wrap them around his waist. "You are something else. Would you accept the fact that you helped make this happen? In fact, I want to do something special for you when we get out to L.A. to express my appreciation for all your hard work."

206

"Is that right?" His eyes lit up when he heard that. "How will you be expressing yourself?"

"I'll let you know when it happens, and no sooner, baby." I kissed him a few more times before I broke from him to stand up. "You made my dreams come true, it's only fair that I help make one of yours come true, too."

"Lexi, you just got signed, I don't want you—"

He was interrupted with another kiss across his lips. "You don't have a choice in this matter, Mr. Lowery. I'll let you know when it happens, and not a moment sooner, do you understand me?"

Devin relented, trying his best to figure out if he wanted to press the issue or not. "Okay, baby girl, I'll wait. Now, go and celebrate with your girls, I'll be home later tonight around ten, just in case you want to come by."

Oh, I'll do more than just come by. I'll do much more than that.

But I had another idea in mind after a text came in from Laura. A grin spread when I realized where we would be later. "We'll be at the Mansion Elan to celebrate. Come by after work so we can have a reason to come back to your place and cap off this night properly...please?"

I felt his body shift after I bat my eyelashes and flashed my eyes at him. "You know by now that I can't refuse you, so why would I try now. I'll be there by eleven."

After leaving the studio, I got a text message from Natalia that made me smile even bigger. *Congratulations, baby, I told you! We need to celebrate properly when I get back in town.*

I sent a text back in return, *Yeah, I know, and I can't wait to find out what you have in store when we do celebrate.*

As I headed down to the main floor to get to my car, I smiled as I wondered about the possibilities that lay ahead. The sky was the limit, and I couldn't wait to get started.

Deion

Chapter Twenty-Nine: Lose My Mind

Tina stood in the doorway of my office, dressed in an outfit that intensified the laws of attraction, and that was my way of saying she meant to be inappropriate and she had no business being as such in my presence. Even though it was a warmer-than-usual day, it wasn't the time of the year to show that much skin. She looked like she was ready to hit the club scene, but it was only early evening at best. I could understand if it were after eleven or so, but not seven in the evening.

I tried to avoid stealing glances in her direction, but my curiosity won out. The skirt she wore rose dangerously high on her hips, hugging her frame like the material was painted onto her skin. She'd filled out in all the right place, I had to admit, as she'd matured, but I still didn't want to give her any inclination that she could get it. "Aren't you supposed to be in class? And shouldn't you be wearing a little more than that on campus?"

Tina stared at me like I'd insulted her intelligence. "Did

you lose track of time or something, baby? It's nearly ten o'clock."

I checked my watch, amazed that I'd let the rest of the evening get away from me. I'd been immersed in concept designs for *Envyye*, trying my best to erase the images of the other night from my memory the best way I knew how. The incident with Anton still had me shook up pretty bad, and in hindsight, I should have taken the advice of everyone involved and taken a day to myself to grieve and get this post-traumatic stress out of my system.

Tina seemed oblivious to my inner struggle. "Why don't you stop working for tonight? You can take me to the *Envyye* signing party at Mansion Elan so we can shake it up, take your mind off whatever this project is doing to you."

"Tina, seriously, tonight is not the night for all that." I tried to level with her as best as I could, so I did my best to be as candid as I could. "I'm in a relationship now, so, you're gonna have to find another dude to pester about taking your precious V-card, okay?"

She frowned for a moment before she giggled to herself. "I get it, you're trying to throw some trick in my way, like that's supposed to deter me. Look, D, why don't you do both of us a favor and simply do what comes naturally so you can stop struggling. I told you I got you the minute you get me off."

"I'm nobody's manwhore, alright?" I barked. "I'm not doing what you think I'm supposed to do. I work for your father, and you are off limits, got it? For you to even pull this type of shit on me is bordering on the ridiculous right now. Stop this madness, Tina."

"Look, you're grouchy, let me rub your shoulders and

take some of that stress away." She moved toward me, intent on invading my personal space. "Besides, you and Talia dated for a while and you didn't seem to worry about your job back then."

"Talia and I grew up together, leave her out of this." I stepped away from her reach, keeping the chair between us to keep her from advancing any further. She pouted, acting like she was about to roll into one of her infamous temper tantrums whenever she realized that she wouldn't get what she wanted. "You're too young for me, Tina, and I have to consider the repercussions if I even let something like that creep up in my mind."

"I'm willing to keep the secret if you are, baby."

"Stop calling me baby."

"D, you're being a bit over the top about this aren't you?"

"Let's see…I sleep with you, I take the chance on getting where I need to go based on a promise that you say you can deliver on to make my dreams come true. How do I know that you can coax that kind of capital out of your father?"

Tina regarded my incredulous look before whipping out her smartphone and keying in a few pads on her screen. A few seconds later, she showed me the screen. "That amount is the sum of what has been saved in my account since I was in middle school. Daddy wanted to make sure I was taken care of while I was in college. It's all yours, all you have to do is make my dreams about you come true and all your dreams can come true."

The near eight-figure amount I saw on the screen were enough to make my knees buckle. I tried my best to hide my obvious awe of that much money being in one person's account, much less someone I'd known for the bulk of her young adult life.

Her eyes caught my crisis of conscience, until she said something that snapped my mind back into reality. "I'm surprised Talia never tried to help you get things started. It makes you wonder why she didn't. Does she trust you like I do, D?"

Now she's gone too far. "You need to leave. Now."

I ushered her out the door as the text messages chimed on my phone. Tina was dismayed by my sudden irritation with her. "Get your hands off me, what do you think you're doing? You can't rush me out of here like I'm some trick off the street!"

I slammed the door once she was in no danger of being harmed, slumping against the wall, wondering how in the world I managed to get myself into this mess. I looked over at my phone, noticing the texts were still there.

Yo, D, you need to get down here ASAP! Some dude from MNPL is harassing Alexia. The text from Quinn woke me from the haze I was in, kicking in my protective senses. *Some dude named Dryl or something.*

TramaDryl and his boys were at the party? And how the hell did he know Alexia?

I texted Quinn to let him know I would be breaking land speed records to get to the spot. *Keep that fool busy until I get there. I'll be there in twenty minutes.*

Bet. You want me to cue your girl that you're on the fly?

Nope. I want this entrance to be a complete surprise to everyone in the spot. If he so much as lays a hand on her, I'll drop him where he stands.

I made one more call as I rushed to the truck. If the connects I had at Mansion Elan were still there, I would be able to get away with a few things tonight. This fool wouldn't know what hit him until it was too late.

Alexia

Thirty: We Like to Party

The signing party at the Mansion Elan was crazier than anything I'd ever dreamed it would be. RPK pulled out all the stops, bringing the Atlanta elite in film, music and radio all in one place to get things rocking, and we were at the epicenter of it all. The only thing that was missing was having Devin there to get all boo'd up with in one of the corners in the VIP section. It was getting close to midnight, and I tried not to look disappointed that the one person who meant the most to me wasn't here to celebrate the biggest event in my career to date.

I avoided the ballers trying to get my attention everywhere I turned, while answering questions from the radio personalities about how it felt to be the next big thing that RPK would be bringing out to the public. I was on a high all night until I heard a commotion coming from where I saw Keri had been camped out on the other side of the VIP section.

"Why the hell are you here? Who let you and your crew

in here anyway? This is a private party." Keri's palm was pressed against a figure I couldn't make out due to the dim light in the club. He looked like he was trying to get through her to get to someone, but she was adamant about making sure that didn't happen.

I got up from where I was having drinks with some of the other fans that were celebrating with us in the VIP section, heading in the direction of where Keri was, in case I needed to bring some backup to the mix. The closer I got to Keri, the more I dreaded the inevitable drama that would be heading in my direction, whether I wanted to avoid it or not. Seeing L-Dove in his usual spot next to him didn't help matters, either, and it was all I could do to keep the resting bitch face from making a permanent residence with no possibility of relocation.

I hadn't seen him since that incident at my apartment. I had all but written him off as "out of sight, out of mind" so I didn't have to worry about whatever hold he thought he had on me. Seeing him with the rest of the group made things even more complicated. I wouldn't be able to tell him to leave without having to make a scene with the rest of their ghetto asses. With all the cameras around, it was just a matter of timing and opportunity for someone to try to make this a viral social media moment.

"Relax, Keri, we heard over the radio that y'all got your deal done with RPK. The fellas and I wanted to say congratulations and kick it wit'cha, shawty." Troy's smug look only amped up the anger I felt for him. "You know we about to do a collab with Offset, so having us in the spot might help the cause, you feel me?"

"Well, thank you for the congrats, and now you can

leave." The ice-cold nature of my response could have kept the chill on the margarita I was still sipping on. "I'm gonna enjoy my night with my girls without you and your crew trying to fuck things up."

"Damn, Lexi, why you gotta be so cold?" Troy seemed to feel like he had every right to be there with us. "I thought making it to the big time would put you in a better mood than this."

Camryn jumped into the mix, placing herself between me and Troy. "Please, Troy, you weren't any more interested in Lexi's career than you were in the last presidential election. That's how Trump's bum ass got elected. You're on some next level bullshit right now coming here to begin with. Leave."

"Oh, so you got bodyguards now, Lexi? Is that how it is now, after all we've been through?" Troy was frustrated now, but the smirk on my face only fueled his irritation that he couldn't have me alone to talk. "I wanted to see about my girl, but it's obvi to me that you still wanna act like you ain't rocking with me no more."

I didn't see the point anymore. He wasn't worth the effort, and I took pride in my new-found courage by tapping Camryn on the shoulder to tell her that I could take things from here. Camryn moved out of the way, but she stayed behind me, cutting her eyes at the rest of his crew, daring them to say something.

"Troy, I can't tell you how much of a favor you've done just by being here right now. It makes it easier to say this to you face to face." I was thankful that the music wasn't as loud in the VIP so that I didn't have to shout. "There's nothing left for you here, Troy...nothing. You can be a fan from afar, but I'm not feeling you up close anymore. Goodbye."

I turned to walk back to my seat, and Troy had the nerve to grab my shoulder to spin me around to face him. His jaws were clenched, which in the past would have made me pause, but that was when he had power over me. His sneer showed his bad intentions. "I'm not done with you yet, Lexi. Do you know who I am? You don't get to say it's over, trick, I do."

My eyes darted away from him for a split second as a familiar face caught my attention, the strobe light catching it for a few seconds. For a minute, I thought it was my eyes playing tricks on me, but when the light flashed and confirmed my suspicion, a grin spread across my face. It was about to be a very interesting night after all.

My girls must have seen it, too, because Keri tapped my shoulder so fast, I could feel the excitement on her without looking back to see her face. I heard a fit of laughter behind me coming from her and Camryn, and it triggered a laughing fit of my own.

"Oh, y'all think this shit is funny now? I'll show you how funny this shit is." Troy cursed as he tried to raise his hand back to hit me. Too bad he never connected.

It was over before it started, and I didn't care that this made it to TMZ or not, it was worth the price of admission.

Devin looked like he was possessed, the way he did when he came at Quinn the night Anton died. I might have been worried about what might happen then, but this time I was looking forward to it. To be real, it made me hot as hell for him in an instant. I wanted him to cut loose; he had so much pent up aggression from getting shot that I couldn't wait for him to unleash it all. The only thing I worried over was whether he would reinjure his shoulder.

"Do you care to show the ladies just how funny this shit is?" Devin spat as he caught Troy's arm and twisted it so hard it caused Troy to yell out in pain. Troy had to do a double-take for a minute before he realized who stopped him. Devin was undeterred. "I think I asked you a question, bruh, it might be in your best interest to answer it."

"Oh lawd, it's the corporate, cornball nigga! What the fuck are you doing here, bruh? I thought you were in your cubby hole, trying to get my pictures ready." Troy laughed. "Don't tell me, you're here to see how real niggas handle business, huh?"

What Troy didn't realize was that the club's bouncers had already whispered to the rest of the group that they were causing a disturbance. Long story short, L-Dove and G-Style raised up out of there. So much for group solidarity. Troy was on such a power trip trying to put me in my "place" that he wasn't aware that his backup had deserted him.

Bodyguards from RPK flanked at Devin's sides might have been the reason for the smirk on his face. He winked at me before he turned his attention back to Troy. He was all business. "Hi, baby, I'm sorry I'm a little late, I had to try and come out of my cubby hole before it got too late, and I had to try and convince my imaging editors that I wasn't doing any print work for Animal Planet. You know how hard it is to catch the good side of a subject."

The stare Troy gave him was hot enough to melt metal.

The stare Devin returned was cold enough to freeze molten lava.

"You wouldn't be wild'n out like that with the heavies behind you, partner." Troy tried to flex. "You still a lame ass, corporate, house nigga. I bet them manicured nails hardly ever get dirty, huh, bitch?"

Devin's eyes narrowed, and it wasn't even fair to witness what happened next.

He snapped his fingers, and the RPK bodyguards stepped back about five feet. In the next moment, Troy felt a punch to the gut, which knocked him to one knee. Devin dropped a knee right between his eyes soon after, knocking Troy on his back.

Devin was on top of him before he could get up, keeping a knee to his neck. "Now, unless I missed my guess, I believe the ladies asked you to leave, including my baby. It would be in your best interest to honor that request."

"Whatever, nigga, I ain't going nowhere until your bitch and I finish things between us." Troy tried to move from under Devin's knee, choking through the words he tried to say. "If she thinks this is done, she's got another thing coming."

"It's already done, Troy." I stated. "It was over months ago, there's nothing to finish."

"You heard the lady." Devin told him as he lifted him off the ground. "It's time for you to leave. You might wanna catch up with your crew while you're at it and find out why they were so quick to ditch you when it really mattered."

The bodyguards and the bouncers escorted Troy outside of the club, but he managed to slip through their grasp for a quick moment, trying to rush at Devin while he wasn't looking. I screamed out to warn him, but he turned and caught Troy before he could blindside him. He pushed Troy far enough away to get enough space, throwing a right hand that caught his jaw, dropping him cold. He crumpled to the ground in a heap, causing everyone in the area to react so loud that the rest of the club stopped to figure out what happened.

Of course, cameras were on deck, capturing every sweet moment, and it was only a matter of time before it would hit social media and God knows where else it might pop up in the media circuit.

Devin turned to me with a quizzical look on his face. I was in complete awe of how he'd turned the switch off, sounding normal after he just went "Beast Mode" a few seconds ago. "Any other crazy ex-boyfriends that I need to be aware of? You know, to couple with the crazy females in my life? We sure know how to pick them, don't we?"

"Yeah, you sure do," Camryn chimed in. "Damn, D, I didn't know you had moves like that. And with one arm, too? Hell, I thought you were just a pretty boy."

Keri spit out her drink. "He is a pretty boy, but he got some street in him. I like that a lot. I'm not even into dudes all that much, but after dropping Troy like that, you even got me wet."

"Okay, so now that I've entertained you three, enjoy the rest of your party." Devin pulled me closer to him, kissing my lips. "We've got work to do, starting tomorrow."

Deion

Thirty-One: California Love

I was in deep thought on the flight to L.A, which wasn't too far off base for me. I was in business mode, and the six-hour flight on the RPK jet gave me plenty of time to get a lot of things off my plate. Even with Alexia sleeping in the seat next to me, the only thing it served to do was narrow my focus and figure out how to tighten the itinerary once we touched down.

I had the girls' itinerary cross-referenced with mine, ensuring that the people who needed to be involved in their project were lined up, too. Per Mr. Richton's instructions, their schedule would be filled until after ten at night, giving them enough time to rest and relax and be ready for the next day.

The mansion on the Pacific Coast Highway, with its view overlooking the ocean, could not have been a more romantic locale for setting up some damn good shots. I hadn't had much of a chance to do something on this scale in a long time. Most of the clients that I'd had were male artists, which was fine, but there's only so much I could do for a male artist outside of drape a lot of pretty women over him and let the camera do the work. I had the chance to let my creativity flow, and it would be easier having my baby there with me.

This would be the first time that I would be using the house in a professional capacity, and I was looking forward to finding the spots in the house that would distinguish each of the girls. Lord knows they were not carbon copies of each other, although it sounds that way musically.

I took my time to talk to each of the girls, one on one, since we had six hours before we touched down. I found out that Camryn had a thing for bubble baths, so it was easy to find the whirlpool tub in the master bathroom and have her covered in some very strategic places, just to get the men going.

Keri, for all of her toughness that she portrays when the group is together, by herself I found out that she's quite the sex kitten. A love of lingerie gave me the boudoir experience for her, complete with bedroom poses and seduction on levels that she wouldn't have a clue about.

That left my baby in the living room, lying out against a fire and a tiger skin rug that I remembered was still there. Seeing her in nothing but a leather coat and heels giving me pouty faces and giving me other ideas after the shoot was over left me trying to figure out when my body would betray me.

Oh, and of course a few surprises of my own to shake things up.

The possibilities of this shoot were endless, and it was the type of shoot that could put me on the map on a variety of levels.

But first…we had to touch down and make it all happen.

Ah, there's no place like L.A. We touched down at John Wayne Airport, and as instructed, there were two vehicles waiting, a driver stationed and waiting at one of the vehicles. The Lincoln Navigator limo and driver were for the girls to be chauffeured to the places they needed to go. The Cadillac Escalade was mine.

I needed my space for my equipment, and alone time with Alexia, of course. There was no need for a driver for me. L.A. might as well be a second home for me, as much time as I spent out here for shoots and other business.

The bodyguards rode in the limo with the group, and the driver already had instructions to head up the PCH to Malibu, a little over an hour's drive. Once we got there, it would give everyone a chance to recover from the jet lag a little bit and make calls and settle in.

It would be a good few weeks chilling on the ocean, that's for damn sure. I wanted to see the looks on their faces when they got a chance to see the house that they would be crashing in.

As we loaded all of the equipment and the baggage into the trucks, Alexia slid her arms around my waist and slipped in a few kisses. I couldn't resist the urge to grope her butt. "I take it you're enjoying the journey so far?"

The answer to my question came in the form of a deftly placed kiss on my neck. "I hope I never wake up from this dream. I can't wait to see what else lies in store."

We finally got everything in and got ready for the ride up to the house. I watched her walk to the limo, enjoying the view as she turned her head to wink at me. "You know I love you, right?"

"Yes, and before this trip is over, I plan to show you how much I love you, too." She blew a kiss before disappearing into the back of the vehicle.

I got a phone call from Mr. Richton as soon as I got in the Escalade, answering it as soon as I could once I settled into the driver's seat. I answered the first question on his mind before he could utter the words. "Yes, sir, we've arrived in L.A. What else can I do for you?"

"There's not much that needs to be done at this point, my boy." Mr. Richton stated through my Bluetooth. "Just do your usual bang-up job."

"Consider it done, sir." I clicked my phone shut as we headed to the entrance ramp to I-405.

The weather was pretty good for mid-January. It felt like early May in Atlanta; not too warm, not too cold. I opened the sunroof and popped *Envyye*'s demo CD in the disc player, letting the girls' voices give me further inspiration as to what to do with their shoot. It was a ritual of mine that had served me very well, and I had no intentions of breaking my ritual.

Hearing Alexia's voice on the lead of one of the tracks had me in a trance. I was glad that the chauffeur had the limo on GPS all the way to the house, I probably would have gotten us lost if I took the point. I indulged, wondering about all the possibilities once the album dropped later in the year. The media blitz would be insane. Posters would be placed nationwide in every possible retail store that can be had. The digital blitz would be amazing to say the least, with the cover being placed on an international stage. Once it hit the Internet, any and every person would be able to view it and pre-order the album.

I had to be on my game, more than I'd ever been, even though I already had three artists who had done some big things under my belt. There was also the added pressure of making the woman in my life look like a superstar. They already had the sound, so the rest would be on me. I was good with that, I lived on pressure.

We made it to the Pacific Coast Highway coming off I-10. Having the ocean as the backdrop for the ride all the way to the house was exactly the serenity that I needed. Well, I needed something else, too, but there would be time for that after work had been done.

My cell phone began singing to let me know text messages were coming in, and even though I wasn't supposed to answer while I was on the road, I picked up my phone to see what came in.

Alexia's smiling face graced my screen first, in addition to other pictures of her kissing at the phone, acting a fool with the girls while in the limo. It was fun to see them finally enjoying themselves for a moment or two. Her naughtier messages telling me what she couldn't wait to do to me were worth the risk. Some of the things that she suggested would make a good girl blush.

Fortunately for me, I liked my women naughty.

I texted back that I had some things in store for her, too, and she should be ready for whatever I had for her. By morning, work would begin. In the meantime, I enjoyed the ride up the Pacific Ocean all the way into paradise.

Alexia

Thirty-Two: Glamorous

"Oh my God, look at this place!"

It felt like forever after we turned off the PCH to get through the winding roads that led to the beach estates that Deion described to us during the flight. We got to the driveway to where the home was located, and it felt like drive within a drive just to get from the main road onto the estate grounds. It was well worth the wait, though. It looked like something out of a Hip-Hop video.

We drove up to the front of the house, and it looked simple enough; we could see that it had two levels and that it was pretty sizeable, which worked for me. I had hoped to have my own space to do what I wanted to do with my baby.

Once inside, we had no idea what we were in for. The house was nothing short of exquisite!

Devin studied our faces with this smirk on his face, trying hard not to laugh at us.

"What's so amusing, D?" Keri asked after closing her mouth from looking around her. "We know you high-powered executives are used to this kind of stuff, but us simple girls can't act like we've been there and done that."

"I'm sorry ladies, but I couldn't help myself." He tried to contain his chuckles, but we chalked that up to an epic fail. "Your reactions were exactly what the doctor ordered. Would you like to tour the place, so you can get your bearings?"

Camryn almost knocked us over to let Devin lead the way. "Yes, I want to see this place so that I don't get lost."

I hung on to Devin's arm as he took us from the basement to the second floor, trying to get over the awe of the place became a difficult task as we counted off eight—count them, eight—bedrooms and as many bathrooms, strategically placed around the home.

Every time we got to a window that faced the Pacific Ocean, no one could resist looking out of the window to get another view. It felt so surreal, something out of a dream. I didn't want anyone to pinch me, though. I wanted to ride this one out until someone pulled me from my sleep.

Marble and hardwood floors intermixed throughout the house, glass fixtures on the stairwells and along some areas on the walls, and the kitchen was to die for! What really had us tripping was the sight of the central vacuum system, complete with a robotic vacuum that did the sweeping and vacuuming on its own. Camryn screamed when she saw it heading in our direction to sweep up some dust on the floor.

"Okay, that's it, I gotta get one of these the first chance I get!" Keri yelled after moving her feet out of the way when it rushed past her.

"I'm glad you like the place so far." Devin patted my arm as it intertwined with his. "I didn't want to disappoint when

I made the call to my contact to rent the place out."

"How long are we supposed to be here, D?" Camryn asked. "A girl could get used to being in a place like this. I just don't want to get too attached…well, at least not until the album goes platinum. I guess I'm gonna have to get a sugar daddy or something in the meantime."

"A little over three weeks, but we have the place for an entire month right now, just in case things take a little longer than expected." Devin answered. He sort of did a double-take over her "sugar daddy" comment, but I saw him shake it off after a few seconds to focus on the task at hand. "After we do what we came to do here, the rest of the album will be re-mastered and polished back in Atlanta."

"Okay, cool, then I'll soak all this in for as long as we can, but we might need to come back out here when we're not on the clock." I quipped. "I can see a few parties that can get thrown in here."

"Well, don't get too crazy with it, okay?" Devin winked at me. "I don't have fourteen million to blow to buy the place if we wreck it."

A collective *damn* came from the three of us.

"Okay, so no wild parties, but can we at least have guests?" Camryn was more concerned with someone a bit more familiar than trying to pick something strange up in a new city. "I might wanna see about some people while we're out here."

"I already texted Q the location, Camryn, if that's what you mean." Devin read her query the way the rest of us did. "In fact, I texted the information to your significant other, too, Keri."

Camryn frowned at Devin, folding her arms across her

chest. "Damn, D-Lo, how you know I ain't want someone else to come through? I mean, I know Q is your man and all and you're looking out for him, but you could have at least checked with me first."

"And who did you want to come through, Cam? I'm curious, especially when you know they needed to be vetted before we left the A." Devin's frown matched Camryn's, almost to the point to where he was about to jump all in her business. In the next moment, he seemed to snap out of it and got back to his original train of thought. "It doesn't matter. Whoever they are, they will have explicit instructions to not divulge the location under any circumstances, under penalty of severe punishment by me."

"Don't worry about it, Devin. It might be doing too much to have too many coming to the beach house. I'm sure I can make other arrangements. I wouldn't want to get on your bad side." Cam still wouldn't let the situation go, which seemed to turn down the temperature in the room a few degrees. "Besides, I might want some more space to handle a few things."

"I'd hate to see how that goes down, Cam. We wouldn't want you to wreck this place. Maybe the sugar daddy you're trying to make the come up with can set you up something pretty." Keri smirked as she turned her attention to Devin. "And you, Mr. Crime and Punishment…after what we saw at the Mansion Elan the other night when you took TramaDryl down, I wouldn't want to be on your bad side."

"Okay, ladies, the bodyguards have checked the grounds and they say it's okay to settle in." Laura walked in from the other room to explain. "There are enough bedrooms to accommodate us all, which is a very good thing. According to the itinerary, we have a recording session in the morning, around 8 a.m., so we need to get some sleep, ladies. Goodnight."

"Baby, why are you still up?"

"I'll be a minute, baby, I just need to finish up some stuff." I heard him typing on his laptop, completely enthralled with something on the screen. It wasn't like him to ignore me, even while he was working.

When I moved behind him with the purpose of distracting him, he kissed my hand and kept back at an email that I saw on the screen. The email address was from the detective that was assigned to the case regarding Anton's death. This was not what I wanted him focused on during our first night in this beautiful house. "D, come to bed, baby, I don't want you worrying about that right now. I want you to relax and rest so we can do what we came here to do this week. We'll deal with that mess when we get back."

"I wish I could, baby." He rubbed his eyes. The jet lag was getting to him. "Anton's mother wants me named as the prime suspect and his death ruled a homicide. They're pushing the funeral back until they can complete their investigation."

Another email notification sounded off on his phone, causing him to pick it up. His frown deepened, and he cursed under his breath. "And the hits just keep on coming. Your ex has decided to press charges for assault over what went down at the Mansion Elan the other night."

"That's crazy!" I wanted to shout, but I didn't want to disturb the quietness in the house, especially when I was supposed to be sleeping. "Even the medical examiner said the death was most likely a suicide, and what the hell is Troy talking about, assault? I should have charges brought up for him trying to hit me."

"Yeah, but she's not convinced of the facts and thinks that I killed him, although I can't figure out for the life of me why she would think that. I'm not worrying myself about TramaDryl, though. He's catching it with Black Twitter right now, checking his street cred if he can't even handle himself in a fight." He shook his head, rubbing his hands over his face. "This is a nightmare that I wish would end...soon. I don't want this hanging over my head while I'm out here. I'm supposed to be making you look stunning."

"Come on, baby, you and I both know none of this is your fault." I sat in his lap to shield him from the laptop. "He took his own life. There was nothing you could have done."

"But I deserted him, Lexi!" His eyes welled up with tears. I hadn't realized the guilt weighed him down so badly. "I left him alone. I wasn't the friend that he needed. For God's sake, he damn near tried to kill me before he blew himself away!"

"Listen to me, baby. You can't beat yourself up like this." I reassured him, rubbing the tears away from his face. "We'll get through this, okay?"

"I didn't want you to see me like this, baby." He closed his eyes as he tried to shy away from looking at me. "My emotions have always been hard to control, and *I hate funerals!*"

I realized I was starting to lose him, and no matter what I tried to appeal to his sense of logic, it was his emotions that ruled him at the moment. I needed to get to him that way, and I had a surefire way to do that.

"Okay, I need you to get up from this laptop now." I ordered, pulling him to the bed so I could figure out if there was anything I could do to help. I grabbed my phone as he got up to send a text message. I left one simple message. *He needs you…I need you…how soon can you get here?*

As I watched him stretch out on the bed and lay on his stomach, I fought the initial urge to rape him on the spot. Instead, I straddled the small of his back and began to knead and massage his back and shoulders, hearing a low growl escape from his lips as I worked him over.

We didn't say anything. We simply enjoyed the breeze coming from the ocean and the soothing sounds that emanated from the waves that crashed on the beach in the distance.

My phone chimed in to break the silence for a brief moment. I smiled when I got the return message: *give me 24 hours.*

After ten minutes of working out the tension in his body, he finally loosened up and relaxed. "I know it wasn't my fault, baby, but it still freaks me out to have to go through the process. I did some crazy shit when we were younger, some really dumb, crazy shit. Dealing with the cops on this level was something I would have never imagined."

"It's all right, baby, the cops will get things taken care of, and then we can move on to bigger and better things." I whispered in his ear as I felt his breathing labor, which let me know he would be sound asleep soon. I slipped off his back and slid to spoon against his chest, grinning as he slipped his arm to caress my hip.

"Thanks for ignoring me tonight, I really needed you," he whispered, grabbing my hip and giving it a squeeze. "These next few weeks should be fun, if you can call work fun."

I snuggled deeper against his body, feeling the warmth taking over, enjoying the cool breeze from the open window, and waiting patiently for the seduction of the sleep that would soon claim us. I couldn't wait to see what the morning would bring, and more mornings to come.

Deion

Chapter Thirty-Three: No Ordinary Love

We were getting back from running a few errands throughout the day. The girls were at the studio putting in some more preliminary work while I did some scouting in the area to see what I wanted to use for location shoots. I had no real reason to expect the day to go any other way but business as usual, except for an unexpected guest who I wasn't aware was arriving at the property.

Natalia had two weaknesses: chocolate and Corvettes, so the fact that I saw a pearl-colored beast in the driveway tipped me off to her being in the city. What threw me off base was that I expected her to be on location in Barbados on a film shoot.

I couldn't take my eyes off her. The tan gave her skin a darker, cocoa-rich hue that mesmerized me. My curiosity was piqued. "Talia, what are you doing here, baby?"

She smirked, causing Alexia to giggle. "Well, I had to see about my favorite couple and all. Aren't you happy to see me? After all, I left home to see about you."

The look on Alexia's face tipped me off that something else was in the mix. I glanced at Natalia, only to watch her blush and avoid eye contact. Yeah, the conspiracy was in, and I wasn't even an active participant.

We'd been grinding pretty hard all week, with the girls in the studio doing their thing while the tracks were being laid. When they weren't in the studio, we were getting it in with the photo shoots. Mr. Richton did me a solid and flew one of my favorite makeup artists in to take care of the hair and makeup, and she recruited some of the local stylists to help with the three of them. I couldn't have asked for a better setup.

The engineers were so impressed with how the group handled the sessions that they finished everything two weeks earlier than they thought. They express-shipped everything back to Atlanta for the engineers there to put the polish on ASAP. That gave us a couple of days to detox and get ready for the flight back to the A.

I'd planned to do something special, a private, sensual photo shoot, and let things take their natural course. I wanted to wait until Natalia was asleep in one of the other bedrooms to take care of that. Not that she wouldn't object to watching the shoot, of course, but Alexia and I hadn't had a chance to consummate our relationship, and I wanted it to be special.

Natalia gave Alexia the onceover, asking the obvious questions. "So, how are you two doing? How is the superstar life, Lexi?"

"I feel like this was exactly where I'm supposed to be." Even at midnight, Alexia beamed and grinned, showing no fatigue from the sixteen-hour days we were putting in.

I couldn't stop smiling for her, either. Watching them in

the studio earlier this week, I had a new-found respect and admiration for what recording artists went through. As a group, they were in sync. I didn't know how else to describe it, but it was beautiful to watch. I was in awe of it all, and the takes were smooth, like they were waiting to prove that this was in them all along.

Now that things were done and settled, the whole vibe and atmosphere of the house changed, especially since everyone's significant other managed to make it out to the left coast to enjoy the weekend. I guess that's why seeing Natalia here with me and Alexia was such an unexpected, albeit pleasant, surprise.

"Okay, Natalia, seriously, what's going on?" I had to get a straight answer out of either of them, one way or the other. "What brought you out here? Not that I'm complaining, but you know how I am, and the timeline isn't fitting for me."

Natalia looked at Alexia for a moment, and by the time she looked back at me, her eyes told me everything I needed to know. "Your baby told me that our baby needed me."

I tried to find the wall; my balance faltered. I'd never heard the words come out of her mouth like that…definitely not like *that*. "What are you talking about, *our* baby? Did I miss the memo somewhere?"

Natalia grinned, kissing my lips. I felt like I was in some sort of dream state, shaking my head several times to figure out what in the world was going on. She pressed her index finger against my lips when I tried to say something. "For once, baby boy, don't say anything. This was bound to happen, it was only a matter of time."

Alexia shook me out of my haze, her smile as bright as Natalia's. "Yes, that's what I said, baby. We both needed her.

239

There's something that we need to explore, and tonight is a perfect time to figure out exactly what it is between us...all of us."

Watching Natalia and Alexia as they explored each other felt like something out of one of my most intense fantasies, my mind trying its best to convince me that this was not a figment of my imagination.

I sat in a chair next to the bed, taking the whole scene in. I shook my head, still in disbelief at the scene in front of me. My best friend and my girlfriend were so immersed in their own private sensual rendezvous that it didn't matter if I was in the room or not. There was no way in hell that I was going to disturb the connection that they were creating. In fact, it looked like it was stronger than that, which spawned more than a few questions in my head.

In the background, I heard a faint mix of the waves in the distance with the lyrics to 'No, No, No' from Destiny's Child:

You'll be sayin'
No, no, no, no, no
When it's really
Yes, yes, yes, yes, yes
You'll be sayin'
No, no, no, no, no
When it's really
Yes, yes, yes, yes, yes

That song began to mean a lot more in this moment than

I ever gave it credit for. A classic was still a classic.

I picked up my camera as they were undressing each other and started clicking away. Although they were aware I was there, they didn't miss a beat, and I wasn't about to dictate anything to disrupt the flow. I wasn't saying no anymore. Not tonight. Probably not any other night. I wasn't about to lose out on something so right.

Every few moments, either Alexia or Natalia would look into the camera, give me a pouty look or wink, and get back into their flow. It was all I could do to keep from getting in the middle to take things to the next level of ménage.

The song only enhanced the passion of the moment, and the words being sung couldn't have given the scene an eerier sense of serendipity:

Boy, I know you want me
I can see it in your eyes
But you keep on frontin'
Won't you say what's on your mind?
'Cause each and every time you're near me
You give me signs
But when I ask you what's the deal
You hold it all inside

"Come here, baby." The come-hither look and point was nothing more than the sexiest invitation on the planet. I might have been biased, so sue me.

I put my camera down, only to realize that both of them were stark naked and looking at me like they'd been waiting for me for at least the past few minutes. I slipped onto the bed and they jumped on me, two pairs of hands trying to get to any spare inch of naked skin was intoxicating as hell.

"Touch her, baby," Alexia whispered to me over the music.

"What did you say?" I still didn't want to believe this was happening, but she moved my hands, further fueling my desire to believe fantasy and reality were one and the same. "Baby, is this happening?"

Alexia kissed me with an intensity that made me realized I wasn't dreaming. "I said, touch her, baby. It's okay, I want her, too."

"Lexi—"

"Baby, I want this, too. I'm not playing." She caressed my face. Her touch was so warm, and I inhaled a hint of her essence on her fingertips. I wasn't expecting this, I swear to God I wasn't, but it flowed so well. It wasn't forced, it wasn't coerced, and I didn't want to say anything to ruin the moment.

"Touch me, baby, please." Natalia insisted. "It's been so long since you've touched me."

I tried to let myself go and slid my fingers along her waist, feeling Natalia's hips as she moaned and grinded against the palms of my hands.

When I walk up to you, baby
You seem so shy
What's the problem, baby?
Never had a girl like I?
I can see right through you
And you know you wanna be mine
So get your act together
'Cause you're running out of time

"That's it, baby…mmmmm, damn that feels so good." Natalia grabbed my wrists, urging me to move like I knew her body. I tried, but the fear tried to consume me, making me fight her urges and movements. *Stop fighting it, D. Let yourself go, they want it, so let it go.*

Alexia slipped between her legs, which surprised me that she moved to taste her. I didn't want to overthink things, there would be time to talk later. I figured out where my hesitation came from when it came to Natalia. She was right about it being so long. It had been months since we'd been together, right after Jenna left me.

Natalia kissed me, sliding her hand down to my ever-growing length. The softness of her skin against my shaft put me into another zone. I kissed her as Natalia bit my lip and moaned through the kiss. I soon found out why her kisses became so intense.

"Damn, baby…yes, that's it, right there!" Her voice left her as she tried to scream, trying to avoid drawing any attention from the other people in the house. Alexia and I found out the hard way that the acoustics were great and the walls were not the thickest on the planet. Not that we cared all that much. We got an earful from Keri and her girlfriend the night that she flew in to see her.

"Let it go, baby, she wants you to come for her," I broke from the kiss to tell Natalia, even more turned on by the sight of Alexia enjoying her juices like she was a vintage wine that was recently opened to celebrate a grand occasion. Truth be told, it felt like we were celebrating.

Alexia focused a little more, bringing a pitch out of Natalia that I had never heard before. She gripped my shaft tightly as I felt her body trembling from the climax that was coming over the horizon.

"Oh my God, baby, she's gonna…I'm coming!!!" This time Natalia couldn't hold back. Her screams reverberated off the walls, threatening to alert more than the other occupants in the house.

I grabbed one of her hands, and Alexia instinctively grabbed the other one, the two of us holding her down as the waves continued to crash onto the beach outside, competing with the waves that flowed through her body as she continued to lick and lap away. Natalia finally broke free, sliding to the side of the bed to try and catch her breath. She was still shaking from her orgasm, and Alexia pounced on me before I could react.

"Fuck me, baby. Now." She climbed on top of me before I could move to get a condom. She kissed me hard, the traces of Natalia's juices still slick on her lips. I met her aggression, licking the juices from her lips when I felt another pair of hands moving in on me with their own level of furor. The next thing I felt was Natalia's legs straddling my face, grinding her lips against my tongue. I grabbed her hips to get my bearings, feeling Alexia rotating and grinding her hips as she fucked me with an energy that I wasn't sure I was prepared for.

Their voices were muffled, but I could make out through their screams and moans that they were glad that Natalia was able to make it out after all.

"God, I needed this…come on baby…make me come again!" I heard the muffled order coming between moans.

"Oh God, Talia, he's rubbing against my spot! Shit, he's hitting my spot!" Alexia repeated over and over again. "Damn, it's so deep!"

"Give it to him, baby! Take it all!" Natalia screamed, riding my tongue harder.

Hearing their muffled screams as they tore through me was music to my ears. I didn't care if I was sore in the morning or not, it was well worth the delicious torture that I endured right now. I felt my wave beginning to crest, and I needed to hold out a little longer to try and let Alexia know that I was coming.

My body had other ideas.

I growled, unable to speak the words with Natalia still grinding my lips. I dug my nails into Alexia's hips as best as I could, but she lifted off me and started to stroke me with her hand. Natalia got up from my face and moved down to where Alexia was and started licking my thighs, alternating with the head of my shaft. Alexia was on the other side, licking up and down my length, driving me insane.

My climax imminent, I grabbed for anything that I could to anchor myself. I looked down at them, immersed in each other, kissing in between licking and sucking along every inch of my nether regions at the same time. The volcano erupted, and the guttural growl that escaped from my lips scared me to my core. Through my narrowed eyes, I saw both women enjoying the physical proof that they'd gotten me to let go of everything that had been weighing me down the past couple of weeks.

It didn't matter anymore at that point. The exhaustion from that eruption was enough for darkness to claim me quickly. The last sounds I heard were the continuing passionate moans shared between the women that would hold the potential to rule my world.

Alexia

Chapter Thirty-Four: Dirt Off Ya Shoulders

To say the things that happened a couple of nights ago changed everything for me—for the three of us—was an understatement. My head was still spinning. Even as I lay intertwined between the two people who had now become my everything, I struggled to figure out what in the world I'd gotten myself into.

There were so many things that needed to be figured out it wasn't funny. I realized the entertainment industry was a bit liberal in its mindset, but people were still trying to wrap their heads around DeRay Davis and his two girlfriends. I could only imagine what would happen if this managed to get out ahead of the album release. If I'd only realized that it would only the tip of the iceberg once we'd come out of our self-imposed isolation, I would have suggested to stay in bed for another day to get our collective minds right.

"I hate to sound like Beyoncé right now, but how the hell did this shit happen?" Natalia snuggled between me and Devin as she tried to make sense of last night. "Whatever just happened, I don't want this feeling to end."

"I'm still trying to figure it all out. I'm trying to slow my mind down. Last night was incredible." My eyes searched hers, then probed Devin's for some idea of, hell, I wasn't sure at the moment. "This is unlike anything I would have ever considered."

"Honestly, this is the first time I've been caught off guard like this." Devin shook his head, looking at the two of us. "I mean, the most I'd hoped for was that you would get along as friends. This is wilder than any dream I allowed myself to have."

"So, is this real? The three of us?" I needed some form of foundation, something to work from. "I want this to be real, but I don't want to be alone in this, either. Now that I have you both, I don't want to lose either of you."

"Look, we're young, we're enjoying life. We can ride this out to whatever end that comes," Natalia replied. "I'm used to seeing this overseas a lot, so it isn't a foreign concept for me. I want you both, period."

There's the old adage that you couldn't be in love with more than one person at a time, but I felt like I was falling for them both, in uniquely different ways. It's not like I cared all that much to begin with in figuring out the "why" of it all, all I cared about was that I had to have them both.

We had to come back down to earth sooner or later, so, we decided to come clean to everyone else in the house, since we knew they could hear us.

Keri was cool with the whole arrangement. In fact, she admitted that if we didn't take Natalia, she and her girlfriend would have been happy to have her as their third. They were too busy getting each other off from hearing everything we did to worry about the why and the how. I expected that answer from her, despite the majority of her friends in the LGBTQ+ community who were fiercely monogamous in nature. It was part of the reason I was able to confide in her more.

Laura had been holed up in her room for the entire sabbatical, which threw us all off. Under normal circumstances, she was in our faces, trying to keep us on track with whatever we were doing, even during our downtime. We figured she would have her say before too long once she found out.

That only left Camryn and Quinn and finding out what their thoughts were on the matter. In her case, I didn't care either way; she was going to hate on the situation, I felt it in my spirit.

Quinn sort of blinked a few times, trying to make sense of it all. He did his best to save face a little bit, but then he gave me a look like he'd picked the wrong woman. He didn't even hide his disappointment in front of Camryn. I winked at him, knowing that he never had a chance in hell at getting at me. Yeah, it was a bit petty, but ever since the group was formed, I got branded the "good girl" out of the trio.

Camryn didn't disappoint, but that was due to the vibe she picked up from Quinn. "I can't believe you would get into some wild shit like this, girl. You know that's some next level bullshit right there. You ain't woman enough to keep Devin satisfied by yourself?"

"Yeah, you're doing a damn good job keeping Quinn around, too, right?" I was almost to the point to where I was more than ready for her counter attacks. "I should have known you would be the one to play the hater."

"I'm not hating, baby girl, I just know that I couldn't do that shit. I ain't the one to be sharing a man. Who does that?" Camryn sneered. "But I should have known the rest of you were freaks to say you're okay with this mess. It's not even a real relationship."

"Quinn, can you calm your woman down, please?" I looked in his direction, incredulous over why he looked like he didn't want any part of the mess that Camryn was creating. "Didn't you handle that while you were here this week, or were you too busy fantasizing over what was popping in the other rooms?"

"See, that's your problem, Lexi. Sex doesn't cure every damn thing. And for the record, he doesn't have to 'handle' me to get me to shut up. I'll do what I want to do," Camryn lectured, amplifying her attack on me. "Wake up and smell the bullshit! He's having his cake and eating it, too. Don't you see that?!?!"

"Have you thought for one second that I actually want them both, huh?" I threw that nugget out there, which caused her to stare at me. I stepped between Natalia and Devin, returning her defiant stare with a glare of my own. "I want them both, and they both want me. What part of this is not resonating with you?"

"All right, ladies, enough." Laura came in after a few moments of listening in on the conversation. We weren't sure how long she had been standing there, but it was enough for her to set Camryn straight. "Camryn, if you can't handle the relationship that Lexi is obviously happy being in, then that's a personal problem that you need to get figured out."

"But Laura—"

"I don't think you're hearing my words, Camryn." Before

she continued, we saw a couple of men walking out from her bedroom. "The last thing you want to do is judge someone based on what you think you know about them."

Devin took a double-take at the men, who had shit-eating grins on their faces. A silly smirk spread across his face as he realized why Laura had been so out of pocket and not as worried about us as we were used to. She'd managed to keep the bodyguards that we had been with all week long entertained. It was so quiet a pin could be heard hitting the marble floor.

"Well, I'll be damned. I thought you had it in you, love." Devin gave the thumbs up, winking at her before nodding at the bodyguards to acknowledge their discretion.

"So, do you plan to judge me because I had the fun that you wished you had?" Laura's question was like a dagger aimed at Camryn's throat. "Because if you are, I have no problems hitting the speed-dial so that your replacement will be more than happy to enjoy the potential stardom that this group is primed to have."

Camryn was speechless. Hell, we all were, but Laura had a damn good point, and Camryn couldn't argue it. The only difference was we had no clue our manager could get down like that. "I would never get into your personal business like that, Laura. That wouldn't be fair to you. You are our manager."

"Personal business is exactly that, Camryn...personal. It doesn't matter if it's me or your group mates, if you want us out of yours, you have to stay out of ours. You don't have to like it, but you will respect it." Laura explained. "You're not perfect. None of us are. But this holier-than-thou routine has got to stop, or would you like for me to blow up your spot about the videos that you and Quinn have been making when you thought you were alone in his studio?"

Camryn turned bright red when she heard that last part. Her stunned silence tipped the rest of us off that it wasn't more than sex between her and Quinn. I guess everything came full circle this morning.

"How did you know about that?" Camryn cut her eyes in Quinn's direction, watching his head drop to confirm what she'd suspected. "You sonofabitch?! What did you do?"

Quinn shrugged his shoulders, not caring either way. I felt some kinda way about his indifference about it all, until the majority of our cell phones began chiming and ringing almost at the same time.

Laura shook her head as she pulled up her Instagram account on her phone and began to play the first video on The Shade Room's feed. "I'm going to have a time explaining this to our new bosses, Cam. I hope you'll have a good explanation by the time I'm ready to accept the call."

I picked up my phone, watching in horror as the mother of all distractions popped up on my Twitter feed. "Oh my God, Cam, what the fuck is this?"

Devin's face turned to stone the moment he saw the first few seconds. That scared me more than when we were in the boardroom with Mr. Richton and Mr. Parker. This was not going to be good.

Keri said what I believe we were all thinking, in an attempt to break the silence. "So, what the hell just happened, and how in the hell are we supposed to spin this when we were supposed to be preparing for the album launch?"

Deion

Chapter Thirty-Five: Caught Up

This was not good...not good at all. Even in these days and times of social media posts going viral in every type of way imaginable, this was bordering on the biblical of bad. Once the bosses got wind of this, there was no telling how this was going to go.

Sex tapes and such were kind of a thing of the past, but not when you didn't have a reputation established within the entertainment industry yet. This was not exactly the type of publicity that the group needed to garner. The last thing any of them needed was to have to answer questions about something that got loose on the Internet that was in direct contrast to the type of image they wanted to project.

The folks in the RPK offices in L.A. weren't fazed by it at all, despite what I thought would be the opposite reaction. If anything, they were used to this type of publicity, and they knew the way they wanted to spin it, too. They wanted to get Camryn out there ahead of the rumor mill to spin herself as a victim, find a way to get the public to buy into it since she was a no-name and DJ Infinity was the one garnering all the headlines because of his status. I didn't care how much it was part of the hype machine, the group didn't deserve this, and I was ready to wring Quinn's neck for it.

Laura rushed the girls into another area, the bodyguards taking a screaming Camryn as she kicked and tried to break free from them to get at Quinn. Once they were secured outside on the patio so she could help them collect themselves, I grabbed Quinn by his shirt and slammed him against the wall. "What in the bloody hell were you thinking, bruh?"

"D, it's not what you think." Quinn tried to explain himself, but I was already seeing red at that point. He looked down at the grip I had on his shirt, and he put his hands up in a silent plea for me to give him some space. When he realized that wasn't going to happen, he shook his head. "Look, man, the tape got loose, alright? But I didn't mean to have it leak out there. The whole situation just got out of control."

"Okay, you're starting to sound really stupid right now, Q." I backed off him, folding my arms across my chest as I leaned against an adjacent wall to hear him out. "Explain it to me like I'm a six-year-old, please. This isn't looking good for you right now."

Once he had a moment to collect his thoughts, he began to come up with some semblance of an explanation. "I was at a club in Hollywood doing my thing, I figured I could put in some work to get my name back out here in Cali. Anyway, one of my dudes said that the streets was talking, saying that I was playing for the other team and shit."

I softened my stance a little bit, but after hearing the girls shouting amongst themselves and Laura trying to be the voice of reason within the storm the three of them created, that stance didn't last for long. "So, where's the part where you fucked up come in?"

"D, I'm saying, I couldn't have the streets talk like that, so I let dude see the tape of me and Cam." Quinn started motioning with his hands, his tell-tale sign that he wasn't telling the whole truth, but he was trying to come up with as much of it as possible. "I took my eyes off him for a few minutes because this cutie was trying to get my attention, and when I got back to him, he gave my phone back to me. I didn't know he'd dropped the vid to one of his contacts at *TMZ* until about an hour before we all started moving around."

"*TMZ*, bruh?" I couldn't figure out if I wanted to hit him or continue yelling at him like he was some rookie that didn't know how the celebrity game was played. "You're one of the hottest deejays in the country, how the hell are you gonna fall victim to some bullshit hearsay? You haven't been hearing that shit at home in the A, right?"

Quinn hesitated like he didn't want to answer the question.

I shook my head, not accepting the silence. "I need an answer out of you, Quinn. Those girls' careers are in the balance over something they had no control over."

Quinn took a breath and exhaled. "Look, D-Lo, I'm not smooth with the ladies like you are, alright? Regardless of the name I've made, I ain't got it like you, you feel me? So, the rumors started kicking out there that I wasn't into the females like that, that I was at best a switch-hitter. I couldn't get rid of those rumors, no matter what I tried, and it was screwing with my gigs. This was my way to get the monkey off my back, dawg."

"By throwing your girl under the bus, right?"

"Cam and I ain't as deep as you and Lexi…and *Natalia*."

I heard the emphasis on Natalia's name, and it rubbed me the wrong way. "You got something you wanna get off your chest? I suggest you tuck in your skirt and man the fuck up and get it off so we can squash whatever the fuck has you tripping right now."

Quinn saw the heat on me and backed down. That wasn't what I wanted him to do, and it unnerved me. "You know what, D, it ain't even that serious right now. What's done is done, and I'll handle Camryn once we've had a chance to talk. She was with the whole thing, bruh, for real. What you saw was an Academy Award-winning performance just now."

My phone started ringing again. Taking a look at the number, I blew out air as it was yet another number that I didn't recognize. "Lowery…no, I have no comment at this time…I don't care what your sources have told you, I have no comment."

"Yo, D, you ain't gotta take all this on, bruh. I told you, I'll handle it."

"You're doing a damn good job of 'handling it' as it is, dawg." My phone wouldn't stop ringing, so I turned the sound off, I didn't want to feel it vibrating I was so irritated. "The lawyers at RPK want to try and spin this as Cam being the victim in all this, get some sympathy, and at this point, it's going to be her word against yours, and considering she's the newcomer, this thing could be touch and go for a minute. Are you prepared for the backlash when it comes?"

Quinn's demeanor changed. His shoulders slumped, and

for the first time since everything blew up, he looked pissed. He stared me down, moving into my personal space like a man possessed. "Man, you do what you have to do, it's not like you're gonna have my back anyway. A lot of good it did Ant trying to trust you to have his back. I guess in the end, we lose out."

I froze. *No, this motherfucker didn't put the blame on me?*

Quinn put his hands up in surrender, regretting what he'd said in the moment. "D, that was a low blow, I know, but that's not what I meant—"

"I think you need to talk to your lawyer, this is my advice as a *friend*, Q." The anger building inside of me was enough to fuel a few bombs at the present moment. "Once RPK finds out the reality of the situation, they'll be coming for you."

"Yeah, and when the truth comes out about it, not only will Camryn still be with me, but you'll be owing me an apology." Quinn turned and headed for the door. "That girl is not who you think she is, bruh. She's willing to do whatever it takes to get to the big time, regardless of who she hurts. Remember that when it all goes down."

Alexia

Chapter Thirty-Six: Don't Wanna Be a Player No More

I wasn't sure which one of us wanted to rip her a new one, me or Keri. All I could think about was having to give the advance back due to breach of contract or something crazy like that. The ink hadn't dried more than a few proverbial minutes and I was already hoping I wouldn't have to go back to my old life.

Camryn looked more like the cat who swallowed the canary. "Did you see the look on his face? He actually thought I was pissed about it!"

Laura was beside herself. "Camryn, what in the world were you thinking with that stunt you pulled back there? This is not the kind of publicity that the group needs right now."

Camryn was unfazed by the question. "I *was* thinking about the group, and this is the type of publicity that we can use. Do you realize that if we spin this right, we could be superstars by the end of the month? Come on, Laura, you know I'm right. How else do you think I was able to put this in the position we're in? I did what was necessary."

Keri looked like she was ready to slice and dice. "It would have been nice if you let the rest of us know you'd planned on turning us all into video vixens against our will so we could have beaten you within an inch of your life."

I was still in shock over the unmitigated gall she had for doing this. "I know Laura said we needed to sex things up a little bit during our performances, but this ain't Cardi B, either. How are they supposed to take us seriously as artists if they can't get past your legs being splayed all over the goddamned studio with your boyfriend?"

Camryn's eyes widened when she realized her little publicity stunt was backfiring before her eyes. "Come on, ladies, I mean, you're really upset about this?"

"If you have to ask that question, Cam, it's obvious that you didn't get to know us as deeply as you think you did." Keri's eyes conveyed the gravity of the situation. "Do we want to have a little sex appeal? Absolutely. But now every radio station we go into to do interviews, what do you think the first question will be about, huh? It won't be about the first single on the album, that's for damned sure."

Camryn was insistent on sticking to the plan. "This will work out, you have to trust me on this. Besides, this will all blow over in the next week anyway. You know how the news cycles are, even in entertainment circles. Cardi B was on reality television after stripping at the club, and now she's the hottest thing in HipHop right now. She's engaged to Offset with a baby on the way, and everybody is trying to see about them right now. This won't even register worth a blip on the radar screen, come on?"

"Yeah, but we're still talking about Kim Kardashian, and it's been forever since that happened, you twit," I snapped.

Did she really think this thing through or was she really as stupid as she was looking right now? "Hell, she's doing everything she can to stay relevant, popping off all kinds of racy pics on the 'gram, but they always find a way to bring up how she got started in the business, and she's a freaking multi-millionaire. Is that what you want, for your other pair of lips to do the singing for you?"

Camryn stopped for a moment, letting those last words sink in. She began to realize the consequences of her actions. The tears fell, but her cries began to sound off against the proverbial brick wall. "Look, I was trying to put the group on the map, we weren't getting any buzz!"

"Yep, you didn't think this one through at all." Keri's understatement was not lost on the rest of us. "Now you have us all in a sling. I don't even rock like you two do, so it wouldn't have done a thing for me. If anything, it's gonna hurt my prospects within my community."

Laura held her hand up to slow us down. "Ladies, whether we like it or not, we have to roll with the punches. The road to success is not a straight line, and if it was easy, everyone would be doing it. When we get back to Atlanta, we will face this thing as a family."

"Yeah, we won't have a choice now," Keri added. She headed back to the door to head inside. "Besides, we'll catch hell if it got out that she got booted from the group. That's not a good look."

"This will work out, I don't care what y'all are saying right now." Camryn stepped away to take an incoming call. The look on her face when she recognized whoever was on her caller ID was enough to make us pause. She dismissed us like the person on the other side of that call was her whole universe. "If you will excuse me, I need to take this, it's important."

We headed back into the house, finding Devin alone in the living room, a disturbed expression on his face. He was somewhat distracted by the phone call he was on, and from his demeanor, it wasn't a good call to be on at the moment. "Yes, Mr. Richton, I understand. We'll do our best to get on top of this as soon as possible. I'll speak to Camryn about it to see if it was a publicity stunt or not. If it was, I'll handle it, you have my word on that. I have six full hours to get down to it, I won't let up until I find out the real."

It was going to be a long flight back to the A, there was no other way to explain that.

Deion

Chapter Thirty-Seven: 99 Problems

The flight back home to Atlanta was not pleasant, there was no subtle way to express it. I went back and forth with Camryn for the entire six-hour flight, trying to figure out if she was trying to angle for something else entirely, whether the group was her priority now that they'd gotten the deal. I ripped her from every possible angle I could, stopping Laura every time she thought I was being too hard on her. Even Alexia wondered if I was cutting too deep.

"Okay, baby, that's enough. We get that you have to do this, but she's clearly the victim here." Alexia did her best to try to help her groupmate, but I wasn't in the mood to hear it.

"Remember when I said I never wanted to be on your bad side, D? This was exactly what I was talking about," Keri interjected. "Your line of questioning is making it sound like she was a co-conspirator or something, like she was down for the cause."

"Well, considering her boyfriend threw her under the bus

and all but laid the blame and the plan to do this at her feet so they could both help each other, yeah, I'd say this spells out the definition of conspiracy." I realized I was in hostile territory to a degree, but there was a method to my madness. "Camryn, are you sure that you didn't know he was going to drop the tapes?"

"Yes, I'm sure, and I'm insulted that you felt the need to ask." Camryn's attitude shined through as she bristled at the questions I posed. "I know he's your boy and all and we lose out in the end, but I didn't know anything. My group's rep is on the line, and I would never place my desires above the group."

"I ripped his dumb ass a new one for even putting you in this predicament, so I'm going to need you to swerve on that supposed condemnation on the 'bros before hoes' mantra that you think I'm sticking to."

"Then, what's with the third degree, D?" Keri asked. "You've asked her the same questions in three different ways, and it's enough to make me want to choke you out."

"If you think I'm rough, wait until the RPK legal team gets through with you." I rubbed my hands over my face to try to take a breath and lean on my logic of the situation. "RPK has established itself as one of the classiest companies in the music business. That didn't come lightly, and their want and ability to protect that reputation is paramount. If they find anything that they *think* might put us in a scandalous light, they'll find whatever clause necessary to not only terminate the contract, but request remittance of your advances."

The stunned silence for the few seconds after I mentioned the legalities they were facing was enough for me to not say another word about whether I needed to be too hard on Camryn or not. This was business, this wasn't personal, and they had no choice but to respect that by the time we touched down. Although the big men invested a lot of money into them, I'd invested a lot of time and effort to help convince them to get involved.

I'd be damned if I was going to let a poor decision screw up everything that they'd done to get to this point. My career was as much on the line as theirs, and it could screw things up for me trying to get to the next level.

"So, are we clear on the why now?"

Alexia nodded, slipping her head on my shoulder as my cell phone rang for the umpteenth time. "Lowery."

"Mr. Lowery, this is Detective—"

Once we got on the plane, I had to take calls from the police detectives, answering more questions that they had, even though they'd excluded me as a suspect last week. I realized that they were bowing to public pressure thanks to the media campaign Anton's parents waged while I was in L.A. I didn't want to give them any clue that I wouldn't be cooperative, but the interrogation was getting ridiculous.

"I'm going to cut you off right here and now, Detective." I was already agitated, so I wanted this conversation over with. "Here's the summary of the answers I'm about to give to the questions that you and your partner have been asking for the past few days, and I want to be clear that you've heard them clearly. Ready?"

"Mr. Lowery, there is no need to be belligerent—"

"I'm not interested in the back and forth with you, sir. Here's the rundown: Yes, I knocked on the door before I entered. Yes, I saw the house get tossed and ransacked and I headed back to my car to get my gun. No, I did not shoot first. I didn't shoot at all. There was no gunshot residue on my hands, I didn't shoot my firearm, nor did I shoot his. No, I wasn't trying to kill him, I was still there when the paramedics and officers arrived. Yes, I had a concealed carry permit, had it for years, never suspended. Did you get all that?"

I could tell that he was frustrated with my attitude about the whole matter, but the fact that I had been cleared of even pulling the trigger should have been enough to call off the hounds. I was waiting for him to start in on me with the madness with TramaDryl and the incident at Mansion Elan, too.

"And while I have you on the phone, no, I did not throw the first punch at TramaDryl. No, I have never studied any martial arts that might have given me any advantage over him, he just got his ass whooped. I was protecting my girlfriend, who has stated for the record that she needs to get with you to file a temporary restraining order until a court date could be scheduled."

"Mr. Lowery, this isn't going to paint you in a good light if you continue to be glib about this whole thing. We are only trying to get to the truth of the matter in both cases against you."

"And I'm almost to the point to where I want you to go ahead and arrest me when I touch down," I responded. "Once you do, I can go on my own public campaign with regard to harassment charges I'll be filing. Which way do you want this to roll?"

"Have a safe flight, Mr. Lowery. We will be in touch soon."

By the time I was finished with the conversation with the detective and the mess with Camryn and the group, I'd come to two forgone conclusions: first, I was better off in film. Not that film was any better or worse, but it was more my speed. Second, I was not looking forward to going to Anton's funeral.

Deion

"I don't care what the police said, you killed my son!"

I didn't have time to even view the casket before Anton's mother, Mrs. Peyton, began her verbal assault. I had gotten out of the truck, with Alexia at my side, trying to keep some form of an emotional balance since I didn't want to make a scene.

I was surprised that she didn't slap me first. "Mrs. Peyton, I didn't kill Ant, the medical examiner—"

"My boy never used drugs until he ran into thugs like you!" She spat as I watched Anton's casket lowering to the ground. "In my mind, you're responsible for him being in that damn casket! It should be you down there, not him!"

It was all I could do to keep my emotions in check. Even though the last few moments were rough between us, Anton was still my boy, cradle to the grave. I didn't expect the grave to come before we hit thirty. Watching her make a spectacle of things was too much to deal with, and I needed to get things under control before something else happened.

Mrs. Peyton wasn't done with me, that was obvious. Before I could adjust, she let me have it. "I regret the day you came into his life! You took everything away from him! You took his jobs, you took his spot on the team—" she took one look at Alexia, she really lost it. "—and you even took his girlfriends!"

Wait a minute, I did what? That was the straw that broke the camel's back. I was ready to explode, the only thing keeping me from doing it was feeling Alexia squeeze my hand to calm me. "Ant was *never* as perfect as you thought he was. You kept your eyes blind to what was going on, ma'am. He screwed his own life up, and I refuse to stand here and take abuse for your son's mistakes."

Mr. Peyton walked in on the conversation as I was done talking and caught what I said to his wife. "Son, you know better than to talk to your elders with that tone. I would suggest that you apologize right now."

"No, sir, I won't apologize for taking abuse and not standing for it." I continued to try to bite my tongue. "I'm not in the mood for your madness right now, especially when you walked in on the tail end of this conversation and jumped to the wrong conclusion…as…usual."

"D, come on, you'll have another time to pay your respects, okay?" Alexia grabbed my arm, giving a cold stare back in Mrs. Peyton's direction.

"Not before I say my peace first." I returned the glare that Mr. Peyton gave me, daring him to say another word before I really went off. "With all due respect, sir, your wife sees only what she wants to see, and in hindsight, I should have realized that by now. I'm sorry for your loss, and I sincerely mean that, but I am not to blame for his death."

As we walked away, Mrs. Peyton yelled out, "You're gonna get what's coming to you, Devin Lowery! I promise you that, as God as my witness!"

Part of me wanted to read her the riot act for trying to vex me. The other part knew that it wouldn't do anything but give more fodder to an already crazy day. The cameras were in my face as the reporters tried to get a statement while I was with Alexia almost provoked me into a "Kanye moment." Alexia did her best to ignore the cameras, too, but they were relentless in their pursuit.

Quinn walked up with Camryn, noticing the dejected look on my face. "What the hell happened? You look like someone tried to rip your heart out."

Alexia answered for me, knowing I didn't want to talk at that moment. "Ant's mother did a number on him, blaming him for his death. Having to deal with these camera crews hasn't been easy, either."

"Speaking of the camera crews, it looks like someone else has their attention." Quinn pointed to the familiar maroon Corvette rolling into the parking lot. The unmistakable roar grabbed everyone's attention, including the camera crews.

Natalia got out of her car, taking the attention in stride. She posed for the cameras in as pensive a mood as possible, mouthing something about being here for her boyfriend and respecting the privacy of the family in such a difficult time.

She noticed something was wrong the moment she saw me. "What happened? Did she try to lay the blame at your feet?"

I nodded as she caressed my face, trying to get me to look in her direction. "Everyone knows that it wasn't your fault, that's all that matters. She never could handle the fact that

Ant was always trying to compete with you over any and everything."

"I wish I could share your faith in me, Talia." I told her. "You remember how I was in high school. I was ruthless, even when it came to the crew. Player's code, remember? Take no prisoners. Every man for himself."

"But you are not a thug, baby." I heard Alexia say. "I don't deal with thugs anymore, even the wannabes."

"She called him a thug?" Natalia raised an eyebrow. "Now I've really heard everything. Your parents live in the Mount Paran area, what the hell is she talking about?"

"Listen to me, and Natalia can back me up on this," Alexia stood in front of me, her perfume taking control of my senses. "We would not be in your life right now if you were anything less than what you are right now. You are not the man that she tried to paint you as."

Natalia chimed in, "She's right, baby. I love you to death, but if you were anything like what Ant had become, I would have dropped you after that incident with Samantha."

"I hear what you're saying, both of you." I tried to shake off the words that I worried would haunt me for a long time to come. "Right now, I want to take my favorite ladies to dinner, if that's okay with the two of you?"

Natalia looked at Alexia and smirked. "Be careful what you ask for, D, you just might get your wish."

We were about to head back to the car, when I heard a voice that shook me to my core. "Long time, no see, Devin."

I guess it was going to be one of those days. What's the old adage? *Into everyone's life, a little rain must fall.*

Seeing Jenna Whitmore standing in front of me was a little more than rain. More like a hurricane would be more appropriate. I felt like I was in the twilight zone. I tried hard to figure out why she was there in the first place. She and Anton were not close...in fact, I could've sworn she hated him.

I had to blink twice to believe she was there. "Jenna, what are you doing here?"

"Yeah, I would love to know the reason for this myself," Natalia chimed in, irritated over the sight of my ex-girlfriend. "What, we're resorting to opportunistic swoop-ins now? You like the glare of the cameras now?"

"Same old Natalia, forever protective of your pseudo-boyfriend. No wonder we never got along," Jenna snapped. She winced for a second before patting her stomach and resuming her aggressive stance. "I guess I should have known better than to think you would be the slightest bit happy to see me, but that might have had a lot to do with the fact that you probably were part reason we didn't last anyway."

"Yeah, I need you gone from here right now," Natalia replied. She narrowed her eyes, looking like she was about to go through me to get to her. "If you weren't worried about upgrading to what you thought was something better, you wouldn't have been putting all the blame on a figment of your imagination."

"I didn't come for you, I need to speak to my ex alone," Jenna explained, trying to grab my arm to pull me away from the group.

I ripped my arm away from her grasp, wondering where she thought she had the right to even put her hands on me to begin with. "Whatever you need to say, you can say it with them present. I have nothing to hide from them, just like I had nothing to hide from you. You're the one who decided I wasn't good enough for you."

"Have it your way, love." Jenna shrugged like she didn't have much to lose by speaking what was on her mind. The next words might as well have felt like a nuclear bomb was dropped in the middle of my life. "I just found out from my doctor that I've tested positive for herpes simplex virus, type two. Since I wasn't with anyone else at the time I tested positive, I think you were the one who transmitted it to me. You'll be hearing from my attorney in the morning."

Alexia

Chapter Thirty-Nine: Deuces

"That's not possible. I don't know what type of crazy you're on right now, but I need you to come to your senses, for real."

I watched Devin as his face contorted in ways I didn't know were possible. He shook his head so hard I wondered if he was trying to spin the information we'd all heard from his psyche.

The dead-serious expression on Jenna's face gave a whole other vibe I wasn't in the mood to acknowledge. I didn't care about anything else in that moment, except for the answer to one burning question in my mind. Until she answered it, anything that came out of her mouth was immaterial.

Jenna noticed the scowl on my face and decided she needed to see about it. "I wonder what's in that head of yours? Not that I really care all that much, unless I need to make sure you're going to be helping him with the settlement I'm going to win from him for putting me in this situation."

I wanted to choke her within an inch of her life. How the

hell was this trifling ass woman gonna stand here and drop something like this on my man's lap out of the fucking blue? "You won't be getting a dime out of him or me, not until we get some legitimacy out of the way first."

Devin was as cold as ice. His body language was as rigid as I'd ever seen it. "I'm calling bullshit, Jenna. How do you expect me to even believe what you're saying right now?"

I stared at her, taking in the physical manifestation of the woman that Devin had once loved, and I couldn't say I was impressed. He upgraded when he got with me, even more so when Natalia was added to the mix. She was right, he could have done better than her, considering all of the women that I've seen him photograph and film.

"You can call bullshit all you want, D." Jenna's ice-cold stare in my direction seemed like a direct challenge, and I was more than happy to oblige her. All she had to do was say the word and I would give her every bit of business she wanted. "I have the results in my hand from the past six months to confirm my status. One is from a month before we broke up, the other from three months ago. My suggestion is to get tested. I'd hate for your new woman to suffer from your bullshit."

"He doesn't have to, Jenna." Natalia interjected. "Now you're coming back for what, sympathy? A payout? You got caught out there and now you want him to pick up the pieces? Do you think this is supposed to bond you because you think he's HSV-2-positive?"

Jenna gritted her teeth, pursing her lips when she looked in Natalia's direction. She turned her attention back to Devin in an attempt to ignore us. "Do you want to see the results for yourself?"

"I'd rather get that from your doctor, if you don't mind?" Devin shot back. I felt the heat on his skin, and that temper was about to flare. "I prefer to have legitimate results for myself. I can't put anything above your ability to not want to see me happy."

"I told you this nigga wasn't worth a shit, all sloppy about his business," Camryn inserted, which had everyone looking in her direction. We were so engulfed in the matter at hand that we didn't realize that she was still there. "How many other tricks do you have in the mix, huh? I'm not about to let you get my girl caught up."

"I think it's time for you to leave, Camryn. You have no clue what you're talking about." Devin cut his look in her direction, turning his attention to Quinn. He was in full Alpha male mode, and it was only a matter of time before the collateral damage would spread from his wrath. "Get your woman under control, Q or I'll do it for you."

Jenna started laughing after hearing that. "Still taking orders from D, Quinn? You're the one with the juice in this city, and you got your boy still handling things for you? I thought you would have stepped out on your own by now."

Quinn gave her a look that almost shut Jenna down. She started to say something to him again, but her eyes shifted away from him seconds later. I didn't want to speculate over why, but I tucked it away for further questions for Devin once we got away from this madness.

"D, I think I'm going to take your advice this time around. We'll talk later." Quinn's surprising statement threw everyone off as he pulled Camryn by the hand without further comment. The look on Camryn's face let me know she was in for the ass-chewing of her life. I didn't know what she was thinking by pulling that stunt, it wasn't her business. I realized she was trying to protect me, but this was the wrong time and the wrong place.

"I don't know what the hell you hoped to accomplish, Jenna, but I expect to hear from your doctor in the next twenty-four hours. If I don't, you'll be hearing from my attorney for a hearing so we can clear this up."

"Well, since you want to roll like that, Devin, but I'd hoped we could handle this privately."

You can't be serious. You show up at a funeral to track me down to tell me this in person, but you want to play like you want to be civil and private? What did you hope to gain with all of this?"

"I was hoping to be the family that we wanted to be, D." Jenna's stance softened, which pissed me off even more. She honestly thought she could spin this to where she could have him back? "I know you still love me, baby, and I still love you. I was scared to tell you at first, but if we're both positive, then this could be the bonding moment we needed. We can adopt instead of having kids, whatever you want."

"I didn't want kids when we were together, but I never said I didn't want kids at all." Devin was getting more agitated by the minute. "You're sounding delusional about how things ended between us."

"Please, I need you to understand…someone else tried to convince me that you weren't the one for me, but I know now that I was wrong."

"She's an opportunist, she always had been. She's trying to play your heart strings again, baby." Natalia had this look like she was two more comments shy of turning this whole situation into newsworthy fodder. "She waited until now, at

Anton's funeral, to pull some shit like this?"

"Baby, let's just go, okay?" I tried to pull him out of his aggression toward Jenna, even though I wanted to run through her myself. "We'll figure this out together."

"Together? Wait a minute…you're his new woman? And why is Natalia still defending you like she's the woman in your life, too?" Jenna raised her eyebrow as she looked at me, trying to put her own puzzle pieces together. Once the light bulb went off in her head, she scoffed, "You have got to be kidding me, D. Are you serious? You've upgraded to a harem, now?"

"It's in your best interest to leave my women out of this," Devin threatened. His stare was as venomous as hers tried to be earlier. "I'm leaving now, but you will not be able to lie your way out of this one. I promise you that."

"I'm…there's no way…I get tested regularly, my doctor would have told me something if there were any irregularities." Devin put his head in his hands, trying to make sense of what happened at the church earlier. "She knew I didn't want kids yet. Hell, I wasn't sure I wanted to marry her because I suspected she was cheating on me."

"D, what was she talking about earlier? And for that matter, why did she shut down when Quinn checked her?" I asked, trying to get him to focus. "Why would she even respond to him like that?"

Natalia scratched her head, trying to recall that moment. "She had no reason to react to him like that unless there was something going on with them. Could it be possible that Q might be caught up in this, too?"

"I don't want to even think about it right now. My head is still swirling that she might have gotten me infected," Devin replied. "To think that I might have you both at risk is more than I can bear right now."

"Baby, listen, you said it yourself. You get tested regularly, there's no way she could have transmitted anything to you unless you backslid and saw her behind our backs." Natalia turned his head to meet her gaze. "I refuse to believe that. Even when you were with Jenna, you never once cheated on her. That's not the man I know and the man we're in love with."

His cell phone sang that a message came through. He picked it up and his expression changed. "Jenna's doctor left her number. She wants me to call her as soon as possible."

"You're not going over there by yourself, do you understand me?" I tried to be as clear as I could with my language. "We're with you, no matter what."

"She's got a point, baby." Natalia held his hand as she spoke. "We are with you, we always have been."

As I watched him get up to speak on the phone to the doctor to set up the meeting to get to the bottom of things, I texted Camryn to let her know we weren't finished and we needed to get things straight, once and for all.

Deion

Chapter Forty: What You Know About That?

I wanted to scream. I thought it was safe to exhale for a few minutes, and now I gotta deal with this godforsaken mess. In light of what happened to Usher and the women who had accused him of the same thing, I had to play this by the book. The difference between his current situation and mine was that I wasn't community property. With all his money and stature, for him to sink this low was disappointing.

This was not what I had in mind after the amazing time that we had in California. Coming down to earth came with a landing that should have broken my spirit, to be real, but I wasn't weak like that. I knew my status. It was going to take a helluva lot more than what Jenna tried to throw at me to drop me to my knees. Besides, I had my resources, and I damn sure knew how to use them.

First thing I did was hit up one of my connects at my doctor's office to pull my testing records from as far back as high school to prove that I got tested on the regular. He had me taken care of within hours, with the promise that I take care of his fiancée for their upcoming wedding. She wanted to do something sexy for him as a personal wedding gift between them. For this, I had no problems doing that for free.

The next thing I did was get with RPK Legal and put them on retainer. I had a feeling I would need them and then some. The other thing was to have someone to help with the upcoming media swirl over this latest revelation. I was convinced that Jenna would do her best to put the spotlight the best way she could.

My cell phone rang, breaking my thought process as I left my doctor's office. I cursed when I saw Jenna's smiling face pop up on my cell screen. I had to remind myself to purge my phone or at least put her number on auto reject or something. I answered the phone, intent on making this sound as business-like as possible. "Yes?"

"D-Lo, I know I'm the last person you want to hear from—"

"Talk woman, what do you want? And you don't get to call me that, period. Those are reserved for friends and business contacts, and you're neither of those." I didn't know what was worse, answering the phone or not answering it and having to hear the voicemail message. At this point, being in on this conversation was winning out, big time.

"I saw the look in your eyes. Even through all that hurt I still saw the love you have for me." Jenna kept up the onslaught, and it was killing me. She couldn't be serious about what she was saying to me. "I know you love me, D. I know you're trying to replace me, but you don't have to anymore."

"Jenna, I don't love you anymore," I declared. I wanted to hear myself say it out loud to see if I could say it. "I can't love you anymore, not after what you did to me. We can't go back, no matter how badly you think we can. You just accused me of giving you herpes."

There was a brief second or two of dead space over the connection, and I wasn't sure what to expect. I prepared for one of Jenna's patented diamond-cutting rebuttals. If I'd learned anything about her, it was that she was a creature of habit.

Some things never changed. "Fine, since you don't want to do this the easy way, I guess I can tell you that you should be served with papers to appear in court within the next few days, you sonofabitch."

Who was she trying to bluff? I wasn't about to sit there and take her nonsense any more than I had to, and I had the trump card to prove it. "I've actually beaten you to it, love. You should be served before the end of business today. But I do want to thank you, you've made things easier for me. I won't have to hear from you until we get to court."

"You're gonna be sorry, Devin Lowery!" she screamed over the phone. "By the time my lawyer is done with you, you're gonna wish you'd tried to keep me instead of the bitches that you're with now! Once those test results become public, you'll be lucky to get anybody!"

Sooner or later, she was bound to bring up my relationship with Natalia and Alexia. She was predictable and her jealous streak was still as strong as ever. One look at Alexia was enough to send her through the roof. Realizing that Natalia was still in the picture even after all this time was too much for her to take.

"I hope your lawyer is good, love, because she's going to need to perform a miracle or two once it's all said and done."

I tried to put as much bravado in my voice as I could before I disconnected the call, but the problem with taking that stance was the uncertainty that was hidden behind it. If I was wrong, it would change everything.

I needed some air, and I wanted to get some work done to take my mind off. So, I headed to the RPK building, thinking that maybe a couple of hours work might clear my head. I had to get with the producers for the video concepts for the group's first songs anyway, so I could bury my troubles and be productive at the same time.

A couple of hours turned into two in the morning, trying to finish *Envyye*'s marketing project. There were some ideas that I wanted to toy around with for the Internet buzz, and I was lucky to find a few video concepts to run by the producers after all.

I put the package together and emailed it over to them with specific instructions to talk in the morning to figure out the particulars before we presented them to the girls. Having the ability to work in the building after hours was a perk that I loved the most. The building was quiet and I could get some work done in peace and solitude. I did my best work that way.

I sent a text to both of my girls, letting them know that I would be in the studio, in case one of them—or both of them—wanted to stop by to help me "relax" a little more. Yeah, I was going to enjoy being spoiled by two women that were into each other as much as they were into me. I could get used to this.

I got the text back from Natalia about twenty minutes later, telling me that she might stop by after hanging out at the club, and Alexia texted that she was still in the studio with the group finishing up another track, but she would meet me at home. I was good with both of those plans. I needed to release a lot of tension, in as many ways as possible.

As I studied the images in front of me, my mind started to roam a little bit, into territory that I didn't want to delve into, but I didn't care. In my mind, I looked forward to a summer vacation with my girls, probably in some tropical location, preferably at a nude only beach or something like that. I wanted as little clothing as possible to be worn, day or night, and just indulge in the decadence and sensuality that they would help create.

The thoughts were so exquisite, so intoxicating that I struggled with my focus on what I needed to do. I figured that a power nap might do the trick so I could get back into the mix and head home to enjoy the first one to get to me before going to sleep. I didn't have to be anywhere the next day, so I could sleep in and be lazy for a change.

My cell phone chimed as I put my head down on the desk in front of the computer. I didn't care who it was at that point, I would get back to them after I had gotten my twenty-minute nap in.

Alexia

Chapter Forty-One: The Girl is so Dangerous

I managed to get out of the studio early, but I wasn't ready to head home yet. I was too wired to sit and wait for Devin to get home, so I called Natalia to find out where she was. It was Thursday night, a prime night for the club scene, and I wanted to strut my stuff as a new and hot upcoming artist, show off a little bit, and enjoy the attention. It might be something I need to take the edge off before I took Natalia home and made sure we wore each other out while wearing him out.

"Hey, Talia."

"Hey, baby. Where are you?" Hearing her voice was music to my ears, adding heat to a cold evening.

"Coming out of the studio. We got done early, where are you?" I had a clue she might be in Buckhead, but I wanted to make sure before I got in my car. I slid into the driver's seat, listening to the roar of the first purchase with my signing bonus, a Lamborghini Aventador coupe, and smiling as the rumble of the engine vibrated against my body, making me tingle.

"I'm at the Sanctuary enjoying the music and the energy of the place. Are you coming?" Natalia asked. "On second thought, I want you here, now. These butches are really acting a fool trying to holla, and I'd rather you be here with me to keep the wolves at bay. I'll make it worth the trip, I promise."

She didn't have to say another word. "I'm there."

"Good. Tell L.J. that you're with me when you get to the valet so he can take care of your new ride."

"Gotcha, baby. I'll see you in fifteen minutes."

"What are you doing here? I thought you would be in the studio for another hour."

I was curious as to why Tina was in my personal space asking about my whereabouts. I found it strange that she wanted to even be in my personal space, considering the last time we were around each other, she wanted to fight me over Devin.

I regarded her demeanor, noticing she was a bit fidgety, trying to look like she wasn't nervous about something, but looking like she was coming unglued at the first possible moment. I shook my head, figuring I needed to make nice. After all, she was the boss's daughter. "We got done with the session a little early tonight, things have been rolling pretty well as of lately, and we should be ready for the album release as scheduled."

"Cool, I'm looking forward to the listening party soon." Tina looked over my shoulder before her eyes connected with mine again. "I hate to cut the convo short, but I have to head out and take care of an important appointment that just popped up. Talk to you soon?"

"Yeah, no problem." I watched her rush out the door, wondering what in the world that was about. As I got to the VIP area and approached the table where a few of Natalia's actress and model friends were, and I began to realize why Tina might have been so harried.

"I can't find my phone. I left it right here." Natalia moved like finding the phone was a life-and-death mission, barely noticing that I was there. Once she noticed me, she rushed over to hug me, trying to stop shaking. "Hi, baby, I'm glad you're here. I'm trying to keep from freaking out. My phone is missing."

"Here it is." Trisha, one of the models in Natalia's company, retrieved the phone out from between the cushions on the sofa. "I told you we would find it, girl."

"Thanks, Trish, but I'm still confused over how it even got over there in the first place." Natalia picked the phone from Trish's grasp, scrolling through the phone for a minute to check it out. Everything seemed in order for a moment, but her eyes widened when she got to her text messages. "Tina, I'm gonna whoop your ass!"

"What happened?" I tried to understand her anger, but I was late to the party, so I had to ask for my own benefit. "What does Tina have to do with this?"

"She was here in the VIP earlier," Natalia explained. "I was on my phone, taking a selfie to send to you and D, when she showed up. I needed to go to the restroom, so I dropped my phone in my purse and headed there for a few moments. I thought I locked my phone, but I guess I didn't."

One of the other girls in the group, Lori, snapped her

fingers like she remembered a detail that they might have missed. "Talia, I didn't pay it any mind at the time, but it makes sense now. Tina had your phone, but she flipped out when I asked her what she was doing with it. She rushed out before you got back to the area."

"I ran into her before she headed out, too," I added. "She said something about an important meeting she had to make. At almost midnight, I assumed she was trying to keep from saying it was a last-minute booty call, the way she acted."

"Yeah, she had a last-minute booty call all right." Natalia showed me the text that was sent a few minutes ago, and I gasped at the message. *I'm on my way to see you now, baby. I'm horny and I need you.*

"What the hell?"

"Tina's obsessed, and I need to finish this once and for all."

"Let's go. I need to handle her, too. She can't get away with this."

Natalia kissed me in the middle of her circle of acquaintances and friends. It was reassuring, almost protective, with a hint of sensuality that left me breathless. "I can't risk that. If she sees you with me digging into her, it could jeopardize your contract. Tina can't touch me, I have too much dirt on her as it is because she's been so freaking sloppy all these years. I'll handle it. Trust me, baby, okay?"

I was reeling from the kiss, my face still flushed from blushing at the scene we made. The women around us seemed unfazed by the public display, and the majority of them actually smiled from watching us. I caressed Natalia's face, nodded, and moved in for a final quick kiss before sending her off. "Okay, baby, take care of it. I'll be at D's, waiting on you both to get home."

"Now I know I need to get this done. We'll see you in a few, baby. Don't fall asleep, this won't take long."

Deion

Chapter Forty-Two: The Boy is Mine

Being kissed while half asleep was one of the sexiest things in the world to me. Natalia was aware that I loved that, and she did it often when we were together and I'd fallen asleep after one of our more rigorous interludes. Her text said she would be by any minute now, but exhaustion won out, so I thought I would take a quick nap and let her "wake" me up.

I let myself go, enjoying the kiss, trying to get a feel for Natalia's lips, opening my mouth to feel her tongue slide inside my mouth. The scent of her perfume took me deeper inside my fantasy, the faint hint of berries from the drinks she probably took from strangers at the bar coated her lips.

Damn, you feel good, baby…oh my God, I needed this.

She climbed on top of me and started to grind against my crotch. I was glad that I wore sweatpants for easy access, and even more turned on that my baby wore no underwear under her skirt. She kissed me deeply, pulling my pants down far enough to free my ever-growing length. "I've been waiting for this for so long."

"Mmmm, you just had me earlier this week, baby." I started to wake out of my grogginess, ready to take this late-night rendezvous to the next level. "I missed you, too."

She was about to slide in for the ride of her life when I heard someone yell, piercing the haze and breaking the spell that my baby had on me. There was only one problem. It wasn't my baby that had the spell on me.

"You have three seconds to get off my baby, Tina." Natalia gritted her teeth as she stood in the doorway, watching. "I should have known you were up to something when you swiped my phone when you thought I wasn't around."

I panicked in a desperate attempt to focus on Tina above me, half-naked, with her lipstick smeared and her hair tousled from the brief moment of passion that we'd shared. I tried to slide from under Tina, but I didn't realize how exhausted I was. Even though she was light thanks to her petite frame, under normal circumstances I would have lifted her like it was nothing. In my weakened state, she might as well have felt like a sack of stones. I tried to regain some strength in my arms, but Tina seemed intent on not moving from where she was.

Before Tina could say another word, Natalia snatched her by her hair and threw her across the floor, standing over her like a boxer daring her opponent to get up so she could put the beat down on her.

I scrambled to an upright position, my eyes wild as I found myself in an indefensible compromised position. "Talia, baby, I...it's not what—"

"Don't worry, baby, I got this." Natalia cut me off, directing her attention toward Tina. "Care to explain?"

"You had to ruin it, didn't you?" Tina scoffed, deciding it was best not to budge from her spot under Natalia. "All you had to do was let me have what I wanted, and you could have his trifling ass afterward. You always ruin shit, Natalia. Damn."

SMACK!

The next thing I focused on once my vision cleared was Tina holding her eye and Natalia coming close to hitting her again. Her fist was balled tight and shaking like she had real intentions of hurting her.

She pulled Tina from where she sat on the floor, digging her nails in to Tina's shoulder, causing her to scream out in pain. She forced Tina to look in her eyes to get her point across with all the force of a Mike Tyson punch. "If you don't want your father finding out about you breaking your curfew when your ass was supposed to be on campus at school being a good little girl, you might want to find the quickest way back, do you understand me? If you think I'm bluffing, I have a video you might be interested in seeing. I know for a fact that you aren't a virgin anymore."

Tina's eyes narrowed. "You wouldn't dare."

"Oh yes I would, girlie." Natalia sneered. "And it's enough to ruin your pristine image in your daddy's eyes. Now, get out of here before I decide not to be so charitable."

Tina ran out in tears, leaving me and Natalia alone in the studio. My shocked expression didn't seem to convey the truth of the confusion over what happened only minutes before.

"Relax, baby, and let me explain." She sat in the same spot that Tina had occupied, caressing my face to get me to realize it was her and I wasn't dreaming. "The girls and I

295

were hanging out at the Sanctuary for the set that one of the radio stations usually did, so I could get *Envyye*'s single on the floor and the set could get jumping. I saw Tina and her crew show up, and she called herself trying to holla for a minute after she saw me coming off the dance floor."

"So how did she know I was here?" I asked, trying to get my mind to work.

"The little trick took my cell phone while I was in the restroom." Natalia said, shaking her head at it all. "By the time I realized it was gone, she was already out the door, on her way to see you."

"So, it wasn't you flirting with me before I passed out at the computer?" I deduced, closing my eyes and putting my head down. Damn. "I must have really been out of it to not realize it wasn't you."

"Baby, relax, I'm here, and I got here before something could really go down, okay?" Natalia kissed me to settle me down. "Lexi told me that she would be at your house in about twenty minutes, so, you wanna go so we can take care of our baby, please?"

Deion

Chapter Forty-Three: I Don't F&$# With You...

I sat in the doctor's office with Alexia, waiting for the nurse to call me to give my DNA sample for the STI testing. The past few days had been nerve-racking to say the least. First, there was the mess with Tina that could have gotten me into some serious trouble. Next was the craziness with Camryn and the aftermath over the sex tape leaking and trying to do damage control to try to calm that down, and now, I have to deal with this stupid shit with a false claim of giving my ex herpes.

The lawyer that I was referred to told me that she couldn't represent me, citing a conflict of interest on her end. The truth of the matter was that when she met with me and she saw Natalia and Alexia sitting with me to get the details, she saw the writing on the wall and realized there would be no real "perks" that her girlfriend told her about.

After leaving her office, Natalia made a few calls and we hooked up with Kelli. She was one of the ladies in the legal department at RPK that had been trying Natalia for the longest time, until she found out that Natalia wasn't only into women. All of a sudden, it was all about protecting the brand. I didn't care about the sexual politics of why my baby was somehow tainted in that moment, I was interested in clearing my name.

The conversation between Kelli and Jenna's attorney was contentious, and that was an understatement. She kept the line open and on speakerphone so we could hear the conversation and we could hear her attorney trying to come up with every possible roadblock imaginable when it came to doing the final testing. The thing that kept bothering me was that I'd heard that voice before, but I couldn't place my finger on from where I could have recognized her voice.

They went back and forth for about ten minutes before Kelli made it clear that if the test was not done that she would go to the judge in the morning to file a motion to dismiss the civil suit in its entirety. After a brief silence on the other end, her attorney relented, explaining that the location would be at Jenna's doctor's office, and that we could have witnesses to attest to the validity of the test, to avoid any "impropriety."

So, here we were.

I tried to find ways to occupy my time, and even with Alexia there with me, my anxiety level wouldn't drop much.

"It's just a formality, baby, don't worry, okay?" Alexia tried to calm me, but my fingers wouldn't stop shaking. "After we do this, it will only be a matter of days and we'll know the truth."

Yeah, the truth. I wasn't sure what the truth was any more. In my mind, I trusted my instincts that I had been careful the entire time that we'd been intimate. That I had been careful even before Jenna and I had met.

I was on some Big Sean shit in that moment, wishing I had never dealt with her in the first place. My life was moving at a positive pace, and it was going well—extremely well—and she was not about to derail all of that because it suited her needs.

The nurse made her way to the front area after what felt like an eternity of waiting to call me back to give the blood sample. "Mr. Lowery, I will take your sample now."

I kissed Alexia and patted her hand. "I'll be out in a few. Will you still be here when I get back?"

She looked at her watch, feigning being in a rush. "Unless I have an award show to attend in the next hour or so, I doubt I'll be gone when you are done. I'll be here, baby…always."

It only took a few minutes for the blood sample to be collected, but the nurse became more concerned with the commotion that the receptionist had to handle. After finishing up and rushing to the front, I could understand why she was concerned.

My current girlfriend and my ex-girlfriend were in the midst of a very heated argument. They were face to face and toe to toe, but thankfully there were no punches thrown. Otherwise, we would have been witnessing Armageddon.

I pulled Alexia away from Jenna, listening to her shout obscenities the entire time. "You wish you could still have him, you conniving ass trick!"

"You might need to be worried more about what's gonna happen after we get out of court, bitch!" Jenna shouted back as she was being forcibly held at bay by the receptionist. "I got enough to deal with going through this HSV crap to worry about your insecurities!"

"Ms. Whitmore, please control yourself." The nurse cautioned her as she helped to restrain her. "You're not supposed to be here. You're going to violate the terms of the agreement."

"Yes, Ms. Whitmore, calm your fucking nerves." Alexia seethed through her words, still trying to break free from me. "You didn't need to be here for this anyway, but you had to find whatever excuse to be here to see *my* man, didn't you? Aren't you under a restraining order anyway? You aren't supposed to be here."

"Alright, calm down, baby." I pinned her against the wall to get her to focus. "She's not worth the trouble. She's doing this to get in your head. You're bigger than that."

"Yeah, I'll say she's bigger than me, alright." Jenna smirked as she popped off her insult. "I didn't know you liked them that thick, Devin. Had I known, I would have worked out a little more to put the curves on for you."

"I think you've caused enough trouble simply by being here, Jenna;" I swung to face her, catching her and the other women off-guard. "My baby is right: you are under a restraining order, one that I should call law enforcement to explain that somebody has violated."

Jenna quieted down in seconds, unable to find a snappy retort that wouldn't trigger me further. She dropped her head, and the water works began soon after, causing the nurses to try and console her to keep her from stressing herself out any further.

I took Alexia by the hand and headed out of the office, ignoring the insults that Jenna and the nurses hurled at me. We got to the truck, and it was obvious that she was emotionally worn out from dealing with Jenna. "Baby, I'm sorry about all that, I didn't know she would just pop up like that. I understand if you need some time to relax from all that bullshit."

Alexia laughed at me like she expected me to say something like that to her. "I don't know what weak females you've been dealing with in the past, D, but I'm not about to let some toothpick of a female think that she can run me away from something that I know is a good thing. Besides, I remember a certain man in my life who—damn, I'm getting moist thinking about it—put my ex-boyfriend on his ass when he got up in his feelings. I'd say we're even now."

She kissed my lips, feeling my heart beating against her hand. She grinned after she broke from the kiss, whispering in my ear, "Even though I'm sharing this with someone that I'm falling for, too, I know who this heart beats for, and that's all I need to know. Now, if you make this up to me by giving me a massage when we get home, I'll forgive you anything."

Alexia

Chapter Forty-Four: Get it Together

Riding up to the Parker estate was one of the most nerve-wracking things I'd ever gone through. A lot of Mr. Parker and Mr. Richton's high-powered friends and associates in the music industry would be there, fueled by the hype machine that guaranteed a performance unlike anything they'd seen since TLC. No pressure, right?

It was safe to say we were ready for the spotlight, but it was also safe to say the anxiety levels shot through the roof. We'd worked too hard to not be ready. We'd been together for so long, it felt like we were sisters for real. There was nowhere to go but up, but first, I had some things to take care of.

Even though Natalia and Devin told me about the situation with Tina and how it got handled, I still felt the need to put a scare into the little twit to make sure that she stayed out of grown folk's business. So, I took the video that Natalia had of Tina and threatened her with it. And not simply any threat, but something that could have gone viral. With the new-found two hundred-thousand followers I'd had on Instagram, Twitter and Facebook, it wouldn't have taken long at all.

The look in her eyes was priceless. She had no idea that I would go so far, but the pampered princess thought that good girls always played fair. The message on my keychain said it all: *51% Angel, 49% Bitch.*

The next thing I needed to do was to have a "Come to Jesus" meeting with Camryn. It was obvious that she hadn't learn her lesson the first time around. The wildest part of that was we wouldn't be able to have that issue resolved until we got to the release party. One way or another, something had to give, and I wasn't about to be the one to do the giving. For the good of the group, there was no other choice in the matter.

That left one last person to deal with. Troy.

He really didn't give up, even after the issue at Mansion Elan that night when Devin embarrassed him. Despite the fact that he'd tried to press assault charges that ended up getting dropped, he felt that he still had a chance to win me back. He kept leaving messages, on my cell phone, on every social media platform I was on, it was crazy. So, I did the one thing that I didn't think I would need to do until we started hitting the circuit or on tour: I went to the DeKalb County PD and filed for a restraining order.

I had the saved messages, and the behavior at the club was caught on a cell phone and sent to me by Keri. By the time I was done with the chat with the police detectives, including one that had been following the group since we were doing the underground parties, Troy wouldn't be able to come within fifty feet or be in the same venue as where I was going to be without violating the restraining order.

It wasn't as hard as I thought it would be, but when he threatened to hit me when I walked away from him at the club, there was no other alternative. I wasn't about to become that chick that couldn't make up her mind that she wanted an ex-boyfriend out of her life or not. I wanted Troy gone from my world, without the possibility of return. I was a little worried that the entertainment blogs would get wind of this and try to make this more than what it should be, but my safety was more important. If I was going to be a star, I had to start thinking like a star.

Dealing with Camryn would be something different, and a little harder to handle. We were supposed to be closer than the way things turned out. She'd been standing in my backyard way too long, throwing stones when she'd been living in her own glass house. She needed to be aware that— for the good of the group—it had to come to an end, and ASAP was not soon enough.

I'd been to release parties before, but not like *this*.

Mr. Parker's estate was situated up in Milton, which was a little less than an hour north of Atlanta. And I thought Mr. Richton liked living lavish and large? Mr. Parker was even bigger about his palace. The place was set on I didn't know how many acres, and most of it was flattened out with cabanas and gazebos all over the place. The house itself looked like something out of an architecture magazine, complete with tall bay windows and a balcony over the front door. And that was the outside of the house.

Keri was as awestruck as the rest of us, after she finished

viewing the pictures of the house. "Okay, we need to get the stars out of our eyes and act like this is just another gig." That was kinda hard when he sent for all of us in the stretch Cadillac Escalade limousine to ride up to the place.

On at least three different radio stations—believe me we all checked—the deejays made mention of our album release party happening, even though it would be invitation only. But what we didn't know was that Mr. Parker had released some rare invitations to be given out to people who called into the radio station to be a part of the event. The stations loved the hit single that we put out in advance of the album release and the public kept requesting it on the radio station countdowns.

Despite all the highs that we were going through, and that was all happening before we even got to the party, I still had to get the last of my to-do list taken care of.

While Keri was up front flirting with the female driver, who I had to admit was a cutie, Camryn and I sat down in the back of the limo. I broke the silence between us first. "Talk to me, Cam, you seriously bugged out back in Malibu. Is there something that I should know about? Do you dislike my choices that much that you have to be so damn vocal about it?"

Camryn exhaled and closed her eyes before she shifted her body to face me. "Fine, you want me to say it, I'll say it, Alexia. Springing that situation, or relationship or whatever, on us out of the blue was crazy as hell. I'm still trying to figure out what to make of it all."

"But it's not causing strife in your life, and I'm pretty damn happy in mine. So, why are you stressing so much about it?" I shifted my body to close off the distance between us.

"Because I'm supposed to be the freak of the bunch, not you." The tone in her voice caught me off guard. She couldn't have been any more blatant about what her thoughts were than she was in that moment. "Those nights you spent with Devin and Natalia...I'm the one that's supposed to have those experiences. I'm the bad girl of the group, not you. Why else do you think I let the tape loose on the Internet?"

"So, you mean to tell me that your temper tantrums are coming out because you think I'm stealing your persona or something?" I was in complete shock over that revelation. This was my life, my romantic life, not fodder for the Internet boards. If I was honest with myself, it probably would be once the spotlight hit us. Her revelation that she meant for the sex tape to get out floored me, though. "You proved your status with that damn tape, girl. All we've been talking about before getting to the music has been that damn tape."

"You're not stealing anything, Lexi, I'm a little pissed at myself right now, okay?" Camryn's tears softened me up a little bit. "This thing with Blake, it's not working out, he's too fucking clingy. Once the tape got out, he started acting brand new. Now, he doesn't want 'his woman' doing all the things that them freaks he was fucking with before we got together were doing. It was fine when it was just a fuck buddy thing, but now this dude's talking about getting serious and shit. I didn't ask for all that."

Hearing her talk like this took me back damn near two years, when I was having this same conversation with Keri when I had the switch-a-roo happen to me with Troy's crazy ass. "Cam, I know you didn't, but was that a reason for you to blast my relationship like it was nothing? I'm really trying my best to figure out whether or not I want you to even know anything more about anything going on in my life."

"Lexi, I've been trying to find a good time to say that I was sorry for that outburst, but there'd been so much tension between us, I didn't know if I would ever have a chance to." Camryn admitted. "I promise, I'm happy if you're happy, but I'm not happy with mine right now, and now I understand why you weren't through with what you went through when you left Troy. Can you forgive me?"

"Forgiven and forgotten." Now that I understood the root cause of all the craziness that was going on, it was easier to deal with her.

Her cell phone rang, and my eyes dropped to the screen when I saw Mr. Parker's face pop up. What had my mind blown was seeing "Daddy" ascribed to his number. My eyes shot up to search hers as she rolled the call to voicemail, eyebrows raised the whole time. "Is there something you might need to tell me and Keri? What in the world is Mr. Parker calling you for, and why is he being listed in your phone like that?"

Cam's eyes narrowed and her body stiffened, letting me know a cold shoulder was on the horizon. "If I have to stay out of your business, you have to stay out of mine, Lexi."

"Okay, but it's starting to make sense now." I shook my head in an attempt to erase the puzzle pieces that filled in over her clandestine disappearances while we were in LA recording. "I hope you know what you're doing, our careers could be on the line because of the way you're moving."

Keri watched on while we thought she wasn't looking, and the grin was silly, to say the least. "So, have you two finally buried the hatchet? I'm not gonna lie, you two are wearing me out."

"Yeah, we're good. I just need help trying to figure out how to get rid of some high-profile dead weight." Camryn answered, wiping the last of the tears away. I couldn't tell if they were real or crocodile, but I wasn't about to go into this party with any stress on my shoulders. It was time to put our names on the entertainment map tonight.

"Good, because we're here. We can figure out the other drama between you later." Keri looked out the window to see we'd arrived at the front entrance of the house. "It's show time, ladies. Let's do this."

Deion

Chapter Forty-Five: A Party Ain't A Party…

Being at the Parker estate was, from my personal perspective, a whole different experience. The house and estate were a lot larger than what Mr. Richton preferred, although Mr. Richton's tastes were more of the four-wheeled and two-wheeled variety. Whenever we had release parties, Mr. Parker's spot was ground central, and with the radio and television commercial spots that broadcasted *Envyye's* arrival, it brought all the ballers looking for the top-shelf booty and the top-shelf booty looking for the ballers with the pallet racks of green in the bank.

Quinn didn't seem to notice me standing next to him as he continued to survey the landscape. "Damn, look at all the potential out here. This could get very interesting."

I looked at Quinn like he'd lost his mind. Regardless of the scattered beauty walking around and enjoying themselves in this unseasonably warm Georgia weather, he really had no business trying to act like he was a free agent. "Earth to DJ Infinity, whiskey-tango-foxtrot, dude? Your girlfriend will be here in t-minus ten minutes, could you put your tongue back in your mouth before you get caught up in some serious bullshit?"

"You the wrong man to be coming at me about being faithful, bruh." Quinn tried to cut me, bringing up my current relationship as some way to make his point. "Real talk, I don't know how you pulled that shit off with Natalia and Alexia like that, but I want some of the shit that you drugged them with, and I want your supplier, too."

He'd been snippy for a minute, ever since we got back from LA. He was avoiding my calls, even going so far as to avoid wherever I was going to be, even if he was obligated to appear. Jealousy could be a bitch, but damn. This man was acting like I took his girl from him or something. "You make it sound like I convinced them to be a part of things, bruh. Since you wanna yell real talk, okay. Real talk, I had nothing to do with it. Natalia flew in to L.A. that night, rode up to the beach house and surprised me by being there. Lexi already knew because she set the whole thing up."

"Oh, so you're there by accident now? Ain't that about a bitch?" Quinn's heat toward me amped up. "I'm really starting to understand Ant a little more now, post mortem. You wanna act like you ain't have nothing to do with nothing, like you can rock a dine and dash and not catch no heat from it, huh?"

Low blow…and the irritating part was, he meant what he said this time. I watched his nostrils flare, and I wanted to crack his jaw for stooping to that level. I raised my eyebrow, wondering if he cared that he touched a nerve with his last statement. "Oh, it's like that, now, Q? So, what are you saying? You think you're a sidekick now, is that the company line? You can't catch nothing because they all checking for me on the regular?"

"Look, D, I'm amazed at your streak of luck when it comes to these thots, that's all," Quinn countered, trying to take the edge off of things for a moment. He gave me a curious look, sending a weird chill down my spine. He'd never looked at me with such indifference before. "Except for that mess with Jenna, you've had better luck than most dudes we know, and most have more juice than both of us put together, plus some. Maybe this STD thing might be where your luck finally runs out."

He had to bring Jenna up again. I figured he needed to know what was going on with me on that front, if for anything to at least close the subject and move on to something else. "I might as well tell you. I'm taking her to court to prove that I didn't give her herpes."

"Well, I'll be damned…the great Devin Lowery actually has women troubles like the rest of us mere mortals. But damn, dude, you burning bitches?" Blake laughed. "Break out the Cristal, bartender, this muhfukka's human after all!"

"I'm glad that you think I'm perfect or some shit, Q." I was irritated at his sudden smugness. "Have I evened the playing field for you now? Do you feel better?"

A group of women walked past us, and they looked in our direction, like they were trying to recognize us. Well, not exactly us, as they were looking more at Blake than they were at me. Finally, one of them smiled, looking at Quinn with sex in her eyes. "Are you DJ Infinity?"

The shit-eating grin on his face confirmed her and the group's suspicions. That grin soon faded when a scowl washed over their faces.

"Yeah, we heard about you. Word on the street is that you been burning women."

The other girl snapped her fingers and then pulled out her cell phone. "Yeah, the clubs been spreading word, other deejays been clowning you all night."

"What the fuck?" Blake pulled out his phone to see what the women were talking about. His face lost all its color as B. Scott's website spilled every drop of tea. "This is some bullshit, they're trying to ruin my reputation."

"It can't be ruined if it's true, bruh." The first young lady remarked. We didn't even get a chance to find out her name, and she didn't seem to have an interest in giving it, either. "I feel sorry for your girl. I hope you tell her before someone else does. That's not a good look."

I'll admit she had him shook. If anything, it had me shook, too. I half-thought that they were coming for me with the rumor mill. I tried to be a friend as best I could, offering to run interference. "Cam doesn't deserve to find out this way, bruh. Be a man about it and let her know so she can get tested and take her own precautions."

Quinn gave me a look that could have melted steel. "You got a lot of nerve coming at me with that shit. I'll handle mine, you handle yours. Which reminds me, where are your females, anyway?" Quinn questioned. "I figure I already know where one is, but where is the other one?"

"I was wondering why my ears were burning," Natalia popped up, sliding her arm inside of mine before kissing my lips. "Was another hater talking about us today, baby?"

I laughed at that snarky comment as she continued to stare in Quinn's direction. "Hi, sexy...yeah, someone else has been wondering why I'm so lucky to have such lovely women in my life, and he's wondering if I've been drugging you or something like that. I figured he needed to hear it from the horse's mouth. Have I been slipping you and Lexi mind-altering drugs?"

Natalia rolled her eyes and faced Quinn so that she couldn't be misunderstood. "Okay, that's a good one, Q. Let me see if I can figure out why you can't keep my name out of your mouth. You're pissed off that I never gave you the time of day, and you're thinking that it's because I've been in love with D this whole time, does that about cover it?"

Quinn sat there with his mouth hanging open, which put the brakes on my jokey-joke fest, too. I wanted to see how this was going to play out.

"All those times we danced together at the clubs, I gave you clues that I was interested. I remember a time when you tried to grab my ass while you were making eyes at the other two females that wanted a turn at DJ Infinity." Natalia recalled. I saw the look in Quinn's eyes, and it was easy to see that he remembered it, too. "I kept a mental note of all of that to see if you would, or even if you could, decide that it was time to grow up."

Quinn tried to counter as best he could. "I knew I never had a chance with you, Natalia, so quit flexing like I did. Everyone knows you were always into D-Lo."

"But I still dated other dudes that had the balls to ask me out, so, what happened to yours?" Natalia challenged his logic, which made me take a step back. This was an argument that I was going to make sure I saw my way clear of any collateral damage, even if my name was all up in the mix. "Or were you too busy trying to chase after every pair of legs willing to open wide for you? And before you answer that question, don't think for a minute that I didn't see that last situation you put yourself in before you got into a relationship with Camryn. You were really on some next level shit doing that, all to prove a point, huh?"

Quinn gave up after realizing that arguing with Natalia was pointless. But the look on his face gave me pause—and caused chills down my spine. "You know what, Talia, it really ain't that serious. On God, I knew what time it was, so there was no point in embarrassing myself."

"And that's why I'm with D right now," Natalia remarked, pressing her ass against my crotch. "If you had half the juice that these people in the scene think you did, you'd be in this man's shoes right now, and you wouldn't have to chase women that are trying to upgrade. Even that stunt you pulled with the sex tape isn't gonna get you a better-quality female, bruh. Unless I missed my guess, it didn't calm down the rumors, now, did it? How's that for embarrassing yourself?"

"Okay, baby, that's enough," I kissed Natalia on the cheek as I squeezed her hip. "Eventually he's gotta learn like I did, and he's still my boy, even though he's all up in his feelings about some shit."

"I'm good, playa, you ain't gotta worry about that no more. Y'all got all this shit figured out," Blake snapped before taking his drink and downing it in one gulp. "Now, if you'll excuse me, I have some partying to do before I get all domesticated."

"What am I gonna do with that dude?" I asked.

"Well, we could always neuter him." Alexia sashayed in, making a comment to join in the conversation. She kissed Natalia before getting a kiss on my lips. She caught a glimpse of Quinn, oblivious to Camryn walking toward him and the scene that was unfolding and shook her head. "That is, if Camryn doesn't castrate him first."

I watched as Camryn approached, catching Quinn with his hand on the inside of some random woman's thigh. What came next was a cussing out that anyone within earshot could hear even if they didn't want to hear. Camryn walked away, with Quinn in pursuit, looking like he wanted to explain himself further. So much for the "I'm a badass, I can do what I want and my woman will be okay" attitude.

I headed toward the bar to get something to drink, the situation with Quinn no longer in my circle of concern. As I approached, Mr. Parker intercepted me with a smile on his face. He almost never smiled unless he had some good news to give. "Just the man I wanted to see. D, we need to finish the conversation we started a few weeks ago."

I watched Natalia and Alexia move through the crowd to socialize a bit, so it wasn't a problem to finish things. "What's on your mind, Mr. Parker?"

"Well, kid, for starters, I wanted to make sure, as I promised, to compensate you for the groups that you helped sign over the past year, including your new girlfriend's group." Mr. Parker noted. "After taking a look at the record sales, digital and physical, of the last three groups, Rich and I found a way to get you the proper compensation for helping bring in the millions in revenue that we have enjoyed thus far this year."

He handed me a sealed envelope. From the size it, it wasn't hard to figure out that it was the size of a paycheck. Upon opening the envelope and reading the contents of the statement and the breakdown of the amount of the check, I fought the urge to hyperventilate. By the time I got through all of the particulars and the percentages for the finder's fees and the commission for the album sales that had been certified, the bottom line was a seven-figure payday. This was beyond surreal.

"Mr. Parker…I'm completely speechless…I didn't realize…I mean, is this for real?" I fumbled through my words as I fought back tears. I never expected to see money like this in my life, ever.

"Yes, D, it's for real. Those acts made a killing for us, both here in the States and overseas." Mr. Parker grinned even wider now. "It was only fair that you were taken care of for the money that we've made with those groups, and I'm sure that *Envyye* will be another hit machine also."

"I want to yell right now, but I think I'll wait until the party has calmed down a bit before I start dancing on the ceiling or something." I had already begun figuring out what I was going to do with the money. "Thank you, thank you so much. I'm still trying to find the words right now."

"I know how you must be feeling, youngster, but we take care of our own," he replied, grabbing a glass of wine from the hostess that walked past us. "You've been like a son to me, to Rich, too, and it was a treat for both of us to do this for you."

"I will have to make sure to thank Mr. Richton the first moment that I see him before the night is out." I stated, still trying to figure out my emotions over this unexpected turn of events.

"I don't think you'll have to wait that long, my boy," Mr. Richton walked up after seeing us at the bar. "I take it Parker has given you the check? I believe that it might take care of a few things you've been putting off for a while."

"Okay, now you're just playing with me, gentlemen," I joked. I wanted to play things cool, but I couldn't hide the grin on my face. "What did you mean by that?"

"Well, kid, Natalia confided in us about a year ago that you wanted to own your own film studio, and that you wanted to direct and produce movies one day." Mr. Richton explained. "We knew that your pride wouldn't allow you to accept seed money, so we had to come up with a way that you would feel like you'd earned it. We also talked to the film producers on the other end, and, if you're willing to go through their mentoring program for young filmmakers, they are willing to guide you to eventually direct and produce some videos and films for us."

Damn, they had me dead to rights, and there was no way I could deny what they were saying. I would have balked at the first mention of the word "investment." The part they added about going through the mentoring program to learn the craft of film production and directing threatened to cause me to pass out.

Every dream I thought I would have to defer came rushing like a flood, washing away every obstacle that was in front of me. "Okay, okay, I understand, and I will still say thank you, gentlemen, for helping to make a few dreams come true in the interests of playing tricks on my mind so that I wouldn't give you too much grief."

Mr. Parker and Mr. Richton left me to my private celebration to continue mingling with the guests. I ordered a bottle of Cristal and looked up into the night sky for a moment as I pondered what the past few months had been for me. I had gone through highs and lows, getting through some things in one piece, while other things I wondered if they would haunt me forever. For now, I was going to enjoy the hell out of this high, and I didn't want to come down from for a good week or two at least. I didn't think anything would be able to bring me down, until I turned around and saw Camryn making her way in my direction.

Deion

Chapter Forty-Six: I'm So Sorry…

The wall between us couldn't have been higher. I thought she couldn't have had a better use for me, to be honest. I wasn't in the mood for any type of confrontation to where the bloggers on site would have a field day talking about the next morning.

She wasn't ready to chop my head off. That was a good sign. "D, can we talk, like, for real? We need to clear the air between us."

I didn't know if I should be nervous or outright fearful. There was only one way to find out. "Sure, Camryn, we can talk. What's on your mind?"

"I would rather we spoke in private, D, I don't want any ears trying to leak anything out to the press. I'm sure you can understand that after the mess I made of things with the sex tape scandal."

I could sympathize with where she was coming from with that. The media could be a bear sometimes when they thought there's a story to be had, and tonight was no different with all the big names in the industry socializing at the house. The tape fiasco caused a media storm for a few weeks, until a slew of celebrity breakups and other scandals eclipsed Camryn's faux pas as the hot stories of the moment.

I found a gazebo not far from the house out front, since everyone would be out back doing their thing. We sat down, and Camryn faced me, looking as defenseless and unguarded as I'd ever seen her. It actually made her look damn good.

She forced herself to look at me as she twirled her hair, the universal sign I learned about women whenever they were nervous about something. "D, I know I've been hard on you ever since you and Lexi got serious, and I want to apologize to you for that."

"It's all right, Camryn, I've been treated worse by overprotective friends before, so, I'm used to it." I chuckled to help loosen her up, and it worked as I saw a slight smile spread across her face.

"Thanks, D, you didn't have to make all this so easy, I appreciate it." She straightened her back, leaning against the bench to get comfortable. "I don't know if you've noticed, but things aren't as hot between your boy and me right now."

I was a little disturbed by her admission, but the scene that she would have made under normal circumstances after she saw Quinn acting like he wasn't in a serious relationship spoke volumes about where she was in her head. "To be honest, Q doesn't talk to me about jack these days. I don't know what the deal is with him, and we've been boys for a long time."

"Well, it was fun for a minute, but it's time to move on." Camryn exhaled, listening to the words that she spoke and realizing their finality. "Damn, I guess I needed to say it out loud. I just hope he understands that I don't do well with being put in a box."

"The way he's been rocking the field tonight, there's no telling if he will even care all that much. Especially with the rumors about some women accusing him of the same thing Jenna's accusing me of right now." I wondered.

A frown spread across her face. "Yeah, that would be the other part of the reason things aren't so hot between us. Some chick hit me up on Twitter and said Q burned her and that she was going public to blast him."

"Wait, so, you knew about this? I just got wind of it tonight."

"Yeah, she said she wanted him to pay her off to shut her up, but I guess he decided not to. It's not just her, it's like several women." Camryn shook her head. "I'm just glad I made him wear a condom the few times we did have sex. After I got that message, I got tested out in LA to make sure I wasn't infected."

"Who was the woman that hit you on Twitter?"

"It came from some ghost account, why?"

I checked my watch and realized that we'd been gone for about twenty minutes. "We'd better get back to the party. The last thing we need is someone trying to figure out where we've been and what we're doing."

Camryn smirked a little before kissing me on the cheek. "It's not like I would mind all that much, but I know a couple of women in your life that might not be too keen on that."

Out of nowhere, Camryn slipped into my personal space, staring into my eyes for a brief second before she kissed me hard and slow. I wasn't sure if it was the shock of it all or what, but I pushed her off, rubbing the lipstick off my face. I glared at her for what seemed like an eternity, wondering what possessed her to do something like that. She sat across from me, her eyes searching mine, trying to find something there that would have given her the access to try again. The moment she didn't find one, she dropped her head, refusing my attempts to get her attention.

I still wanted answers. "What the hell, Cam?"

"I know, and I'm sorry, D. I thought I saw something there, and I'm so tired of being locked down. I just wanted…forget it, let's just go before someone sees us." Camryn got up and took off toward to backyard.

I did my best to catch up with her as we headed back to the backyard to rejoin the party, but she ignored my attempts to get her attention. I caught Alexia out of the corner of my eye, turning my attention to her to figure out why she was yelling in my direction. I stopped walking, confused for a brief second as to why she looked so worried.

In hindsight, I should have kept my head on a swivel and been aware of my surroundings. Even Camryn trying to pull on me didn't tip me off to the force that headed toward me with a fury that I never expected in a million years. Everything seemed to move in slow motion after that.

The first thing I felt was a fist across my jaw that put me on the ground. I tried to get up and was met with another fist to the same spot, followed by a slew of profanities and shouts of betrayal and threats of finishing what Anton started. I tried to protect myself as best as I could, but I was already dizzy from the blows to my head.

I caught a few kicks to my ribcage, which limited my ability to breathe. I wanted to say I didn't deserve what was happening in that moment, but there was nothing I could do to justify it. He must have seen me and Camryn coming from the front of the house and snapped.

The last thing I saw and heard before I blacked out was a size twelve boot and the Timberland tree insignia connecting against the side of my cheek and Camryn screaming for Quinn to stop kicking me. I wasn't sure if I was relieved that I blacked out or fearful that I wouldn't come out of it once I did. One thing was for certain: I guess he cared a little more than he let on.

Alexia

Chapter Forty-Seven: Mama Said Knock You Out

"Damn, did someone get the number of that truck?"

I was so glad to hear Devin's voice once he came around that I was able to ignore the black eye and bruises on the left side of his face. Natalia, Camryn and Keri were busy trying to replace the ice packs on his face and his ribcage while we were in one of the main level guest rooms after Quinn lost his mind.

I tried yelling for security first while shaking Natalia to get her attention. We tried to get to him, but it was too late. He was already on the ground and Quinn was stomping on him before we could get enough security personnel to break things up.

Camryn even tried to pull him off, but Quinn shoved her so hard that she went flying into a group of partygoers. In all, it took three men to get Quinn off of Devin, and when he didn't move, Natalia and I panicked and feared the worst. The whole scene played out like a bad drama.

Mr. Parker had the rest of the security team shield Devin

as three other men helped block the photographers trying to get pictures of him while the paramedics that were on station at the party were summoned to assess his injuries. Quinn was secured on the ground, face-down with his arms held behind his back until Milton police could get to the house to take him into custody for the assault.

The ultimate insult to injury was when he looked at Camryn for help to explain the situation, only for Camryn to look at him like he was a complete stranger and walk off in the other direction—and into the waiting arms of Mr. Parker! Natalia was shocked beyond words, but I was more focused on helping to get Devin conscious instead. The incident itself was caught on tape, so it was only a matter of time before social media would be ablaze with the video from the news cameras.

Mr. Richton was in the area with us, checking on Devin's status for himself. He was a bit confused over why his daughter was more animated than usual over his current situation. Natalia took the opportunity to explain the nature of her new relationship. After a moment of confusion, he hugged his daughter and said that they would talk later once Devin was up and around.

The paramedics worked over Devin, using smelling salts to bring him back around and checking his abdomen to make sure there were no other surprises other than the bruised ribs that they felt. He turned in my direction as Natalia rushed to my side to get in on the conversation. "Ma'am, it looks like your boyfriend will be okay, but his ribs are badly bruised. We need to take him to the hospital for observation."

"That won't be happening." Devin protested. I watched him try to get up before he started wincing in pain, holding his ribcage. "Nothing's broken. I'm not going to the hospital."

"You are not about to sit here and pull the pride card, youngster," Mr. Richton said, leaning over to grab his shoulder. "You were knocked unconscious, and you're going to get checked out. If they say you can go, you can go, understood? And in light of your new status as my daughter's boyfriend, your pride is not about to have my daughter worrying over you, and you are not about to have me do the same thing."

"Damn it…all right, sir, understood." Devin relented, realizing the boss was not about to be disputed. He was caught off guard that he was told about us, but there was nothing he could say. "You and Mr. Parker have been like father figures to me, the last thing I would want to do is go against your orders."

"Good man. I will have Talia give me and Parker a status update when you leave the hospital." Mr. Richton kissed Natalia across her forehead and kissed my cheek before he took his leave.

After Mr. Richton left, Devin slumped as they lifted him onto the stretcher. "What the hell got into Q? He acted like I'd stolen his car or something."

Camryn shook her head in disgust. "He was pissed because he saw me with you. He has a temper when he sees me talking with or in the company of any man, regardless of who it is. It was one of the other reasons I didn't want to be with him anymore. I never thought he would hit you, much less try to beat you into oblivion."

"Yeah, he even threw Camryn into a crowd of folks when she tried to get him to lay off you." Natalia recounted. "I guess there's really no honor amongst players when a woman is involved, huh, baby?"

I tried to laugh with the attempt to make him feel better, but the look in his eyes told me that losing another close friend was not something that he expected to happen so soon after losing Anton.

"We can meet you at WellStar North Fulton so we can take you home after the doctors look you over." I caressed his face as he gave a silent nod. "Right now, we have to talk to the officers and give our statements."

"Okay, baby, but try not to be too long. I'm already not thrilled about going down there to begin with, but what the boss says, goes."

Deion

Chapter Forty-Eight: America's Most Wanted

I was still sore from the incident at the release party. I think my pride hurt more than my body, but my ribs would love to beg to differ.

After piecing the details from that night from the RPK security staff and some of the other guests at the party, it turned out that Quinn had been looking all over for Camryn for a good fifteen minutes. His anger over not being able to find her intensified, and a few of the guests overheard him talking to himself and threatening to beat down the dude that she was with. Someone did try to alert the security staff, but they lost track of where he had gone, and by the time they could locate him again, he was already on top of me trying to rearrange the bones in my ribcage.

I got a call from one of the Milton police detectives assigned to the case involving the incident, letting me know that he would be arraigned at noon in Fulton Superior Court. The meeting with Jenna to determine was set for four o'clock at her attorney's office in Midtown. Yeah, this was shaping up to be a helluva day already.

Alexia had a slew of signings going on all day today, and since I was recovering and on leave from work until the end of the week, I had to assign one of the other photographers to handle the PR photos at the different locations. I wasn't happy about it, but I didn't have a choice in the matter.

Natalia had to head out of town on another film shoot out west, which left me on my own to deal with Jenna. I reassured them that I would be okay and I would let them know all the gory details, regardless of the outcome.

I called Kelli to let her know where I would be before texting the girls to relay the same information. I got a message from Natalia first; she must have gotten one of the other models to take a picture of the outfit that she was wearing for the film shoot. The next series of texts I received were pictures and a video text, all to put a smile on my face. The way she looked in the "little black dress" that she had on, it was safe to say her mission yielded the results she wanted.

Alexia texted back, still worried that I didn't have anyone with me for support and upset that she was stuck on the PR tour and couldn't get to me. I was worried that they would have been forced to come to court to testify as witnesses for Quinn's case, but from what the detective explained to me, there were enough witnesses to the incident that they wouldn't be needed anyway, which was a relief to hear.

I sat down on my bed, looking up at the ceiling for a moment or two, trying to figure out how in the hell I managed to be in the position I was in. First, losing Anton, and now possibly losing Quinn to a bid in jail because he couldn't keep his emotions in check. Maybe Anton's mother was right. Maybe this was my karma coming back to take the people that I cared about most away from me to teach me a lesson.

Chills ran down my spine once thoughts about the hearing crossed my mind. My grandfather always told me that good things and bad things always came in threes. Anton dying was the first bad thing to happen to me. Quinn's crazy ass jealous rage and trying to take me out was the second thing to happen. I prayed to God that the hearing would not be the third thing. I didn't think my heart could take it.

A last second video call from both Alexia and Natalia threw me off. Seeing their faces helped a lot, but they weren't smiling as they greeted me. "What's wrong? Has something else happened?"

"D, baby, there's something that Natalia needs to tell you, and it involves Quinn." Alexia looked like she was as pained to be a party to this conversation as Natalia was.

"If it has anything to do with his HSV2 status, Cam told me about that last night during the time we were talking to clear the air between us," I replied. It didn't change either of their facial expressions, which worried me more than I was prepared for. "Wait, is there something else that I'm not aware of?"

Natalia's voice began to crack as she responded to my question. "I didn't want to tell you about this because I didn't know how it would affect you. I caught Q with Jenna at a private party in Miami about a month after she broke things off with you."

My whole world stopped. Quinn and Jenna???

I took a moment to catch a breath. "Why didn't you tell me sooner, baby?"

"I didn't want to be the one to break your spirit even further than you had already gone, baby." Natalia wiped a tear to keep from ruining her makeup. I looked at the other screen, watching her try to keep her composure and failing, too.

"Let's get it all out there so I can deal with this and move on." I was numb. To be betrayed by Quinn after losing Ant was more than I could bear. "I can see it in your faces, there's something else."

Natalia took a deep breath before she continued. "As much as I don't want to say this, but there is a silver lining in this. It means that Q is the one who infected Jenna with the HSV2 virus."

I was so out of it that I didn't realize that she was right. It didn't take away the pain, but it gave me ammunition to take with me to the hearing. That alone was worth the pain of knowing the truth.

"I talked to Cam about the whole situation last night after you went to sleep. She wanted me to tell you that she remembered the name of the account of the woman who came for her on Twitter," Alexia mentioned. "She said it was something like Persephone or something like that."

The rage must have shown on my face because both my girls looked like they were afraid for whomever it was that sparked me. "Jenna couldn't have been that sloppy, but I'm absolutely ecstatic that she was. I'm going to bury her."

"What are you talking about, baby?" Alexia asked. The worried look in her eyes were palpable. "You're scaring the both of us."

"I'm okay, Lexi, I promise you both. Jenna always told me when she was a little girl that she always loved

Persephone when she was a little girl. She was obsessed with her when we were together, including a tattoo of her on her lower left calf."

Natalia grinned like she realized Jenna would no longer be in our lives ever again. "Make that bitch disappear, baby. I only wish we could be there to see the look on her face when you do."

"Am I wrong for getting a little moist over what you're about to do, D?" Alexia blushed as she tried to whisper her admission to keep anyone from hearing her. "Just let us know what happens when you're finished. I want every gory detail."

"That won't be a problem. First things first, I have to take care of Q."

Sitting in the courtroom as we awaited the judge to speak gave me a sense of dread I'd hoped I would never have to deal with ever in life. It was whisper quiet, no one daring to say a word until she decided to acknowledge the people in her domain. I didn't care anymore what happened to him. Any ounce of mercy I thought I had were erased after his blatant hypocrisy.

I looked at him as he tried to make eye contact with me. The contempt I felt was beyond any words I wanted to say. Everything within me wanted to crucify him with the information I was armed with, but I was going to have to be satisfied with the justice he would get for assaulting me.

The judge looked at Quinn, glancing down at her legal pad to scribble some notes. "Begin your allocution, Mr. Hardmon."

Quinn's voice cracked as he spoke, no longer exuding the confidence I was used to out of my soon-to-be former best friend. "I was looking for my girlfriend because she wasn't in my immediate eyesight. When I couldn't find her...I don't know...I kinda lost it."

I thought I would be more emotional, but I felt nothing. I kept my eyes fixed on him, studying his emotions as he re-lived the incident all over again. I needed the closure more than anything, the reason for being on the receiving end of a beatdown that I didn't deserve, all because he had his own demons to deal with.

"I finally saw my boy walking from around the front of the house, trying to get her attention. I saw the smeared lipstick on her face, and her hair was messed up a little bit. I mean, I refused to believe that he would betray me like that, but I saw what I wanted to see because I was already pissed that she disappeared to do God knows what," he continued, tears in his eyes as his body language broke down with his emotions.

"I saw red at that point, your honor. I punched him first, and when he hit the ground, I just...he had to pay for what I thought he did to me." He finished speaking, abruptly turning toward me. "D...God, man, I'm sorry...I'm so sorry, bruh. If you can find it in your heart to forgive me, I'll take whatever punishment the judge gives out without issue."

I couldn't speak for a few seconds. I took a minute to get myself together, but the anger swelled within me, to the point to where I could no longer contain what was in my heart. "I forgive you, but we're done. The things you've done, you'll have to deal with that for the rest of your life—without me in your life."

His eyes widened, confused over what I could have meant. I shook my head, mouthing the words, *you betrayed me. You fucked Jenna*, before I walked about of the courtroom. I did, however, stick around long enough to hear the judge render her verdict and sentence.

As I headed out to the next stop on my emotional gauntlet, I wondered how things would flow during this hearing. Jenna would have no idea what was coming, and I couldn't wait to provide the death knell to her whole world.

Deion

Chapter Forty-Nine: Sorry Not Sorry

I was ten minutes late to the hearing, thanks to the long lines at Underground Atlanta while trying to get something to eat before I dealt with this madness. I had hoped to meet Kelli first to settle my nerves, but the way this day was going, I wasn't about to have my way on anything.

"It took you long enough."

"Let's get this over with. I have nothing more to say to you, Jenna." I walked past her to assume my spot at the defendant's table. I never looked in her direction, it wasn't worth it. "The sooner this is done, the better."

"Suit yourself, D." Jenna replied as she sat with her attorney. "It's your funeral."

I took a good, long look at her attorney, and I couldn't quite place where I knew her from before, but the more I focused on her, the more she tried not to stare at me. The hair was cut differently, and she looked like she got an island tan recently, but the eyes were unmistakable.

Kelli whispered to me, "Are there any surprises that I need

to be aware of?"

I continued to stare at the opposing counsel, and the memories of that night rushed to the forefront of my mind. Damn it. "There are no surprises. In fact, I know I didn't infect her. She slept with both of my best friends, and both of them have tested positive for HSV-2. The other thing is, and I don't think that Jenna knows it, but I had a one-night stand with her attorney New Year's Eve."

Kelli shook her head and stared at Yvonne, whose demeanor changed when she realized that Kelli had been told about our connection to each other. Oh yeah, this day was getting better and better.

Yvonne cut her eyes at me, looking like she wanted to rip me a new asshole, remembering the way I treated her when she left my condo. It wasn't my fault she played me to get what she wanted. I couldn't dwell on that right now, I had to focus on the more important issue at hand.

"Okay, let's get started. I've taken the liberty to have the results sealed and delivered to our agreed upon location and vetted personnel." Yvonne kept her eyes trained on Kelli during the opening dialog. Jenna tried her best to burn a hole through me with her stare.

"I'm certain my client wants to move on from this particular episode in his life," Kelli responded, waiting for Yvonne to show her hand. "Once we have the results, we can move on to resolving any grievances between our clients and close this quickly and amicably."

Jenna scowled at me from across the table, making a throat-slashing gesture with her hand, mouthing the words, *you're done*, before the gentleman walked into the office with a briefcase in hand. He sent a text out, waiting for the respondent as he showed Yvonne and Kelli that the briefcase was locked by code. A few seconds later, the response text was received, and the gentleman used the code sent to open the briefcase and present the sealed envelope to Yvonne before he closed the case and left the room.

Yvonne opened the envelope, taking a moment to read the results of the test. I watched her body language with great interest, wondering if she would give herself away. Whether she wanted to admit it, she had as much of a personal stake in the results as her client.

She turned the results over to Kelli, turning to Jenna to prepare her client. Kelli nodded for a few seconds before she nodded in my direction. My results were negative for any and all possible STDs.

Instead of trying to sound like I wanted to gloat since I already had the information in my back pocket that tipped me off to the results, I remained as even-tempered as I could. I whispered that I wanted to leave now that there was nothing left to discuss.

"My client is satisfied with the results and would like to resolve any remaining grievances at this time." Kelli's demeanor was no-nonsense, awaiting Yvonne's response, never once looking in Jenna's direction.

"I'm not satisfied at all. He infected me, I have no doubts that it was him." Jenna was sticking to her lie until the very end. "I want another test done, period."

"For what reason? So that it can prove that you didn't contract it from me, right?" I never once raised my voice, but the force of my statement rocked them both. "Walk away now with your integrity intact, this is my final mercy extended to you."

Jenna put her head in her hands and wept as Yvonne put a hand on her shoulder. "I bet you're happy now. That's okay, you weren't worth the trouble. Your boys were better than you anyway."

"And you got burned for your troubles. But you did me a favor, though. I can properly say goodbye, Jenna Whitmore, and thank you for freeing me from every tie I had to you."

If she thought her dig at my prowess was supposed to hurt, she had another thing coming. Though, for a moment, I did feel a twinge of empathy for her, but once my mind conjured up the images of her and Anton together, her and Quinn together, all traces of emotion, positive or negative, washed away in an instant. She no longer held me prisoner. I was free from her spell.

Kelli had this look like she'd been forced into the midst of a bad comedy. I didn't blame her for feeling that way. I put my hand on her shoulder to comfort her. "Please understand that my life is nowhere near this chaotic. You've been around me at RPK functions and retreats to know me."

Kelli shook her head, giggling a bit over the recent turn of events. "What really had me tripping was when the parents came in out of the blue. Oh my God, this one is going to top a lot of stories in legal for a good little while!"

I laughed to mask the embarrassment I felt over everything that had happened up to this point. I took some solace, though, since this would be the last time that I would get caught up in some mess like this again.

Kelli patted me on the back as we got ready to leave and continued to shake her head at the madness that was occurring. "I feel sorry for her. I wouldn't wish that on my worst enemy."

I couldn't have agreed more, but I was thankful it wasn't my problem anymore. I needed away from all of this, and with my new-found wealth, I knew where I wanted to go.

Monaco.

Nothing like some time in the sun and away from anything and everything that could have possibly reminded me of anything bad that had happened. I couldn't wait to find some time in my schedule and get the girls away, too.

I heard my name being called, but I ignored the cries. I could have cared less who it was, unless they called out my name formally, I wasn't turning around for anything.

Yvonne caught up with me as I made my way to the front of the building, calling my name the whole time. "Devin, wait! I need to talk to you!"

What the fuck did she want, after everything that just went down in the courtroom? "Okay, so you got my attention, Yvonne, what do you plan to do with it?"

"Look, D, I know the last time we saw each other, I said some things that, looking back on it now, I shouldn't have said." She tried to catch her breath as she spoke. "I shouldn't have lied to you about my relationship with my partner—"

"You said you were separated, not married. Yvonne. Get it together, which one is it?"

Yvonne brushed my comment off, trying to get whatever she wanted off her chest. "Okay, but the point is, I'm divorced now, and despite the looks that I gave you in my conference room, the truth is, I want some more of you."

You have got to be kidding me today! I took my hands to check my forehead to see if it had the word "Gigolo" written on it or something. I really wasn't GQ at all after the day that I just had, so there was no way in hell I could still be attractive at the current moment.

"Look, Yvonne, I'm gonna say it again like I said that night: you were damn good that night, but there are two things that I couldn't do then, and I can't do now, and that's help a woman commit adultery." I wanted to read her the riot act. Who in the bloody hell did she think she was, coming at me with this bullshit? "I helped you do exactly that night, and frankly speaking, I have no time to be anyone's fuck buddy. I'm in a relationship, and for the first time in a long time, I'm happy."

Yvonne's eyes began to mist, her body language shifting as she tried to plead her case. She sifted through her briefcase and handed me a document. "I promise I'm divorced. Here, you can view the decree for yourself."

Sure enough, she got divorced back in February.

Like that was going to change my mind. I had two women that keep my attention and I'm more than happy with. I pushed the door open to head toward the parking garage. "I'm sorry that you're divorced now, Yvonne, and I hope you find someone that makes you happy. Do me a favor and lose my number. I have no need for you in my universe."

I blew air as I felt the sunshine on my face. Too much had happened today—way too much. It was a beautiful day, despite the madness that went on today. If anything, I had no more energy to give to any of the situations.

I needed to hear my girls' voices. Maybe they would help balance the rage and anger that was still inside of me. I was in a dark place, and I didn't want to be there anymore.

As I left the office, I called Natalia and Alexia and put them on a three-way conference as I headed for the truck to head home. "Hey you two, I left from the hearing, and—"

"Baby, don't put us in suspense any longer, please. Just tell us if you buried all the bodies you needed to bury, please?" Alexia didn't mince words. She was dealing with fans that were snatching up the CDs as quickly as they could and taking selfies all over the place.

"Yeah, baby, can we get on with our lives without that bitch being in the picture?" Natalia chimed in right behind Alexia, giving me no room to say anything edgewise.

Hearing them scream and squeal at the same time as I told them that Jenna and Quinn were out of our lives forever was the cherry on what was otherwise a roller coaster day. I didn't think Camryn would care too much anyway; once the news broke out about her and Mr. Parker being a couple, it was over with for him.

"I should be home after this crazy ass PR thing is done around nine, baby." Alexia told me as I turned on to Peachtree Street to ride in traffic to the condo. "After that, I'm all yours."

"Just make sure you save some for me, baby," Natalia told Alexia, which cracked me up for a moment. "I might need to release some frustration from being such a good girl while I'm up here in NYC with all these fine ass men and women on this film shoot. All I want is to curl up with both of you when I get home."

I let them chatter back and forth to do their girl talk thang as I sat in bumper-to-bumper traffic, looking forward to whatever the future held for us.

Deion

Epilogue: God's Plan

The Compound. What better place to celebrate the success of the now Double Platinum-selling group, *Envyye*?

The videos of congratulations from all the heavy-hitters were nice to watch. It was almost as nice as when I had to fly around to the different locales to do the actual videotaping. Kendrick Lamar. T.I. Rihanna. The Migos. Cardi B. The list went on and on.

Even the fellas got in on the videos, although those weren't as fun to do; they tended to be a bit more flirtatious with their congratulations. I wasn't particularly fond of Big Sean and Drake when they singled Alexia out, but I realized I needed to keep my jealousy in check. After all, it's a part of the industry, and it came with the territory, so I had to get used to it.

It was amazing to me to see how much the music community tended to be so tight-knit and positive for one another's successes. Maybe this music thing wasn't so bad after all. On second thought, I planned to stick to my filmmaking ventures; I enrolled in the Savannah College of Art & Design to brush up on my skills. If I wanted next level, I had to prepare like I'm already there.

The heat of the summer gave me the opportunity to enjoy the heat of my women. I was also ready to put some distance between now and what had occurred nearly three months ago.

Things couldn't have been better. It was interesting to see the glances any time we went out to a restaurant or to the clubs in the States, but all we received were champagne or wine gifts from the people who saw us overseas. Funny how that worked out, huh?

Of course, being out with women that had more star-power than I did was an adjustment at first, but I enjoyed the spotlight as much as they did, and it got us tickets to all of the A-list events in the music and film industries. Going as a guest and not as a rising filmographer was leaps and bounds better on so many levels I didn't know where to begin.

Even Mr. Richton warmed up to our relationship. Being a widower, he had no interests in getting married again. He even did his best to get over the relationship Mr. Parker was in with Camryn, but he couldn't be one to talk. Being in a "friends with benefits" situation with Laura and a few other women around the city tended to keep him from being critical of others' relationships.

Tina got caught up into someone for the long term, and by the unlikeliest of sources: one of my interns. Even wilder than that, he was as into her as she was into him. It might have had something to do with the fact that she was the owner's daughter, too, but who was I to criticize?

All in all, life couldn't be much better than what it was

right now, but there was still one loose end to tie up. On second thought, I didn't want to invite negativity back into my life by looking into either one of them. They could have gotten together, considering they were both suffering from the same STD status, but that, again, was no longer in my circle of concern.

I snapped out of the thoughts in my head as my ladies found me at the bar. The conspiratorial grins on their faces tipped me off to something that I was afraid to ask about.

"Hi, baby, are you enjoying the party?" Alexia asked, although the party was for her and the group.

"Why wouldn't I enjoy the party? *Envyye* is a hit, and you're on the way to being a superstar. I'm enjoying all of it because I get to see it up close and personal." I kissed her on the cheek.

"Good, because this has all felt like a dream come true for me, and it's only fair that we return the favor." Alexia smiled, giving a knowing wink to her girlfriend.

Before I could ask what the hell they meant by that, Mr. Richton and Mr. Parker walked up on us with their own smiles. "D, we figured we'd find you with your girls."

"Okay, let me in on whatever the hell you all have going on so we can finish enjoying the party, please?" I got up the nerve to say because my bosses were present.

"Yeah, there's no need to put this off any further." Mr. Parker announced. "Thanks to your girls, and some help from us on the location, you currently are the owner of your photography and graphic design studio, with room to expand to your film studio compound, once you've finished with school."

My world stopped moving. I didn't realize that my voice

was trembling. "You wanna run that by me again? My own studio?"

"Yes, baby, your own studio, and the flexibility to do what you want and continue doing business with RPK." Natalia grinned as she snuggled closer to me.

The words escaped me. This was surreal. I'd planned on using the compensation from the acts I was paid for to set things up on my own. "I still don't know what to say."

"Say thank you so we can go back to enjoying the party, baby." Alexia kissed me. "We can find ways that you can personally thank your girls later tonight, alright?"

"Anything for you, baby." I replied, looking at her before I stole a glance at Natalia. "Anything for you...both of you."

ABOUT THE AUTHOR

Shakir Rashaan is the national bestselling author of the *Nubian Underworld* series and the *Kink, P.I.* series. Other projects include *In Service to the Senator.* Projects are in development for later publication under P.K. Rashaan. If you would like to check out more in his catalog, you can visit www.ShakirRashaan.com.

www.ingramcontent.com/pod-product-compliance
Lightning Source LLC
Chambersburg PA
CBHW051120120726
47905CB00005B/1355